ALWAYS CHOOSING YOU

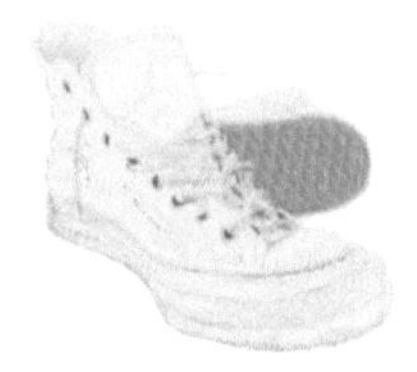

K.SINKO

For all the girls who dealt with messy, confusing high school drama. You don't deserve second place.

And for the bandos, my high school crew.

Prologue

The summer before

RORY STEPPED onto the back porch and slid the screen door closed before scanning the crowd. She found Jay leaning against the railing, watching as he took a pull of his beer.

She brushed her fingers through her thick, mahogany hair and approached him, her stomach doing somersaults at the sight of the smile that curled up his left cheek as he looked out in the distance.

She slowed to a stop. "Hey, have you seen Melanie? I can't find her anywhere."

Jay finally glanced over at her, his expression sly and half-dazed from wherever he'd just pulled his thoughts from. "Nah, been a little distracted."

Rory raised an eyebrow in his direction and leaned against the wooden railing next to him, purposely brushing her forearm against his. "Oh yeah? With what?"

Jay ticked his head toward the lawn, motioning toward a group of girls talking animatedly in a circle, swaying on their feet as they took swigs from a plastic green cup.

Her stomach clenched at the sight of them. She hastily shifted her gaze in Jay's direction, noticing that he was back to watching them with a smirk, like he was on the prowl.

She sighed audibly. "Let me guess," she started. "The blonde one, tall, wearing a shift dress that was probably meant to be a tank top."

"It's working for her," Jay said, his voice thick and devious.

"Typical," she mumbled.

Jay turned, eyes wide. "Come again?"

Crap, she thought to herself. She must have said it louder than she intended, and now Jay was staring at her with that expression he always got when he was raring for a fight. His lips were pinched together in a tight line. The toffee color in his eyes completely disappeared as his pupils dilated, leaving them jet-black, almost onyx, as he stared straight at her.

Usually, when she saw Jay like this, she would try to brush it off with a joke, watching his pupils return to their normal size as he barked out a laugh. With the two of them, it was always teasing and joking and sword fighting with cotton candy–colored spoons at Scoops By The Sea, the ice cream shop they both worked at during their summers in Haverport.

But right now, she didn't have the energy to fake it. She was angry at him.

Rory squared her shoulders in his direction, facing him full-on, and crossed her arms. "You just have a type, that's all."

"Is that wrong?" he snipped at her.

"It's unoriginal," she bit back, cocking her hip.

Jay took the last pull of his beer, balancing the empty

bottle on the railing without looking back at her. "What does that mean?"

"Your interests just fit the stereotype perfectly," she responded, the words flying out of her. She was two drinks in at this point, her filter completely gone. And she didn't care. "Tall, blonde, thin, typically in some kind of skimpy outfit that shows off a sizeable rack."

"Things you clearly don't have," he responded with an icy tone.

She froze.

"Finally, been looking for you guys everywhere."

Tyler, their friend and Scoops coworker, approached the two of them from behind, a plastic water bottle clutched in his hand. "Ry, have you had any water yet? Found this in the fridge, miraculously unopened."

She hardly registered what he'd said, her eyes still focused on Jay, who was now glaring at her.

Tyler slowed. "Yo...is everything good?"

"Apologize," Rory whispered.

"Ry, what's going on—"

"Apologize," she repeated. "You have no right commenting on my body."

"Yet you have every right to comment on someone else's?" Jay hissed back, a small speck of spit flying from his mouth as he pointed to the crowd of girls completely oblivious to the scene taking place on the porch. Not like it was anything interesting compared to the rowdy party around them, the blaring music echoing off the river beyond the house.

"I was just stating a fact," she said tightly.

"And I was *too*," Jay said, emphasizing the last word. "You're clearly just jealous because you look absolutely nothing like them."

"Hey, this is getting out of hand," Tyler said coolly, reaching his free hand to gently grab Rory's wrist, his face sternly on Jay. "You've both been drinking—you're saying things you don't mean."

"Oh, I mean it," Jay said.

"I hate you," Rory said curtly.

"Only because I speak the truth."

Without thinking, she jerked her hand away from Tyler's grasp and lunged at Jay, slapping the same left cheek that held a coy smirk just minutes before.

She was seething—the ringing in her ears overpowering whatever Jay was now screaming at her, muffled only by Tyler, who now stood between the two of them. He barked something in Jay's direction before snatching her hand and pulling hard. Her vision was blurry from the tears pooling in her eyes as he led her down the porch steps and around the house.

Tyler wrapped an arm tightly around her waist and lifted her up into the passenger seat of his Jeep, slamming the car door next to her. He hopped in on the other side, shoving the water bottle right at Rory's chest. "Drink that. Now."

She silently obeyed as Tyler switched on the ignition and pulled out at lightning speed, climbing back up the road they came from just an hour earlier. She remained silent as he turned onto Main Street and drove past Scoops and Grampy's and sleepy late-night moviegoers stepping out of Haverport Cinemas.

Moments later, they rolled through the main entrance of the Misty Bay beach community. Tyler turned the car down Chestnut Road, then pulled into the driveway of his house and killed the ignition. Rory didn't say anything as she twisted the empty water bottle in her hand, the popping and cracking sound of the plastic satisfying her need to squeeze and break something.

"He didn't mean it," Tyler said as if reading her mind.

"Yes, he did," she whispered. "And he's right; I'm nothing like them."

Tyler twisted in his seat, now facing her. "So what? Why do you care so much? What's the—"

But then he stopped. She watched as understanding shifted his expression. His eyebrows furrowed with this new truth.

"He's an idiot," Tyler said, loud enough that she was almost worried they would wake his parents, his voice carrying from the open car window to his house in front of him. Her own was right next door, but it wasn't like it mattered much for her—her mom probably wasn't even home. "Why do you bother with him? He's an asshole to literally everyone."

"Not always to me," she responded, her words coming out short and tight. She was trying not to cry in front of him again.

"And what? He's nice to you five percent of the time, and it's worth the rest of the time he's a complete shithead? You don't deserve that, Ry."

Her nostrils flared. "Why do you care so much about what I deserve, huh?"

Tyler rubbed his hand over his face and let out an exhale before continuing. "Because...because I do."

She huffed. "You don't see me chewing into you about the girls you like."

Tyler lifted his arms in frustration. "*What* girls? There are none!"

"Yeah right," Rory said, opening the passenger door.

"Do yourself a favor and stay out of my personal life, 'kay? Because you're not invited."

"Oh, so the whole 'best friends forever' thing was all bullshit to you then?"

Rory threw the bottle at him, but the action had no effect on Tyler as it lightly bounced off his broad shoulder.

"Best friends are supportive," Rory spewed. "And right now, you're just being a dick."

First Semester

Chapter One

FOUR OF THEM STOOD THERE, staring at the ice cream shop. Everything was completely bare; the shop was spotless for the first time since opening in March. The walk-in fridge and ice cream cake freezers were empty. Candy containers and hot fudge canisters cleaned and stored away. No more rainbow jimmies or crushed-up waffle cones scattered on the floor. No more snaking lines or bulging tip jars or music blasting in The War Room. Just silence, and the faint smell of bleach.

It was November first, the day after Scoops By The Sea's annual closing...and the day Rory dreaded the most.

She faced the front of Scoops, watching as Calvin rounded the corner after locking up the back door leading to The War Room. It's what they called the small room in the back of the shop that customers couldn't see, the place that belonged to the Scoopers and the Scoopers only.

Calvin slid up next to Melanie, curling an arm around her neck and kissing her forehead. But Melanie kept her hand firmly in Rory's, holding on tightly.

"I can't believe it's over," Melanie whispered.

"Just for now," Calvin said. "We'll be back before you know it."

"Not soon enough," Rory huffed.

"You guys are bananas," Blake said. "I, for one, will not be sad about having a few months off."

"Says the boy who doesn't have to work a second job," Jess said tightly.

"School is basically a job," he complained. "The worst kind, actually."

"Not as bad as having to refill the wet nuts container," Rory quipped.

"Or pressure cleaning the sticky ice cream from the sidewalk," Melanie added.

"Or dropping an entire ice cream cake and trying to clean it out of the rug," Jess said.

Rory winced. "Okay, that was *one time*, Jess."

"One is still too many," Jess mumbled back, shaking her head.

Rory sighed. "It's weird," she confessed. "Not having them here."

No one had an answer for her...and she understood why. It was her fault everything was so weird between the seven of them. Without Tyler and Jay, it felt like a massive hole in their family. And now, after another wild summer season at Scoops, they were all going their separate ways.

Rory truly hated this day.

"I've gotta go to work," Jess said curtly, and it was enough to break the awkward silence. She turned on her heel and went for her car, not stopping to look back.

"There's our Jess," Blake said as they watched her pull out of the Scoops parking lot. "Always the most sentimental one."

Rory heard sniffling and turned toward Melanie, who

was now crying. Calvin tightened his arm around Melanie's shoulders. "Ready to go?"

She nodded. Rory squeezed her hand one last time before letting go, watching the two of them walk over to Calvin's truck.

She sighed, turning toward Blake. "Need a ride?"

"Nah, Zach's picking me up," he said, his face flushing slightly at the mention of his boyfriend. He stepped closer to her. "Hey, is Melanie, um, doing okay?"

She felt her heart twist in her chest. "I-I don't know."

Blake's brows furrowed. "But aren't you guys, like, best friends? Shouldn't you know this stuff?"

She tried to steal a glance through the window of the truck as it pulled away, catching Melanie as she nuzzled her head against Calvin's shoulder. "I'm not really good at the whole 'best friends' thing."

"But—"

"Blake," she snipped. "Drop it, 'kay?"

Blake nodded, his face bright pink from embarrassment.

Rory knew it was probably the polite thing to wait for him to get picked up, but she wasn't feeling particularly polite at the moment. So, she mumbled goodbye and walked toward her car.

He wasn't wrong; she knew that. It *was* strange that her newly proclaimed best friend barely talked to her about the fact that her twin brother died a mere two months ago. Yet... she also knew part of the reason they never spoke about it was her own fault. She probably should make more of an effort to be there for Melanie.

But her mind was a little too preoccupied these days. Mostly over the fact that her final season on Haverport's varsity soccer team was about to come to a close and she had no idea what to do with herself the rest of the school year—

let alone after graduation. And maybe more importantly, she still had no idea how to get her other best friend of over ten years to talk to her again.

RORY PULLED into her driveway on Chestnut Road and let out a low curse. After the emotional roller coaster she just went through at Scoops—the high of being at work with her friends, the lows of realizing it was the last time until March —she hoped to come home to an empty house. Her plan included pouring herself a giant bowl of Lucky Charms, ignoring her Calculus homework, and watching *Peter Pan*. She was making her way through all of the Disney animated movies again, but this time in the order they were released. *Alice in Wonderland* was her Sunday night watch when her mom had to work a double at the Haverport Diner, leaving Rory home alone with the Mad Hatter, Cheshire Cat, and a frozen pizza. Tonight was supposed to look similar, but her mother's bright red Prius parked outside of their house pointed to her perfectly planned evening being doomed before it could even take shape.

Which, of course, made no sense. Thursday was trivia night at the diner, and Gabriella always worked the late-night shift for those extra tips. And yet, here she was...and Rory really didn't want to deal with it.

She groaned as she climbed out of her car, slamming the door behind her and slinging her backpack over her shoulder. The day was surprisingly warm for mid-autumn, and the heat from the sun caused a bead of sweat to trickle down her spine. She huffed, ignoring the front door and what faced her inside as she walked to the edge of the lawn. It was magically covered in more campaign signs even after purging some that same morning. She pulled them out one by one, not daring to look at the gleaming smile of Garner Clark. The man was bound to win first selectman, just like every other election year, yet that didn't seem to slow down his campaign fairies from littering the neighborhood with his horror-film-worthy smile every day.

After tossing the last one in the dumpster, she straightened and surveyed her handiwork, then trudged her way up to the house. She took a deep breath in a pitiful attempt to try to calm herself, then opened the door.

"Hi, sweetie!"

Rory blinked twice as she took in the scene in front of her. The living room had been completely transformed. A massive sheet hung from the ceiling and cascaded down to the floor into a canopy. A few strands of twinkle lights draped down the sides, disappearing into a mound of pillows on the floor. The coffee table was pushed to the side, but you could barely see the surface of the wood thanks to the endless number of bowls filled with all kinds of junk food covering the top. Cheetos and Hershey Kisses and Twizzlers and tortilla chips next to a steaming bowl of hot queso.

"Gabi..." she began, no small amount of concern lining her tone. "What's going on?"

Her mother huffed. "You know I really hate that you call me that."

She ignored her. "Did you take all of the pillows in the house and make a massive pile in the middle of the living room?"

She smiled. "Yes! It's a little slumber party surprise for you."

Rory crossed her arms, pushing down the hope that was

starting to bloom in her chest. "Why aren't you at the diner? It's Thursday."

"Well," Gabi started, hesitating as she crossed the room to get closer to where Rory still stood by the front door. "I remember how hard this day was for you last year, so I thought I would do something to cheer you up."

"With a slumber party and lots of junk food," Rory said flatly. "Just like *Gilmore Girls*."

Gabi crossed her arms. "Hey now, you're not being fair. I'm trying to do something nice here."

She shook her head, not surprised at her mother's lack of denial. While some parents got their parenting advice from books written by actual professionals, Gabi used the show *Gilmore Girls* as her rulebook. Sure, their stories were similar, Gabi had Rory at 19, her father didn't stick around, and they lived in a small Connecticut beach town where everyone knew everyone's business. But for Gabi, the show was like a religion in itself...hence how her name came to be.

Rory detested it. She hadn't watched much of it, but from what she gathered from the show, Rory was nothing like the fictional one on screen. Fictional Rory had no idea what to do when it came to boys. Real Rory was not above making out with someone, even if it was just for fun. Fictional Rory never really went to parties or drank. Real Rory had her first sip of alcohol at 14. Fictional Rory was always the smartest in the room, the top of her class, and an aspiring journalist bound for Harvard (or, apparently later in the show, for Yale). Real Rory was average in the classroom, had yet to apply to any college, and had absolutely no clue what she wanted to do with her life.

But that didn't stop her mother from working extra

hours and late nights to save up for Rory's education. Which meant she was always out of the house.

Rory was used to being by herself at this point, used to the disappointment that had made a home in her heart. So the fact that Gabi was *here* with an absurdly over-the-top sleepover setup didn't sit right with her. There was no way her mother was choosing her over work.

"You know, if we really want to live out your fantasy, Rory Gilmore would say no and go straight to her room to do homework instead of succumbing to her mom's whims," Rory reasoned.

Gabi shifted uncomfortably. "Actually, um, the sleepover isn't for me."

There it was. Her stomach sank as she dropped her backpack to the ground with a thud.

"I was thinking you could invite Melanie over, if you want?" she continued. "I know it's a school night, but I called her mother and she said she didn't mind."

She blinked. "You called Mrs. Albertson?"

"Yeah, just to make sure it was alright before you offered," Gabi continued. "And I was—"

"Wait," she cut her off. "So you are going to work?"

Gabi wrung her hands, a nervous tic Rory was aware she'd developed in recent years. "Yes, but not at the diner."

She stood there in silence for a moment, staring at her mother, who was now looking down at her shoes. "Did you lose your job?"

Gabi coughed out a chuckle. "God no, they need me. I'll still be working there, but only during the days. I took a second job."

"You took...a second job?"

Gabi nodded. "Yes, as a bartender over at Wilson's Pub," she started. "Remember how I said I was getting my bartending license? Well, I finished, and now I'll be working there to make extra money."

Rory shook her head, pacing back and forth for a moment as she let all of this sink in. Second job. Bartending. Working nights. "You're already not home that much."

"I know, sweetie. And I'm sorr—"

"Why?" Rory cut her off again. "I don't get it. We're doing fine. You said the house is paid off."

Gabi's shoulders dropped. "Because you're a senior bound for college. And I don't want you to have to take out too many loans."

She lifted her arms out at her sides. "That is *insane*! I don't even know where I want to go to college, let alone *if* I want to go."

"Rory, you're going to college."

She stopped pacing and stared at Gabi, who now had her arms crossed against her chest. Her face was stern, a look Rory had honestly only seen a handful of times in her life. The time she came home drunk. The time she flunked out of chemistry and had to take it again the following year. The day she told her she took a job at Scoops, even though Gabi told her countless times not to get a job and to focus instead on studying for the SATs.

It made no sense why her mother was so obsessive about her going to college. Was it because Rory Gilmore was desperate to go to college? Was it because Gabi never got the chance to go herself? Whenever she tried to broach the subject, she always got the same answer: *Because it's just what you do.* But she knew there was more to the story.

She shook her head and crossed her arms, looking away from Gabi and out the sliding glass door leading to their backyard.

"Sweetie, please try to understand."

"Whatever," she said tightly. She charged for the back door, only pausing to deliver what she knew was a harsh and probably unfair blow. "You do what you need to do."

She didn't listen for a response as she slid the door closed with rattling force. She kept moving down the back porch steps and onto the lawn, her mind reeling as she charged for the play set. She sank down on a swing and placed her face in her hands.

She knew it was stupid to be so mad about this. She should be happy to have the ultimate freedom to do as she pleased. More movie marathons and cereal for dinner, more chances to avoid her homework and stay up late. But instead, the entire situation made her feel like a giant dark cloud hovered over her, blanketing her with a deep sadness she couldn't make sense of. She didn't want to give Gabi the satisfaction of knowing she was lonely, that she missed spending time with her. And yet, a tiny part of her wanted to say *screw it* to her pride, charge back in that house, and plead for her not to take the job.

The soft ping of a net next door pulled her out of her head. She peeked out from her hands and looked out to the lawn next door as a shirtless Tyler retrieved a football from the ground. He walked a few paces then turned back to face the net, posturing himself again for another perfect throw. He tightened his shoulders and turned to the side, clutching the ball tightly to his chest. He paused, his eyebrows knitted together as he homed in on the tiny red square at the center of the net. Then, in one swift movement, he made the throw, the ball spiraling effortlessly through the air, making the same pinging noise as it hit dead center of the target before bouncing down to the grass.

She watched as Tyler's shoulders relaxed, his expression one of satisfaction. She couldn't help but take in the smooth ridges of his bare chest, his sweat making his light brown skin gleam beneath the unseasonably warm sunlight.

When did Tyler get so...ripped? Gone was the boy she used to play with in the backyard, all scrawny bones and lanky limbs as he chased her around the lawn. Now he was all muscle and brawn, his shoulders and pecs chiseled like a Greek god's, his hair trimmed into a fresh fade. He even had a set of abs that she'd never noticed before, even after spending countless days at the beach together that summer.

Maybe I just wasn't looking, she thought to herself.

Tyler turned then, his gaze shifting toward the swing where she was perched. She glanced away quickly, feeling her cheeks get warm, and wondered if he could sense her checking him out.

Her...checking Tyler out.

For years, he'd been the brother she never had. Rory vividly remembered the day he and his family moved in next door from New Orleans. She watched from that same swing as Tyler jumped out of the car, immediately running for the backyard, his mother steps behind him with a toddler at her hip—a little girl with two poofy pigtails tied with bright pink bows at the top of her head. Tyler ran up to the swing set and asked if he could join Rory, and she nodded enthusiastically, if not a little surprised. She would never forget how hopeful she felt that day, swinging next to her new friend, realizing she wouldn't be so alone in the neighborhood anymore. They were seven.

But now here she was, a decade later, no longer looking at the boy next door as her brother, but something more. She physically shook the thought away. What was wrong with her? Was it because of what happened this summer? The party? The vile words she'd said to him? Or, more likely, was it the confession that had brazenly come from Jay's lips?

Rory felt the phantom crushing in her chest, the same one she felt when Jay had screamed at her that summer at Scoops. He'd wanted her to pretend to flirt with him to get the attention of some girl, and she completely lost it. She screamed back, telling him how absurd he was in his mission to constantly get into someone's pants. And in their back and forth, he just *told* her, like it meant nothing. Like having Tyler standing right there wasn't a big deal as Jay confessed Tyler's feelings for her after a decade of harboring them in his heart.

She remembered the awkward silence as Melanie watched from the sidelines before Calvin sent him home for the night. She remembered bolting herself moments later, afraid to look Tyler in the eyes, afraid of what she would find there.

She hadn't spoken to either of them since. But it seemed, as a shadow cast above Rory, blocking out the sunlight above her, that their bout of silence was about to end.

She looked up to find Tyler right in front of her, a bead of sweat trickling down his forehead.

"How'd it go today?" he asked.

She just shrugged, finding a spot above his left ear to focus on. "Fine, I guess. How was practice?"

"Awful, as always."

They were silent for what felt like eternity. He *really* needed to put on a shirt.

"May I?" he asked, pointing to the swing next to her.

Rory smirked. "If you can fit."

He moved to the side and grabbed the chain of the swing. "You making fun of me, Ry?"

She smiled at the use of her nickname. That first day on the swings all those years ago, Tyler told her to call him Ty. As a joke, she told him to call her Ry— pronounced like "rye" to rhyme with Ty. They instantly became best friends, Ry and Ty. He never told anyone else in Haverport to call him Ty. Just Rory. A nickname only for her.

"Pretty sure your shoulders are wider than the swing," she quipped.

He chuckled as he sat down, the swing hanging low to the ground under his weight.

She laughed at how absurd he looked. "I honestly think you're going to break this thing."

"If I did, Bea would probably kill me in my sleep. She's been out here every day."

Rory smiled, thinking how, just the day before, she saw Tyler's little sister out here, swinging while she listened to music. "I know."

Tyler glanced up at Rory, his expression soft and kind. Just like the boy she'd always known. Even if he was hidden behind a massive set of muscles now.

"I've missed you, Ry."

Rory nodded, glancing down at her grubby sneakers. "Me too."

They swung back and forth in silence for a few moments, listening to the trees as a cool breeze brushed past them, golden brown leaves falling off branches from the force of the wind.

She didn't know where to go from here. She desperately wanted her friend back, especially now that she was going to be home alone even more. But how exactly were they supposed to go back to what they'd been before everything went down?

How do you win back your best friend when you know he may actually be in love with you?

Okay...*love* was a strong word. She actually had no idea if Tyler was in love with her. As far as she knew, it was just a crush. One he'd had for a very long time.

She looked up at Tyler, noticing that he was staring at her like he was trying to read what she was thinking.

He took a deep breath. "Ry, I—"

"Wait."

He stopped, his mouth closing around unspoken words.

"Gabi took another job," she confessed. "A bartending gig. She's going to be working days and nights, and I'm just going to be alone. All the time."

His face was now etched with concern. "I'm sorry."

"I don't like not talking to you," she continued. "I need my best friend in my life. These past few months have been torture."

"I know," he said, his voice lower than she'd ever heard it.

"Can we just..." She paused, hoping beyond all hope that he wouldn't be offended by what she was about to say. "Can we just forget any of it happened and move on?"

Tyler looked down at his hands, thinking it through. The seconds ticked by slowly as she waited for him, wondering if she did the wrong thing by suggesting it.

"Is that what you want?" he asked gently.

She nodded. "Yes, that's what I want."

His dark chocolate eyes wandered her face, searching for something. What, exactly? She couldn't be sure.

A blink later, his expression shifted, a smile brightening up his face. "Then we're all good, Ry."

She exhaled and tilted her head back to look at the now-darkening sky, relief flooding her chest. More silence stretched between them, but this time, it felt a little more comfortable. The kind of silence that was easy between two best friends who knew each other inside and out.

"Do you think, if he were here, that my mom would be around more?" Rory asked, her voice soft and vulnerable.

"You mean your dad?"

She nodded. When they were kids, Rory would talk to Tyler about her father—extensively. She shared what she imagined he was like, from the kind of job he had to the personality traits they shared, even down to the kind of food he probably ordered for takeout. Tyler always listened to her, dreamed with her. He knew how much Rory yearned to know the man. One who celebrated a good grade, fixed her beat-up Honda Civic she bought with her Scoops money, scolded her for coming home tipsy, looked uncomfortable when she got her period for the first time. In her head, he was the perfect dad—always attentive, always around.

But besides paying regular child support, he wasn't in her life. She didn't even know his name.

"Ry."

She glanced over at him, noticing the hand he was holding out to her. She smiled, taking it like she always did when they sat on these swings.

He squeezed it tightly. "Just because she takes these jobs does not mean she doesn't love you or doesn't want to be around. It's more like the opposite."

She nodded, brushing the tears streaming down her cheeks with her free hand.

"And you know you always have us," Ty said, cocking his head toward his house. "You're never alone. We are always here. *I* am always here."

"Promise?" she whispered.

He dipped his chin, that familiar confidence having returned as he squeezed her hand again. "I promise."

They swayed lazily, still holding hands. Her eyes seemed to have a mind of their own as they drifted to his chest again. He didn't seem to notice, his own gaze down at the football near his feet.

She cleared her throat, then pulled her hand away from his. "Practicing for the big game?"

He sighed. "Yes."

"Need an opponent?"

He looked at her with a menacing grin. "Maybe one who's a little more challenging—"

Before he could finish, Rory lunged for his football, running to her end of the lawn for a touchdown.

"Oh no you DON'T."

She heard Tyler sprinting behind her as she charged. He quickly caught up though, wrapping his strong arms around her waist as he lifted her from the ground and threw her over his shoulder, and then turned and ran in the opposite direction.

"Oh my god," she screamed, kicking her feet in protest as he carried her. "CHEATER!"

Tyler laughed as they reached his end of the lawn, dropping her down on her butt so he could celebrate his victory. He threw out his arms like an airplane and jogged around her in a circle, just like he always did when he scored a touchdown against her.

She chuckled and shook her head, feeling at peace at the sight of having Ty back in her life.

Chapter Two

"YOU NEVER CALLED LAST NIGHT."

Rory glanced over at Melanie as she shut her locker tight.

"Yeah, sorry. Tyler came over and within an hour there was no junk food left," she said. "It was like watching a human garbage disposal at work."

"Takes a lot of calories to be Haverport High's star running back," Melanie replied with a laugh. "Wait"—her eyes went wide and she tilted her head—"you and Tyler are *talking to each other?*"

Rory nodded, shifting her gaze away from her friend's inquisitive one. "Yeah, we're, um, all good now."

"Okay but..." Melanie started, then hesitated. "Did you guys talk about, like...the fact that he *likes* you?"

"Uhhh, not exactly." She opened her locker back up and shuffled things around for no particular reason. "I just kind of told him I wanted to forget everything that happened and go back to how things were."

Melanie frowned. "Can he even do that? Can *you* even do that?"

Could she? "Everything seemed fine last night."

Melanie tapped an index finger to her cheek. "Interesting."

She closed her locker once more and pointed to Melanie's jeans, desperate to change the subject. "Miss Mel, do I see a rip in the jeans you are wearing today?"

Melanie sighed. "Unfortunately, yes. They got caught in my bike gears the other night riding home from Calvin's."

"He made you bike home? God, he's getting lazy."

She rolled her eyes playfully. "Noooo, he just needed to study for a test, and I left so he wouldn't have any distractions."

She wiggled her brows. "Too much of a distraction then, huh?"

Melanie blushed. "Oh, shove it."

She laughed. Never in a million years did Rory think someone might actually be interested in Calvin. He was the guy everyone loved to hate at work—always bossing people around, treating every aspect of the job like it was the damn military. Sure, it made sense why he was the way he was; Ron Parsons, the owner of Scoops, was Calvin's only father figure. Hence why Calvin made the decision to take over Scoops from him someday. But still—was refilling hot fudge canisters or having enough homemade waffle cones really a matter of life or death?

All it had taken was Melanie moving to town for Calvin to become a whole new guy. His goofy side made a surprise appearance every once in a while, and he could not keep his hands off the girl. It was sickening sometimes; she and the rest of the Scoopers had to constantly yell at them to knock it off or kick them out of the tiny bathroom in the back of The War Room where they would meet to makeout between shifts.

Rory took her friend in for a moment, noticing how much Melanie had changed since she'd first met her back in May. Gone were the preppy clothes and the perfectly straightened hair. Haverport seemed to have taken hold of her; she now sported a pair of baggy light-washed jeans, a big knit cardigan over a flowy white tank top, and a pair of chunky sandals. Her beachy waves were held back by an elastic blue headband, and the faint glow of a tan still lingered on her skin.

Melanie frowned. "What?"

Rory shrugged. "You just look like you belong here now."

Melanie gave her a shy smile, her eyes starting to mist over. "Yeah?"

Rory pummeled her in a fierce hug. She still didn't know how to talk to Melanie about the fact that Duncan was gone—an event that'd undoubtedly and irrevocably changed her friend's life. It had been clear to most people over the span of the previous summer that Duncan had a drinking problem, but the fact that he was taken so soon because of it? It just didn't seem fair.

She wanted to say something to Melanie, something comforting or encouraging. But she couldn't string together the right words, so she just hugged her tightly, ignoring the bustle from students heading to their homerooms.

Rory felt her phone buzz in her back pocket. She pulled away slightly, using the back of her sweatshirt sleeve to wipe away the tears on her friend's cheeks before reaching for her phone. She swiped open the screen to a text message.

JAY

Hi

Rory's stomach dropped.

"What?" Melanie asked, sniffling. "Who is it?"

She didn't say anything, just turned the phone so she could read it.

Her brow furrowed. "That's...odd."

"No kidding," Rory huffed.

"Have you guys talked at all since—"

"The day he shouted for all to hear that Tyler has a crush on me? Nope, not a lick."

"Weird," Melanie said. "Did you guys ever text before the—um, you know..."

"No, never," Rory said. "I'd try to get him to, but he always gave me some dumb excuse, like how he's horrible at texting or he didn't see it or whatever else."

"Well, clearly he's not so horrible at it now."

Rory stared down at the single word. Jay was three months into his freshman year at the University of Connecticut, and no one from Scoops had heard from him yet. He just up and left at the end of the summer, leaving all of them in the dust. Leaving her without saying a proper goodbye.

Not like she deserved one—they were never an item or anything. Even though she fantasized about it pretty much every day since meeting him during her first shift two years ago.

"What do you think it means?" Melanie asked.

Rory felt herself get flustered. "I—god, I have no idea."

"What are you two staring at?"

The two of them jumped at Tyler's sudden appearance. He was wearing his football jersey, just like the rest of the team did for Friday football games. And tonight was a *big* one—the game that could qualify Haverport High for the state championship. And, to top it all off, it was Homecoming.

With Tyler's huge frame towering over them, Rory almost didn't notice Blake stealthily creep up to her side and try to peek at her phone.

She quickly switched the screen off, then shoved it back into her pocket. "Oh, nothing, just a silly TikTok."

"But how silly?" Blake asked. "Gimme, I'll be the judge of that."

"No." Her face heated. "Only girls would really understand it."

"Why?"

"It's about vaginas."

Melanie laughed out loud, causing a few heads to turn toward them in the hallway.

Blake winced. "Yep, pass."

Tyler leaned in, looking slightly uncomfortable. "Can you guys *please* not scream about vaginas so early in the morning?" he whispered.

"Aww, does someone think his rowdy, inappropriate friends are going to cause him to lose votes for Homecoming King?" Rory teased.

Tyler shook his head. "No, stop—"

"Wait, you call that screaming?" Blake asked. "I mean, I could show you screaming."

"Vaginas," Melanie said instantly, her voice steady, her eyes dancing with mischief.

"Vaginas," Blake said louder, causing a few more heads to turn.

Rory inhaled dramatically, eyes dead set on Tyler. "VAG—"

Tyler lunged for her, throwing his hand over her mouth, his palm practically covering her entire face. Melanie and Blake burst out laughing as a teacher approached them, telling them to lower their voices.

Rory tried biting Tyler's hand as he pulled away. He shook his head at her. "You're a menace sometimes, you know that?"

She grinned. "Menace is my middle name."

The warning bell rang, signaling them to get to their homerooms.

Tyler started backing away from the group. "See you guys tonight?"

"Wouldn't miss it!" Melanie cheered.

"I'll be the one in navy!" Rory quipped.

"Aren't we all supposed to wear navy?" Blake asked, looking confused.

"That's why it's funny, Blakey-boy."

Blake frowned. "I don't get it."

"And that's why I didn't show you the silly vagina TikTok—you never understand my humor," she teased, meeting Melanie's eyes and sharing a grin with her.

Blake shook his head as he walked away from them. "You are a strange, strange human."

Once Blake was out of earshot, Melanie placed her hands on Rory's shoulders. "Update me on this little situation at lunch?"

Her stomach twisted, realizing she still hadn't responded to Jay. What were you even supposed to say to an out-of-the-blue *Hi?* Who did that?

"If I have an update by then," she responded.

"And I think you now owe me a sleepover."

"Oh, trust me..." She pulled her backpack over her shoulder. "There will be *plenty* of opportunities for sleepovers now. Gabi picked up another job, so I'll constantly be in an empty house. Want to come over, I don't know, every night?"

"Don't tempt me."

The second bell rang, letting them know they were both sufficiently late for homeroom.

"Look at you," Rory teased. "New wardrobe, no AP classes, getting in trouble with a teacher, late for class. Who are you, and what have you done with Melanie Albertson?"

Melanie cocked her head as she backed away, that grin still on her face. "She moved to Haverport."

JAY

Does this mean we're still ignoring each other?

RORY SAT down on the metal bench next to the high school's soccer field, drenched head to toe in sweat. It was the second to last practice before their final game next week, and this one was especially brutal. Coach Konicki had them run their winning plays over and over again, and by the end of it, her legs felt like goo.

She huffed, grabbed her water bottle out of her bag, and squirted the top of her head. She had yet to respond to Jay, going back and forth on what to say to him. Would a simple "hi" back be enough? Or was it alright to jump right in and tell him off about how angry she was that he left Haverport without saying goodbye?

She looked down at her screen and decided to be cordial. At least...for now.

RORY

Sorry, been busy

Hi back. How's college?

Rory sat there and watched the little gray dots dancing.

JAY

Fine

How was the last day at Scoops?

She shook her head. He left the way he did, yet he actually wanted to know how things were going? It didn't make sense. He was always the one complaining at work about how much he hated it and that he wasn't making enough.

RORY

Don't tell me you actually care

JAY

I do care!

RORY

Sure didn't seem like it when you left
without saying goodbye

She couldn't help herself. He made her *angry*—especially when it really didn't seem like he cared about any of them.

JAY

Can't a man admit that he was wrong?

She shook her head as she typed back.

RORY

That's not on brand for you

JAY

Then consider me rebranded!

Before she could type her response, another text came in. She scanned it, then felt like she couldn't breathe.

JAY

I miss you

She stared at her screen, completely shocked. He...*missed her?* It was hands down the most intimate thing Jay had ever said to her, the closest he'd ever come to expressing some kind of emotion beyond his usual cocky arrogance. While there were a few moments Rory did witness a crack in his facade, it was always gone in a flash—a wall he clearly put up around others to hide whatever was actually going on in that thick, thick head of his.

Yet now, here he was, telling her he missed her.

Rory heard the squeaking of cleats as the rest of her team approached from the field. She switched off her phone and tossed it in her bag, wishing she could go back to answering a text that simply said "hi" instead of figuring out how to approach this massive bomb Jay just dropped on her.

"So who do you think is going to win tonight?" Kayla asked as she plopped down on the bench.

"Haverport," Rory said confidently. Even if they were playing Garrison Prep, who were notorious for having the best teams in the state, tonight's game was a shoo-in. Especially with Tyler out on the field.

"Not the *game*," Kayla teased. "Who do you think is going to be crowned queen?"

Rory rolled her eyes as her teammates burst into a lively debate about which of the school's popular girls was going to be elected for the coveted spot.

"I think Penelope's got it," Kayla said, untying her cleats. "That girl has every single teacher wrapped around her finger."

"Yeah, but so many students hate her," Gina retorted. "Just because she's the class president doesn't mean she's going to win the popular vote. I say Rhianne."

"No way," interjected Helen before taking a swig of her water bottle, the rest of the team collectively waiting with bated breath. "Guys, come on, it's going to be Zoe."

Rory listened to her teammates murmur their approval. Zoe Clark was Haverport High's "it" girl. Cheerleading captain. First selectman's daughter. Tall. Blonde. Absolutely stunning.

But above everything else, Zoe was known for always being the kindest person in the room. With that kind of power, she could be whoever she wanted.

Rory detested her.

"Do you guys think Tyler will get king?" Gina asked.

Rory perked up, leaning in slightly as she listened.

"Against Walker? I don't know, I feel like he doesn't have a chance," Kayla said.

Rory frowned. "Why not?"

Kayla shrugged. "Walker has always been the golden boy. Just because Tyler was made captain and is having an incredible football season doesn't exactly mean he's going to win."

Helen rolled her eyes, tossing her cleats in her bag.

Rory scoffed. "That's ridiculous. Tyler is ten times the person Walker is. And he isn't just having a good season— he's single-handedly *carrying* that team to victory."

Kayla raised her arms in defense. "Not saying he isn't. He's just not that popular, you know?"

Rory pursed her lips. It seemed unfair that Tyler wouldn't get the recognition he deserved because of some popularity contest. Walker may be the quarterback and the team's second captain, but he certainly wasn't as nice or hard-working as Tyler. He'd had everything handed to him on a silver platter...like his scholarship to play football for Auburn next fall, the same university where his father happened to be on the Board of Trustees.

But Tyler, who was *always* in the backyard working on his technique, always the first one to show up at practice and the last one to leave? He deserved to be Homecoming King, deserved a shot at playing college football—something she knew he'd wanted his whole life.

She knew he'd need to be offered a scholarship, which meant a recruiter would have to come watch him play. For some ridiculous reason that made no sense to her, not a single one paid a visit to their school. And with the season coming to an end and college application deadlines getting closer and closer, it seemed to her that Tyler might be running out of time.

Chapter Three

Rory's leg bounced as Calvin inched his truck through the line of cars, trying—and failing—to find a place to park.

"Seriously, just park over there on the side," she said, pointing to an empty patch of dirt next to the lot. "No one cares right now."

"I could get a ticket," Calvin said, voice firm.

She rolled her eyes. "Is it physically impossible for you to break the rules?"

"Yes," Melanie said, a smile on her face.

"*Of course* you would like that," she mumbled. "The game starts in five minutes; we're going to miss kickoff."

Calvin stopped the car abruptly. "Get out and get us seats. I'll keep looking for a spot."

Blake threw open the door and hopped out of the truck, not needing to be told twice. Rory grabbed Melanie's arm and pulled her away from the unnecessarily long smooch Calvin was giving her.

In a small town like Haverport, there really wasn't much else to do this time of year. Here, everyone lived for the summer. Between Memorial Day and Labor Day, the town population practically tripled in size as all of the "summer people" inundated the Port for a vacation by the beach, renting out any available cottages and cramming the public beaches with coolers and beach chairs and plastic buckets. The townies call it their "busy season," given the profit turnover—Gabi's words, not hers—that small businesses made between May and September compared to the rest of the year. Some were even able to take an extended break during the off-season, or in the case of Scoops—and to Rory's dismay—the entire winter.

As the last of the summer people left and everything slowed down, the people of Haverport turned their attention to the next big thing: Friday night football games. It was a well-known fact that you would run into everyone you knew at a game; it was just the thing the townies did on Fridays, even if the team absolutely sucked.

Which, of course, wasn't the case this year. Everything *felt* different. The energy in the stadium tonight was electric; fans were buzzing with anticipation. Rory glanced up at the sea of navy, white, and hints of gold in the stands, everyone there to cheer on their boys to a promising victory. Haverport High hadn't been in the running for the state championship in over fifty years, and if they actually won, it would be their first championship win ever.

She linked arms with Melanie and Blake as they zigzagged their way through the crowd. The line at the concession stand was already astronomical—the heavenly smells of salty fries and sugary funnel cakes causing Blake to drift from Rory's grasp. She held on to him firmly, dragging him past that stand and the pop-up booth where students submitted last-minute votes for Homecoming King and Queen.

"Do you think there's a chance he'll win?" Melanie asked.

Rory sighed. "I really hope so."

She groaned when they came to another traffic jam. "We're never going to find a spot."

"Melanie! Blake! Rory!"

The three of them looked up toward the top of the stands and found Dan and Jan Fletcher waving furiously at them. Dan gestured toward some vacant seats at his side, as if they were waiting for them to show up. Rory followed Melanie and Blake as they climbed to the top, each of them getting barreled into a bear hug from Jan, who was matching Dan in Haverport crew-neck sweatshirts. They were dipped in blue tie-dye that matched the sea of navy in the stands flawlessly.

"Did you kids eat?" Jan asked, opening up a cooler next to her. It was stuffed with cream sodas and peanut butter and jam sandwiches, probably made with the coveted homemade jam the Fletchers sold at the farmer's market during summer.

"Wow, you guys came prepared," Rory said, taking the sandwich Jan handed her.

"We've been here for a couple of hours," Dan said proudly. "We're going to be state champs!"

The crowd around them cheered loudly as Dan fist-pumped the air.

Rory settled down next to Melanie, who was already unwrapping a sandwich on her lap. "Okay, I have to ask," Melanie started, pointing to Rory's head. "Why do you always wear that bright green bandana to the games?"

She touched it proudly, a smile creeping onto her face. The rest of her outfit matched the colors of their team— navy-blue Haverport crew neck, white jeans, and the number *17* painted obnoxiously on both cheeks. But the bandana stuck out like a sore thumb...which was kind of the point.

"So he can find me," said Rory. "I've worn it to every single one of his football games."

"But doesn't he know you're here?"

"Well, duh, I would never miss a game," she responded. "But there was this one game in eighth grade when they finally let him start as running back. He was really nervous, so I told him anytime he felt that way to look up in the stands and find my green bandana, and know that he's not alone."

"That's fucking cute," Blake said.

She grinned. "Blake, I love it when you swear."

He flushed. "Again, you're strange."

"That really is cute though," Melanie said. "It's almost like you guys were meant—"

Ding.

Rory swiped her phone from her back pocket at rocket speed, wondering if it was another text from him.

It was.

He sent a picture of two plastic spoons on a table.

JAY

Come fight me!

"Oh, right. I almost forgot," Melanie whispered next to her. She leaned in, looking at the string of messages on Rory's screen. "Hold up, did he say he—?"

Rory flipped her phone over quickly. "You didn't see anything."

Melanie's mouth fell open. "He said he *misses you*."

"Who misses you?" Blake asked.

"No one," Rory said flatly, turning her attention to the

team now spilling out across the field, the crowd screaming as the players jogged to the center for a quick huddle. Rory scanned the navy jerseys for number 17, but it didn't take long to find him. He was dead center, hyping the team up in a chant with a massive grin on his face, the whites of his teeth gleaming under the bright stadium lights.

"God, he's going to miss this," she said.

"I'm not done with you," Melanie said, tugging on her sleeve. "Want to tell me what's going on?"

Calvin came bounding up the metal stands, hugging Dan and Jan before tucking in between Melanie and Blake.

Saved by the bell, she thought. "We'll talk later," Rory murmured.

But truthfully, she hoped Melanie would just drop it. Apparently, Jay missed her. So much so that he was texting her constantly to get her attention. She...loved it. Loved that he was finally paying attention to her. And yet...she had no idea what to say.

THE TEAMS WERE neck and neck by the time they reached halftime. Rory watched as Tyler kept encouraging his team-mates in between plays, patting them on their backs and likely saying something inspiring that had his teammates nodding their heads and cheering along with him.

He was a good captain. A natural-born leader. If her peers couldn't see that, if they really wanted to vote for someone like Walker—who was currently stomping around on the sidelines and arguing with the assistant coach—to be their Homecoming King, then good riddance. Rory didn't want to associate with a town that couldn't see something good when it was right in front of them.

The referee blew the whistle, and the players sprung to action. She watched as Tyler jogged up to Walker as they headed back onto the field. He reached for Walker's shoulder, but Walker shoved him off, clearly still riled up from whatever conversation he just had with the coach.

Tyler's shoulders sagged. He then turned to the crowd, his gaze scanning the stands above them. She watched as he finally froze, his eyes set on where she sat. She stood up in her seat, just in case he couldn't see her properly.

If she wasn't mistaken, a grin pulled on the corner of those lips underneath his bulky helmet. Tyler lifted his arm and pointed in her direction, causing a few people in the stands to look over at her with curiosity painted plainly on their faces.

Rory turned slightly, her eyes still on him as she lifted her arms, holding an imaginary football. She "threw it" in his direction, watching as he jumped and caught the invisible ball in his gloved hands. A few people laughed and cheered at the gesture as Tyler returned to his team, setting himself up for their first play of the third quarter.

She plopped back down in her seat next to Melanie. "And *that's* why I wear the bandana."

The marching band blasted the school fight song, the crowd going wild as they sang along, pouring all their energy and hope to the field below and hoping beyond hope that it could give them a little luck. That the 14-14 score glowering down on them from the board across the field would miraculously change, that those numbers would look a lot more promising with just a few more dazzling plays.

The cheerleaders danced along with the song, their gold pom-poms glistening beneath the stadium lights. Zoe Clark stood at the center, her perfectly curled blonde ponytail bouncing with each peppy move.

Walker stood at the center as the boys lined up, yelling a few commands at the team. Tyler stepped a few paces back, bouncing slightly on his feet as he waited for Walker to finally scream "*HIKE!*"

Walker held the ball briefly, his gaze focused on Tyler who was sprinting to the right, dodging past a defenseman from Garrison before reaching the other side of the field. Walker pulled his arm back and threw the ball, and Tyler jumped and caught it with his left hand.

The crowd went *nuts*. Rory stood up and screamed as Tyler tucked the football under his arm, holding it tightly as he charged past the 30-yard line, then the 20-yard line, before getting tackled at the 15.

The band started blasting again, the cheerleaders chanting as the boys huddled together to chat through the next play. Rory sat back down, her leg bouncing at the anticipation of it all.

Melanie patted her knee. "He's got this, no question about it."

"I can't imagine how he's feeling right now," she said. "The pressure is killing *me* and I'm not even out there."

"Tyler is so chill though," Blake said. "He never loses his cool."

Rory's mind flashed to the night of the party that summer, at the fierce way Tyler had pulled her into his Jeep, shoving a water bottle at her chest. "I beg to differ," Rory mumbled.

She noticed Calvin studying her briefly, almost like he was trying to read her mind. She glared at him before turning her attention back to the field, watching as the boys lined up at the 15-yard mark. Tyler was now heading for the side of the field closest to the stands and the cheerleaders, setting up in a runner's position.

The cheerleaders were about finished with their cheer, briefly stepping into one of their stunts. Zoe was at the center again, bracing herself on the shoulders of her two squad mates before getting hoisted up into a hold. They held on to her ankles firmly as she stood at the top of the pyramid, waving her pom-poms and hyping up the crowd. She lifted a leg and turned into an arabesque. But before she could shift and stick the landing, one of her base's knees gave out, his body slowly crumbling to the ground.

Fans gasped as Zoe fell back. Tyler sprinted from his spot, the ref whistling furiously at his early start. Only he wasn't running down the field but a few feet off it as he beelined for the cheerleading squad, lifting his arms out and catching Zoe before she could hit the ground.

Rory watched in stunned silence as the crowd went absolutely apeshit. She stood alongside the other Scoopers to get a closer look, watching Tyler on his knees as he held Zoe. He was speaking to her as he got to his feet, Zoe still cradled tightly in his arms. She looked panicked for a moment as she glanced up at Tyler, but he gave her a reassuring smile, saying something else that had her visibly relaxing. Then she flashed a huge grin to the stands and waved, letting them all know that she was okay. Everyone was chanting "TY-LER CHAP-MAN" like he was their hero.

Rory realized how tightly she was holding her breath. Zoe fit perfectly in his arms, the two of them a shiny spectacle on the field.

"Well, there's no question about it now," Blake said. "We're about to lose him to royalty."

Chapter Four

Haverport won the game. Of course they did, right? After a moment like that, where the football captain catches the damsel-in-distress cheerleader falling from the sky? If high school were a test, this kind of cliché outcome would earn an A+.

And all the while, Rory was forced to sit in the bleachers and watch.

She kept the facade up throughout the rest of the game, cheering as Tyler immediately scored another touchdown, even after his five-yard penalty for running early to catch Zoe. Haverport was able to hold off Garrison's offense for the rest of the game, almost as if the team had some kind of collective jolt of energy making them downright unbeatable on the field. Then, in the last quarter, with just thirty seconds left, Tyler faked a play as Walker darted from behind the line of scrimmage. Tyler defended his run, blocking any player from getting to Walker so his teammate could score the winning touchdown.

Everyone in the stands went nuts—*again*—screaming and blowing air horns and dancing to the marching band's songs. Rory clapped her hands and hollered like everyone else, but inside, she didn't feel like celebrating. Especially as she watched Tyler like a hawk as he ran past the cheerleaders. He lifted Zoe around the waist with his right arm, spinning her in a hug before returning back to the team.

High school, she thought bitterly. The story was just writing itself.

She *should* be happy for him. Wasn't she just moments ago thinking that Tyler deserved this kind of recognition and praise? Yet she couldn't shake the nausea roiling in her stomach and the bitter taste filling her mouth.

It's really not a big deal, she tried telling herself. *This will all blow over.*

After the teams lined up to shake hands and the marching band blared their final few songs of the evening, everyone in the stands cheered as they watched Penelope Fairweather strut onto the field, clutching a microphone. It was tradition for the senior class president to announce the Homecoming King and Queen—even if she was the one to win herself. Which, if Rory read Penelope's tight and cordial smile correctly, it seemed Madam President wouldn't be taking the crown.

"Haverport High, it's the moment you've all been waiting for!"

Cheers exploded in the stands. Rory clapped as the football team line up behind Penelope. Tyler was laughing at something his teammate just said to him, looking elated after their win.

"It was a tight, tight race this year," Penelope said. "But after an...*influx* of last-minute votes," she continued, her words blanketed with subtle resentment, "we were able to determine a clear winner for this year's Homecoming Queen and King."

The crowd silenced as they watched Penelope dramatically open a navy-blue envelope like it was an award show. Rory rolled her eyes.

"This year's Homecoming Queen is..." A sigh broke up her speech. "Zoe Clark."

Everyone whooped and howled as Zoe nodded and gave her sweet-like-honey smile. One of her squad mates reached over and removed the white bow in her hair to make room for the tiara a quivering freshman delivered. She graciously let the girl place the tiara on her head, her ponytail bouncing playfully as she stood up and twirled for the crowd.

"And now, our king," Penelope said, her words cutting off the *oohing* and *aahing*. "And this year's Homecoming King is...Tyler Chapman!"

Rory didn't think it was possible for everyone in the stands to scream louder than they did when they won the game...but she was wrong. The sound that came from the crowd was like the roar of a beast, their movements just as wild. She screamed along with them, holding so much pride in her heart.

Tyler's jaw dropped slightly at this turn of events. A few of his teammates slapped his back and pushed him forward to receive the gaudy crown now heading his way. On the other side of the line, Walker crossed his arms, his face stony.

But any joyful feelings faded away as she watched Tyler and Zoe in their sparkly crowns join hands and lift them up to the stands. Rory's stomach turned further when Tyler leaned over and whispered something in her ear. She nodded at whatever he said, and in a swift movement, Tyler knelt down so Zoe could get on his shoulders. She raised her arms in triumph as he stood back up, his grin infectious.

They were stunning together.

It made Rory want to vomit.

She felt an elbow dig into her side. "Hey, you okay?" asked her friend.

She turned and grinned. "Oh yeah, so happy. He won!"

"Okayyy," Melanie responded. "Just seemed like you were upset there for a minute."

She scoffed. "Upset? No way! He deserves it."

Melanie furrowed her brow. "Hmm, alright."

She ignored Melanie's curious gaze as they descended from the stands. The Scoopers said their goodbyes to Dan and Jan and waited for Tyler at the side of the field. He kept having to fix his crown from how often he dipped to his new queen's level as they carried on a conversation—oblivious to their rabid fans. At one point, he threw his head back and laughed, the piece of hard plastic falling off his head. A tall middle-aged man with slicked-back gray hair and navy-blue slacks caught it in mid-air. But it was the smile plastered on the man's face that Rory would recognize anywhere.

Zoe's dad, Garner Clark, the first selectman of Haverport, reached his hand out for Tyler to shake. Rory and the Scoopers stood at least thirty yards away, the townies' loud chants drowning out any chance she had at eavesdropping on whatever Mr. Clark was telling Tyler, who stood there listening with a toothy grin, nodding profusely. Zoe stood close enough to Tyler that her arm was grazing his, the small amount of contact causing Rory's head to spin.

"Is Tyler about to get...too popular for us?" Blake joked.

"I'd beat him up before I let that happen," Rory deadpanned.

"I honestly would love to watch you try," Calvin said.

Just then, Tyler said his goodbyes to Zoe and Mr. Clark, Zoe giving him one last smile over her shoulder as she followed her father off the field. Tyler's gaze lingered on her before he turned to the Scoopers and grinned, holding out his arms.

Rory bolted in his direction. She jumped, flinging her arms around his shoulders, Blake and Melanie at her heels as they huddled into a group hug. Calvin stepped to the side and patted Tyler's back.

"Alright, guys, back it up, back it up," Blake said, breaking away from the group. "He's a *king* now, he can't be seen with us peasants."

Tyler chuckled, placing Rory down gently before reaching to touch the crown on his head. "It's all a little silly," he said, glancing down at her. "Don't you think?"

Yes, she thought to herself. But she couldn't bring herself to say it, not with that innocent boy-like look he was giving her. So she just shook her head. "No, you deserve it."

"That catch, man!" Blake said. "That was crazy. She was just falling out of the sky and *BAM*, you were there."

Worry lined Tyler's eyes. "She could have been really hurt."

Desperate to change the subject, Rory snatched Tyler's crown off his head and placed it on her own. "Shall we take the king out for pizza?"

Tyler groaned. "Yes, please, I'm starving." Rory saw him shift slightly, trying to steal his crown back, but she was too quick for him as she ducked and weaved.

"Meet us at Penny's when you're done?" Calvin asked.

Tyler nodded, taking a step back like he was going to leave. But quick as lightning, he jumped, throwing an arm around her and snatching the crown off her head.

"Oh my god, Ty, you *reek*. Get off me!"

He chuckled, tugging on her green bandana before letting her go. "That's what you get for being a menace, Ry."

She shook her head, reluctant to follow the group back to Calvin's truck as she watched Tyler jog up toward the school, holding his helmet in one hand and his sparkly crown in the other.

Rory was taking the first bite of her slice when she saw him approaching Penny's Pizzeria, cleaned up and wearing his letterman jacket. When he stepped into the shop, everyone cheered. Tyler grinned, his eyes wide, clearly shocked by the attention people in town were giving him. He waved and shook hands with townies like he was a movie star before approaching their table, tucking in right next to her.

She frowned. "Where's your crown?"

"Locked in the treasury so little menaces can't steal it," he joked, reaching to steal the slice out of her grasp.

She swatted his hand away. "Mine. Get your own."

Tyler frowned. "But the line is so long. And I'm about to eat my hand I'm so hungry."

"If you had your crown they probably would let you skip the line, Mr. Homecoming King," Rory said.

He shook his head. "I would never skip the line."

"Tyler Chapman?"

All the Scoopers looked up from their table at Penny herself, holding a pizza plate in her hand. The diners around them quieted their chatter, eager to listen in.

"That's me," Tyler said, grinning again. He was grinning a lot tonight. Being popular must be exhausting.

"I just wanted to say, on behalf of Haverport, thanks for

being so good at football," Penny started. The entire shop cheered again. "And here's a pie, on the house."

Rory snorted as Penny placed the pepperoni pizza down at their table in all its cheesy, greasy glory.

Tyler gave his thanks to Penny as Rory reached in for a slice. Without even glancing at her, he swatted at her hand. "Mine. Get your own."

"You're not going to share *one* slice?"

Blake frowned. "Yeah, man, share the love."

"Here, you can have my second slice," Melanie said. "Let him have his pizza. I mean, you did say he was a human garbage disposal these days."

Tyler laughed at that before digging in, half of his first slice gone in one bite.

"I still can't believe you guys beat Garrison," Melanie said. "They made it to State every year I lived there. I think this is the first time in decades they've been booted out of the running."

"So you're basically saying you're the good luck charm," Rory said.

"Sure, that's right, you can hang this victory on me. Not the fact that Tyler kicked their ass," she joked. Calvin chuckled softly, sliding an arm around her waist and kissing her temple.

Rory beamed. "I love when my friends swear."

"It was a team effort," Tyler mumbled, a mouthful of pizza. He was already reaching for his third slice.

She rolled her eyes. "Don't be modest. There's no way they would have won that game without you. They'll be back to being absolutely horrible when you're gone next year."

Tyler frowned. "That's depressing. I hope not."

"Who are you playing at State?" Calvin asked.

"Westford," Tyler replied. "They have a much stronger defense than us. It's going to be a tough game."

She elbowed his side softly. "You can do it."

He smiled down at her. "I hope so, Ry."

His phone dinged on the table between them. She glanced down at it without thinking, noticing it was a text from an unsaved number. Tyler reached for it, hiding the phone underneath the table as he swiped on the screen. She watched as he smiled at whatever it was. Her stomach turned at the sight.

"Who is it?" she asked, leaning in to see the text, but Tyler just brushed her off.

"No one," he shrugged. He slid his phone into his pocket before reaching for yet another slice.

He was clearly hiding something from her, and she hated it. But if he was going to act this way...then fine. Two could play at that game.

Rory grabbed for her own phone and opened up her texts. She turned away from the others and started typing.

RORY

We both know you lose to my spoon-fighting skills every time

Then, after a deep breath, she sent another one.

RORY

And I miss you too

Chapter Five

Rory stumbled down the stairs and made her way to the coffee pot in a zombie-like shuffle. She slept...horribly. Images of Tyler and Zoe kept flashing in her head. Him catching her; the way she smiled in his arms when he comforted her; their bright, shining faces with Zoe perched on his shoulders.

She hated that it bothered her so much, because it shouldn't. They were supposed to be best friends, and she was supposed to be supportive of his happiness. She wasn't supposed to feel dread or jealousy. Maybe she was just being overprotective? She wondered if that was it—that she was worried the guy who was practically her brother was going to get hurt. That he was going to lose sight of every thing he worked so hard for.

Yeah...that made more sense.

"Looks like it was quite the game last night," Gabi said behind her.

Rory frowned and turned from the pot, burning her tongue as she took a greedy first sip of her coffee.

Gabi placed her copy of the *Haverport Courier* onto the counter, pointing to the image on the front page.

Her stomach dropped when she saw the image—actually, dual images, side by side. One with Tyler holding Zoe in his arms after catching her, the other one of her on his shoulders, crowns balanced on both their heads. The headline in big, bold letters almost made Rory spit out her second sip.

Chapman Catches the Crown!

"Jesus," Rory mumbled to herself. "This nightmare never ends."

"I didn't even know we won the game until the third paragraph," Gabi said. "The reporter is a lot more interested in Tyler's little act of chivalry."

"Probably because it's uncommon these days for a high school boy to do something nice rather than think of himself and his dic—"

"*Rory!*"

She smirked, taking a sip of her coffee. "Come on, you know I'm not wrong."

Gabi rolled her eyes, shoving the paper aside. "How late were you out last night? You look like hell."

You don't know the half of it, she thought. "Midnight. We went out for pizza."

"But you slept till ten? You're not lying to me, are you?"

She shook her head. Sure, she'd lied to Gabi a handful of times in the past about parties. But she hadn't been to any since that summer. Since everything happened with Tyler and Jay. And Duncan.

Drinking alcohol just didn't seem to have the same appeal anymore.

"No, just couldn't fall asleep," Rory admitted. "Was up...texting all night."

Gabi smirked. "Texting, huh? Texting who?"

This also wasn't a lie. She couldn't fall asleep, sure, but part of it was the fact that Jay started bullet-texting her after she told him she missed him as well. When it hit four in the morning and he was still texting her, she pretended to have fallen asleep and turned off her phone.

For someone who normally "doesn't text," he was texting her an absurd amount. They texted about college and his classes, about Haverport and closing down Scoops for the season. She mentioned the game but only in passing, changing the subject back to Jay and his female conquests. Which, it turned out, were few and far between—an oddity for Jay. He was always the flirty one, an outright player who constantly gave out free ice cream cones in exchange for phone numbers or a peek down the front of a low-cut shirt. But apparently, College Jay didn't play the same game, and was far more interested in texting Rory on a Friday night instead. And flirting with her. Heavily.

She quickly thought back to his last few texts, the ones that led to her calling it a night.

JAY

My bed is soooo big. Wish you were here with me.

RORY

There's actually room in there with that massive head of yours?

JAY

Which head ;)

If he hadn't been clear before, he certainly was now. For some reason, he wanted her. It was something she'd imagined for so long, what it would be like to *be* with Jay. So why, when she finally had it within her reach, was it making her feel like acid was eating at her stomach?

"Melanie," Rory lied. "She's, you know, still sad and stuff." She felt terrible for using her friend's grief to get her out of a tight spot, but something told her she wouldn't mind.

Gabi nodded, her face turning serious and making her feel even worse. "Makes sense. You never had her over the other night."

"I know. I will at some point," assured Rory.

"Not on a school night though, okay? That was a one-time thing."

She frowned. "And how would you stop me if you're never around?"

Gabi rolled her lips at that but didn't respond. Rory didn't hide her smug expression as she took a sip of coffee.

"Your last soccer game...it's next Saturday, right?"

The smug expression melted off her face. "I, uh, didn't think you'd remember."

"Sweetie, it's marked on the calendar," she said, pointing to the paper calendar Gabi insisted on using to communicate their schedules.

She did write in all of her soccer games, hoping deep

down that Gabi might show up at one. She hadn't yet, of course.

But maybe this time...

"Are you going to come?" Rory blurted, then winced. She had to rein it in. She didn't want her excitement about receiving a smidgen of her mother's attention known.

"I do have a shift at the diner that day," Gabi answered.

Her chest fell.

"But...I was thinking of asking for it off, if you want me to come?"

She schooled her expression, feigning nonchalance. "Could be cool, I guess."

Gabi smirked. "*Cool*, then I'll see what I can do."

She lifted her mug to her face, trying to hide the smile stretching across her lips. She couldn't help but expect disappointment when it came to Gabi. At this point, she welcomed the pain like an old friend.

But maybe this time, she thought, *maybe* this *time she'll prove me wrong.*

HER LACK of response the night before didn't stop Jay from texting her nonstop.

It was eleven, and Gabi was still out bartending. The house was dark, but she was wide awake, lying in her bed. She sighed and flicked on the twinkling lights that weaved through the pictures she'd printed and hung above her bed. All images from the summer before—her and her friends by the beach, at the bonfire after Haverfest, parties, random pictures taken during slow shifts. She also hung up a few of the random sketches she'd doodled during classes, like her favorite Disney-movie moments or ice cream melting off cones. She enjoyed drawing but would never call herself an *artist*. Her drawings weren't nearly as good as what some came up with, especially not the animators who created her favorite Disney and Studio Ghibli films. *Those* people, she admired.

Her phone dinged again. Then again.

JAY

You better not have fallen asleep on me.

Seriously, Rory. You can't leave me hanging.

She rolled her eyes.

RORY

You know, you're getting really needy. I may need to cut you off.

JAY

Please don't do that. I need you.

Her fingers trembled as she held her phone. He...*needed* her? How was she supposed to respond to that?

Changing the subject seemed like the best option.

RORY

Come hang out with us at State and watch Tyler cream everyone.

JAY

Does "us" include Calvin?

RORY

Yes, he and Melanie are a package deal these days.

JAY

Eye roll

RORY

He's gotten…better. Not as much of an ass hat.

JAY

He will always be an ass hat

Rory laughed at that, shaking her head as she watched Jay's typing bubble bob on her screen.

JAY

State is too far away. I can't wait that long. Come visit me next weekend.

Rory sucked in a breath. Could she do that? She closed her eyes and tried to picture the paper calendar hanging in the kitchen downstairs, suddenly remembering the soccer game.

RORY

Can't, soccer. When will you be home next?

JAY

Thanksgiving. We're supposed to travel and see Abuelita. But maybe I'll come early and surprise you. ;)

RORY

It's not exactly a surprise if you tell me about it, you know

JAY

Okay but you don't know HOW I'll surprise you. It'll be epic.

Her phone dinged again, but this time, a different banner popped up at the top of her phone. It was from Tyler. She tapped it immediately.

TYLER

Doom-scrolling again, Ry? I see those lights on. Go to bed.

Rory smiled, sitting up in her bed and glancing out the window. Tyler's room was across from hers, their windows facing one another. His room was also dark, but she saw the brightness of a phone screen through his open curtains.

She leaned back and texted.

RORY

I'm not doom-scrolling. I'm happy-scrolling.

It was a lie. But what Tyler didn't know wouldn't hurt him. Right?

TYLER

No such thing. All social media is doomed.

RORY

Cynic. I actually love watching girls show off their fake lives on Instagram.

TYLER

Sounds like the definition of hell.

She shook her head, wondering what *he* was doing up. He was usually adamant about going to bed on time. Tyler was notorious for being grumpy if he didn't get enough sleep, and he hated being on his phone. Yet here he was, laying in his own bed, also texting.

Her stomach turned. Maybe he wasn't just texting her. Her fingers flew over the keyboard.

RORY

What are YOU doing up so late?

TYLER

Making sure you're not doom-scrolling

RORY

I smell a lie

TYLER

I smell doom-scrolling

RORY

YOU'RE RELENTLESS

TYLER

GO TO BED, MENACE

She sent him a middle-finger emoji, then turned her phone over and placed it on her nightstand. She stayed leaning against her wall for another moment, watching the window across from hers, the gleam of his phone bright in his dark room. He was still up on his phone. Probably texting someone.

And she really, really wished he wasn't.

RORY WAS USED to being alone. Some of her first memories were of her time in daycare, surrounded by other kids her age also ditched by their parents, spending time with a curly, gray-haired woman who smelt like the lemon cough drops she was constantly sucking on. But it was the dread that she remembered the most, that feeling of abandonment that simmered deep in her stomach as she watched her mother leave for the day. She would cry and cry until the lemon-cough-drop lady gave her animal crackers to shut her up. Sometimes it worked. Sometimes she just threw her crackers to the floor.

So she got used to that feeling. The dread that clamored to the surface each time she woke up to an empty house or ate dinner alone in front of the television. Gabi insisted it was all worth it, that she was doing this for *her*. But how could something be for her if she didn't even want it in the first place? Didn't she get a say in what she wanted...which, she always hated admitting to herself, was to simply spend time with her mother?

It was middle school when she stopped calling her *Mom*. Gabi had been an hour late for picking her up, but that didn't stop Rory from sitting on the curb outside in the snow, watching for her red Prius in the sea of white. The after school–care teacher tried coaxing Rory back inside with hot cocoa, but she refused to listen. She just sat there, eyes at the school's gates, hoping the car would round the corner.

When it finally did, the sky was almost dark, the sun set and gone. Rory watched the headlights flash as the car spun around the circle to the entrance, coming to an abrupt stop in front of her.

She whipped the back door open and threw her backpack into the footwell, then sunk into the seat and yanked on the belt buckle to fasten herself in, flurries of snow dampening the cloth interior.

"Sweetie, I'm so sorry, I was—"

"Just go," Rory snipped.

"Do you want to get pizza for dinner tonight?"

Rory shook her head. "I just want to go home, Gabi."

She remembered the look on her mother's face when she said it—anguish, hurt, a hint of realization that things might never be the same again. But she didn't correct Rory, just switched gears as they left the school. It made her feel powerful.

She'd been calling her Gabi ever since.

Rory's distaste for after-school care was what led her to soccer, and eventually, to Scoops. She joined the soccer team in seventh grade and quickly became one of the best players, making Tyler run drills with her in the backyard or taking shots at the net before practice after school. But soccer was a fall sport, and by the time spring came around, the loneliness in her life felt like a gaping hole that needed to be filled. Tyler told her he got a job at Scoops By The Sea. She applied the next day.

Having her job at Scoops and *finally* getting her driver's license felt like her ticket to freedom. She could work and do as she pleased, filling her days with work, parties, and boys. Her lonely upbringing made her bold. She was loud and obnoxious, wore bright colors, kissed boys without a second thought. She painted each of her nails a different color just to stand out from the rest. She wanted to be *noticed*. She wanted people to know that she existed.

There were glimmers of good times, of course. Small moments and sweet memories she could cling to when she missed her mom. Disney movie marathons, big stacks of fluffy pancakes at the diner before school, laughing so hard orange juice flew out of her nose.

But because she was seventeen and needed more than just glimmers, she pushed away every attempt Gabi made to have a real relationship, keeping her at arm's length, not ever filling her in on what was going on in her life. Not wanting to deal with the sting of that disappointment any more than she had to. She was done with it. And thankfully, she had others she could rely on instead.

Even though one of her *others* was now the most popular guy in school.

Rory avoided all social media that weekend and prayed that this would all blow over by Monday. But as she walked through the halls that morning, it seemed the entire school was far from over it. Everyone was still buzzing about the game...and "the big catch." Rory was sick of hearing about it —especially after having to watch a recap on the school's morning show.

Rory was grabbing textbooks from her locker before homeroom when she spotted Tyler heading her way from down the hall. She stood taller and opened her mouth to greet him, only he turned and stopped to lean against another locker. One that belonged to a girl with perfectly blow-dried blonde hair.

The air left her lungs as she watched Zoe smile at Tyler, her teeth somehow sparkling brightly underneath the ugly fluorescent lights of the hallway. He smiled back, saying something to her that made her laugh.

Then he reached for her hand, lacing his fingers through hers.

Rory stopped breathing altogether, the entire world swirling around her in slow motion. She couldn't stop staring at them, at their interlaced hands. People were buzzing again around her, the news already spreading like wildfire. That the Homecoming King and Queen were offi-cially a couple.

She turned toward her locker, forcing short inhalations

through her nose. She looked down at her phone and realized the bell was going to ring in two minutes. Where was
Melanie? She usually always met her at their lockers in the
morning. And right now, Rory needed her. She flicked open
her phone and typed out a text.

RORY

Hey, you coming in today?

She waited for a beat, then two. No response. She
sighed, shoving her phone in her backpack and slamming
her locker shut. She passed the happy couple with her head
turned down and raced to class, feeling her heart pound in
her chest the entire time.

Chapter Six

Rory tightened the laces on her cleats until they dug into the skin at her ankles. She had no reason to be angry, she knew that. Tyler had every right to be with someone who made him happy, especially after she told him she wanted to forget the "big reveal" from that summer. She just didn't think he would move on so quickly...

She sighed and reached for her phone in her backpack to see if Melanie ever replied. She hadn't shown up at all today, which made her worry. Even if she'd changed quite a bit since moving to Haverport, Melanie never skipped school.

She tapped the screen and found a new text. But it wasn't from Melanie.

CALVIN

It's a bad day. She hasn't left her bed.

Rory groaned, placing her head in her hands. She was selfish. Here she was, worrying about a boy she didn't even like, while her friend was in bed mourning the loss of her *twin brother*. How could she bother Melanie with her silly little problems when her friend's plate was already so full? She shook her head, feeling absolutely ridiculous, when another text came in.

CALVIN

You could come see her, you know.
Doesn't always have to be me.

She looked up at the field, noticing her teammates now coming her way wearing athletic shorts and practice pinnies, hair in braids and tight ponytails, all ready for their last practice before the final game that weekend.

She typed back as they approached.

RORY

Yes it does. I wouldn't even know what to say.

CALVIN

She doesn't need words, just company.
Come.

She tossed her phone into her bag and closed her eyes. She needed to clear her thoughts, get her mind off all of it. Off of Tyler and his apparent new girlfriend. Off of Jay and his constant texting and flirting. Off of Melanie and the fact that she'd been nothing but a horrible, horrible friend to her.

Her teammates' chatter grew louder, and she heard the words *Tyler* and *Zoe* ring out. The only person who wasn't gabbing about the budding new relationship was Helen, who seemed far too focused on getting ready for their last practice to care. Helen placed her bag on the bench next to her, rummaging through it for her shin guards. She dared a glance up at the rest of her team and, after noticing the way Gina was looking at her—like she was two seconds from asking Rory if she knew anything about Haverport's new reign of royalty—she decided to take the conversation by the horns and steer it in a completely different direction.

"Can't believe this is the last practice," Rory blurted. "Let alone our final game."

She noticed the way Helen's shoulders visibly relaxed, like having to listen to the constant prattling and gossiping was the equivalent of listening to nails screeching down a chalkboard. Rory didn't blame her.

Kayla groaned. "God, I know. Rehearsals for the dance team start next week and I'm already dreading it."

"Over Coach Konicki's incessant drills?" Gina teased. "I'd much rather shake my ass in front of the basketball boys."

Kayla rolled her eyes. "Then you do it if you're so enthused."

Gina shook her head. "Nah, I'll be slammed with yearbook responsibilities."

Rory's ears perked up. "You're doing the yearbook?"

"Well, not yet," Gina explained. "I'm going to an info meeting for it on Thursday, and then there's some kind of test to see if you're the right fit. But based on the few sign-ups on that sheet, I highly doubt they'll turn anyone away."

Her eyebrows knitted together. "What's the test?"

"I think they're looking for basic photo editing and design skills, seeing if you have the 'artistic eye' or whatever other bullshit Penelope told me."

Rory frowned. "Penelope is in charge?"

"She's the editor-in-chief," Gina said. "Why, you interested in joining?"

It would keep me out of the house, she immediately thought. Things were looking...bleak. If Tyler was going to be busy with a new girlfriend, there's no way he would choose Rory over her during his free time. And with

Melanie struggling the way she was and missing school, Rory was looking at a very, very lonely winter.

She shrugged. "Yeah, maybe."

Gina's face brightened. "Oh, please come with me tomorrow! I need a friend to roll my eyes at when Penelope is being a tyrant."

Rory chuckled. "Well...okay. But only for the eye-rolling."

Gina threw her arms around Rory, squeezing tight.

"You ladies aren't going to want to hug each other after today's practice," Coach Konicki boomed as he set down his duffel bag. "Drills. Now."

They moaned, but Rory couldn't help smiling. No matter how excruciating the drills were or how physically taxing practice would be, she loved being out on the field. A tiny spark of hope flared in heart about what was to come.

"Alright, everyone. Be quiet," Penelope demanded from the front of the classroom. "We only have this lunch period to nail down our staff, so shut up."

Rory took a seat next to Gina in the back. She wasn't wrong, the room was almost empty. Besides the two of them and Penelope, there were about five others at this meeting, which surely couldn't be enough people to put together an entire yearbook. She wondered if she made a big mistake in coming to this meeting and if she was about to sign up for a far greater commitment than anticipated.

She reached for her backpack on the floor, standing up to leave. "Gina, I—"

Gina grabbed Rory's sweatshirt and pulled her back down into her seat. "Rory Michaels, do not leave me here."

"But you *want* to be here," she hissed.

"Something you want to tell the rest of the class, Rory?" Penelope asked.

She looked up at Penelope, who was now at the front of the room with her arms crossed, tapping her peep-toe chunky wedges, eyes wide with amusement.

She slumped, shrugging her backpack off as she shook her head.

"Good, let's get started," Penelope said, grabbing a stack of papers.

"She loved that a little too much," Rory mumbled softly to Gina.

"Just...give it a chance, okay?" she whispered back. "You could always just say no after the test."

Before she had a chance to really think through what the test could possibly be, Penelope slapped down a piece of paper in front of her. A totally *blank* piece of paper.

"Here at Haverport High Yearbook Committee, we are in desperate need of designers," Penelope said to the group, placing a blank paper in front of Gina. "Sean is our photographer," she continued, pointing to where he sat at the front of the room, wearing his signature black jeans, flat-brim hat, and thick-framed glasses. "He has been taking pictures of the different clubs and sports teams, and now it's time to start putting the book together.

"I'll be editing the copy, but what we now need are some artists to bring it to life. Your task is simple—I want you to draw me a mockup of what you think a yearbook spread could look like. I want to see what kind of eye you have, so I know what section I should place you to work on. That's if you're even good enough."

"Is she in a place to turn people away?" Rory grumbled.

Gina rolled her eyes, which had the two of them stifling giggles as Penelope continued to drone on at the front. Gina opened up her notebook and wrote *EYE ROLL COUNT* at the top, starting a tally.

"You have ten minutes to wow me, so give me your best," Penelope finished, floating down into the teacher's seat at the front of the class.

Rory flipped the pencil in her hand as she stared down at her paper, unsure of where to start. She glanced around at her peers, noticing how each of them drew out simple frames with graphics and designs that looked generic, even plain.

But she never liked plain. She didn't spend a chunk of her Scoops tips on different shades of nail polish for no reason. She enjoyed bold colors and loud laughter and animated movies that made you sing. She covered every inch of her bedroom walls with pictures and sketches and posters. She wouldn't want to look back on her high school yearbook as something dull. She'd want it to have lots of color. Lots of life.

She slipped out of her chair and went to the front of the classroom, stepping in front of Penelope. "Do you have any colored pencils?"

Penelope frowned. "This isn't a coloring class."

She bristled, grinding her teeth. "Just...trust me. Maybe something in this classroom? Markers? Crayons?"

"Here," said a soft voice. Rory turned and noticed Vanessa Ramirez sitting next to Penelope. She hadn't even noticed Vanessa sitting there all this time with the way Penelope commanded the room's attention.

Compared to Penelope's blown-out red hair and fancy shoes, Vanessa was her opposite. Her short bob of black curls framed her kind face. She wore no-nonsense combat boots, a black tee with an *Avatar* graphic on the front, and fishnet tights beneath a bright-orange skirt. Her eyeliner was drawn out like a cat, which paired well with her headband that donned black velvet cat ears.

The two crystals placed delicately at the corner of Vanessa's eyes twinkled as she smiled at Rory and handed her what looked like a prized set of colored pencils, the aluminum case covered in cartoon stickers.

"Thanks," Rory said, holding the case with care. She sat down, popped it open, reached for a bright blue pencil, and got to work.

Nine minutes later, Penelope's phone was chiming at the front of the room as she instructed everyone to put their pencils down. Rory placed a purple pencil back in the case and shut it with a soft *snick*.

"Damn, Michaels," Gina said, leaning over.

Rory looked over at her neighbor, noticing a mock-up of what would be the crew team's page. She'd drawn a skinny boat at the bottom with oars on either side and added a few frames above for team pictures. Simple, elegant, clean. She looked back at her sheet, noting that her design was the polar opposite.

Oh no.

Penelope roamed the desks, admiring each person's designs. Rory thought Penelope almost looked bored, until she came to her desk and froze.

She watched Penelope's eyes go wide. "Now that's...something."

Vanessa popped out from behind Penelope and leaned in, taking a closer look at the design. Vanessa's mouth curled into a wicked grin.

She flushed. "It's okay if you hate it, I know it's different—"

"No, no," Penelope said, lifting Rory's design off her desk. The first design she'd touched so far. "This is good."

It was a design bursting in color. Bright bold bubble letters and a page covered in psychedelic colors, with frames for images in all different shapes and designs. A page with personality, something that matched well with the Instagram, TikTok, friendship-bracelet-loving age they were all currently living in.

"I know it doesn't match the school's typical designs," she said. "But in my mind, a yearbook is meant to be a time capsule back to that period in your life, and I think the pages should reflect that."

Penelope turned to Vanessa. "What do you think, Vee?"

Vanessa grinned and nodded, the two of them having some sort of silent exchange.

She whirled around, striding back to the front. "We will send our editor's picks tonight, so please be on the lookout for the email. Our first official meeting will be next Wednesday, and we meet every day after school except Fridays, up until our deadline on May 18."

Rory coughed. "Every day?"

"Is that a problem?" Penelope asked.

She would have to rearrange her schedule with Ron when Scoops reopened in March. She might be able to convince him to only give her night shifts during the week instead of after-school ones. But it was something to do —*every day*. It was going to get her out of the house. It was going to keep her busy this winter.

Rory flashed her teeth in a grin. "Not at all."

Penelope smirked. "Good, check your inboxes tonight."

Everyone started to pack up their things to leave. Rory

lifted the colored pencil case to Vanessa, who was still standing next to her desk. "Thanks," she said.

"Anytime, Rory," Vanessa said, her voice bright and sweet like sugar. "Tell me, have you ever worked with digital design programs? Made graphics or anything?"

Rory blanched. "No, will that be a problem?"

Vanessa grinned, those two little crystals twinkling under the lights above them. "Nope, I was just curious."

She felt a heavy pit in her stomach as she watched Vanessa walk away, wondering what in the world she just got herself into.

THE EMAIL CAME at 10:59 p.m.

The list included everyone from the meeting, which made sense—there weren't many of them to begin with. But it was where Rory sat on the list that had her gasping into her pillow.

Penelope Fairweather, Editor-in-Chief
Vanessa Ramirez, Creative Director
Sean Channing, Photography Director
Rory Michaels, Lead Designer

The rest of the group was listed as generic staff editors, including Gina. But not Rory, who was now in charge of the design for the entire yearbook.

Which meant, starting next Wednesday, she was officially going to be in way over her head.

Chapter Seven

———

THE NEXT DAY AFTER SCHOOL, Rory got a call from a number she didn't recognize.

She flung her backpack onto the kitchen counter and answered. "Um, hello?"

"Rory, hi! It's Vanessa."

"Oh, hi! How did you get my number?"

"You filled out a form yesterday, remember?"

"Right," she said, her chest feeling tight. "Listen, Vanessa...I'm not sure—"

"Don't back out on me," Vanessa interrupted her. "You're about to say you're not qualified for the position, but it's not true. You're exactly what I've been looking for."

Rory's face flushed, thankful this conversation wasn't in person. No one had ever said something like that to her before. *You're exactly what I've been looking for.* "R-really?"

"Oh, totally," Vanessa said. "You have raw talent, and we're about to have the best-looking yearbook in decades."

"I think you're putting a *little* too much confidence in me," she mumbled.

"After what I saw yesterday, I don't think so."

"But I have no idea how to use any of those design programs," she said, feeling panicked, her chest tightening even more. "How am I supposed to do this?"

"Okay, first, breathe."

Rory was silent. *What?*

"Take a big breath in—"

She wasn't sure why, but she obeyed.

"—and now out."

She exhaled, and shockingly enough, felt noticeably lighter.

"This is actually why I'm calling you," she explained calmly. Her voice was like something out of a Zen meditation recording. Rory listened, finding that despite her lacking certain skills, she trusted Vanessa and her calming presence. "Have you signed up for next semester's classes?"

"Uh, no," Rory said.

"Okay, cool, so I think you should sign up for Graphic Design I," Vanessa answered. "They'll teach you the basics there."

"But that's next semester." That panicky feeling was back. "What am I going to do until then? Sit around and let everyone glare at me because I'm their lead designer who doesn't even know how to make a graphic?"

"*Rory.*" Vanessa snapped her out of her spiral with just one word, and she took another deep breath unprompted.

"Good," Vanessa continued. She was the Jedi Master, and Rory was her Padawan. "Thinking through the designs and the art does not require computers. Not yet, at least. These next few months, I want you to design everything on paper. We'll work through the spreads, and then our team can start executing. That's why we have them."

She exhaled, feeling a bit more at ease.

"Bring a blank sketchbook if you have one, and maybe

invest in your own set of colored pencils," Vanessa continued "I'm...protective."

Rory chuckled. "Yeah, I kind of picked up on that. Thanks for trusting me with them."

"I could see the inspiration sparkling in your eyes, and I just *had* to see what you were up to. And prove Penelope wrong."

"Oh?" she said with a smile. "Having a hard time with our editor-in-chief already?"

Vanessa groaned. "Always. But I told her that if we really wanted our yearbook to stand out, we had to do something different. Your design was so out-of-the-box that even she liked it. That means something."

Rory grinned, not sure how to respond. She always found herself doodling, but she never actually considered doing something with her art. Like designing an entire yearbook from scratch.

"And you just said 'our' editor-in-chief," Vanessa continued. "So I'm guessing this means you're still in?"

Rory nodded. "Fine, yeah, okay, I'll do it."

"Perfection," Vanessa said, a cheer in her voice. "Okay, I have, like, two hours to squeeze in some *World of Warcraft* before my parents get home, so I gotta go. See you Monday?"

"Yeah, Monday."

Rory hung up, sliding her phone into her back pocket. She wasn't sure why she was feeling so overwhelmed about it all, but after taking another one of her Jedi/Zen deep breaths, she reminded herself that this was what she wanted. An activity to keep her occupied and out of the house. To keep her mind off of being away from Scoops and slowly watching Tyler slip out of her grasp. It had been four days since she saw Tyler and Zoe together in the hallway, and she had yet to hear anything from him. He *claimed* to be there for her, but already he seemed preoccupied with his new girlfriend.

Pushing the image of *them* out of her mind, she snatched a soda out of the fridge and cracked it open, taking a big gulp as she refocused on the task at hand. When she made the design for the yearbook, she told Penelope and Vanessa that it was meant to feel like a time capsule. Like jumping back into that period of your life and feeling like you never left. She wondered if her mother ever felt that way about her high school years.

Rory set the soda down and bounded up the stairs. Once she was on the second-floor landing, she tugged on the little string hanging off the ceiling and pulled the ladder down. She coughed from the dust in the air as she climbed up to the attic, taking a seat on the edge as her eyes adjusted to the dim light. She squinted at the boxes that'd been tossed up there. Nothing was labeled or organized, just cardboard boxes with lids to store stuff that rarely saw the light of day.

She sighed, wondering if it was even worth looking. Gabi kept everything about her life before having Rory so hush-hush, especially when it came to anything related to her father. Always telling her that it wasn't worth dredging up the pain from the past, and that they should look toward their bright futures instead.

Wasn't the whole *point* of a yearbook to look back at your past, though? To see how far you'd come? How much you'd grown?

She stood up, wiping her sweaty hands on her jeans before flipping open lids to boxes. She knew the ones closest to the ladder would be the most recent, like Christmas decorations or Rory's old toys. So she started in the middle and worked her way back, hoping to find something that looked like it came from her mother's high school years.

She wasn't sure how much time had passed, but when she resurfaced, the sun had almost set, the burnt orange color streaming through the stained-glass window at the other end of the attic. Rory wiped a bead of sweat from her brow as she stepped to the very back, eyeing a box standing alone. She smirked and snatched it up, setting it on a stack of boxes in front of her and carefully lifting the lid so as not to disturb the dust, just in case Gabi came up here and poked her nose around.

Sure enough, out spilled a heap of her mother's old relics. She picked up a few picture frames, recognizing a much younger version of her grandparents in one shot with Gabi, who couldn't have been older than seven. Rory sighed, missing her grandparents deeply. They lived down in Orlando, and Rory only got to see them once a year on Christmas. The reminder had her heart bursting, knowing that it was just over a month away. She placed the frame down and kept digging, past old toys and jewelry boxes, and finally came across a yearbook.

Oak Creek High
Class of 2005

She lifted the book and slowly peeled open the cover. The inside flap was completely covered in signatures and notes from Gabi's old friends. Rory's eyes widened at how many there were, wondering how her mother could have been so popular and yet never talk to or see them anymore. What happened?

She flipped through the pages, analyzing the designs of each spread, which didn't have much pizazz. They were simple and classic, nothing showy or flashy, not what Rory was hoping to find. But as she turned the pages, she became hungry for more images of her mother, who was everywhere. She groaned when she reached the cheerleading page, her mother front and center with a big grin, listed as that year's captain. A few pages down, she found another one of her singing on stage wearing a Pink Ladies jacket, her blonde hair curled and piled up at the top of her head, red lipstick gleaming underneath the stage lights. When she finally hit the senior page and the superlatives, an envelope tumbled out. Rory sucked in a breath as she picked it up and read the front.

She recognized Gabi's handwriting, her curly scroll addressed to some location in Orlando. The return address was for their first apartment in downtown Haverport, where they lived for five years before Gabi was finally able to afford a down payment for their current house.

Stamped in red ink across the front was a return request, letting the sender know the letter had bounced back. And the date on the stamp? May 8, 2006.

Three days after Rory's birth date.

She blinked once, twice, three times, feeling like someone had punched her in the gut. She dropped the envelope and noticed how it landed on a black jersey stuffed at the bottom of the box.

Rory pulled it out and smoothed out the wrinkles. It was a football jersey, with the number one in white on the back and the name BARRY stitched elegantly at the top.

Rory glanced back down at the yearbook, the superlative *Most Likely To Live Happily Ever After* floating above a large picture.

It was Gabi in her cheerleading uniform, held tightly in the arms of a football player wearing the very same jersey

Rory held now. He was sweaty, his dark mahogany hair wet and sticking to his forehead, and he was smiling down at Gabi. Looking at the woman in his arms with familiar seafoam green eyes like she was the most precious thing in the world.

She read the caption below.

Gabriella Michaels & Fred Barry

She sucked in a breath as she looked back at the letter.

It was addressed to Fred Barry.

Rory dropped what she was holding, her hands trembling. She just found her father.

AFTER STUFFING everything back into the box and shoving it in the corner it came from, Rory carefully climbed down the ladder and closed up the attic. Her hands were still shaking as she grabbed her things in the kitchen and headed for her room. Gabi was probably already at Wilson's starting her shift, but just in case, she locked her door. Asking Gabi the truth was too risky, and she didn't have the courage quite yet to take that risk. She would see what she could learn about Fred Barry on her own first.

She plopped down at her desk and opened her laptop, then searched his name. It was generic enough that thousands of results came up, so Rory tried *Fred Barry Orlando* and then *Fred Barry Oak Creek High*.

The results weren't that exciting—just some football stats and a newspaper clipping about him making the All-State team in Florida. But she couldn't find any pictures or links or social media profiles. The guy didn't even have a LinkedIn.

She clicked her laptop shut and cupped her face in her hands. Of course finding him wouldn't be that easy. She would have to try looking for more information about him in other ways.

But...did she even *want* to look for him? Her mind drifted to thoughts of her imaginary father, the one who was attentive and loving and always home and there for her. Yet her real father clearly didn't want anything to do with her, and Gabi sure as hell hadn't shared anything meaningful about him. But what if they were both wrong? What if as soon as Fred Barry saw her, saw how they shared the same thick mahogany hair and seafoam green eyes, he felt he was wrong all along and wanted to actually get to know his daughter?

It was a stretch—she knew that. But maybe...just maybe.

A movement at the window across from hers had her looking up from her hands. Tyler was home and shuffling around in his room, wearing a sky-blue polo and a pair of jeans. He was laughing at whoever was talking to him as he moved around, then stepped aside to make room for a beautiful tall blonde to enter.

Rory's head pounded as she watched Zoe walk timidly around his room, her mouth curled into a genuine smile.

She didn't realize she was staring until Tyler locked eyes with her. She wasn't sure what to do. Wave? Flip him the bird? Cry and pound on her window and plead for him to come over?

All she wanted to do was talk to him about Fred Barry. She couldn't bother Melanie right now—not when she was currently in her worst grief phase yet. She hadn't seen her friend all week.

No, she needed Tyler. Needed to get his thoughts. He had always been the one she turned to when she thought about her father. Maybe he could help her find Fred Barry. Or...maybe he would tell her something wise about not going down that road, about how it would most likely break her heart.

But she didn't have a chance to make any kind of gesture at him. Tyler broke their gaze first as he walked up to his window and closed the curtains, shutting Rory out from his world.

Chapter Eight

She barely slept—again. Thoughts about what Tyler and Zoe were doing alone in his room haunted her all night. She glanced periodically up at his window, hoping he'd pushed the curtain back open.

He never did. Surely Zoe had gone back home at some point. There was no way Mr. and Mrs. Chapman would allow her to stay over.

But Tyler kept the curtains drawn regardless.

Rory now sat on the bus, dozing off and on despite how rowdy the rest of the soccer team was as they traveled to their last game. Avalon was a thirty-minute drive away—not nearly long enough for Rory to get in a quality nap. Exhaustion seeped into her bones, and the piercing noises of her teammates screaming Taylor Swift lyrics didn't help in the slightest. She should be screaming along with them, celebrating their last game together *ever*.

But after yesterday, she didn't feel like celebrating. To be honest, she didn't even feel like getting out of bed this morning.

The bus hit a bump, causing Rory's head to bang

against the window next to her. She groaned and rubbed her head. She'd been told her whole life that senior year was the *best*, that high school was supposed to be the "best years" of her life. So why then did she feel so miserable? And why was it over a guy she didn't even *like* that way?

Gina plopped down next to Rory, shoving her in the ribs. "What's up with you, Michaels? You're usually the one belting 'Cruel Summer' louder than all of us."

"Didn't get much sleep," Rory grumbled.

"Is it because of yearbook?"

Rory sighed. *Right, yearbook.* She still had that to worry about too.

"Yeah, just...feeling nervous," Rory lied.

"Oh come on, you?" Gina said. "You're, like, the most confident person I know."

Rory snorted. "Me? *Really?*"

"Yes, really. The way you demanded colored pencils and then blew them away in less than ten minutes? That's boss bitch energy."

She chuckled. "You know, you really should have considered being a cheerleader, you're good at it."

Gina shoved her again. "Nah, I like grass stains too much, apparently."

The bus rolled to a stop as they pulled into the parking lot. Coach Konicki started belting from the front of the bus, telling them to turn off the music and get their heads in the game.

"I'm going to miss this," Rory admitted.

To her surprise, Gina reached for her hand and squeezed it. "Yeah, me too. Let's make it count."

THEY DID. It was halftime, and already they were dominating six to zero. Avalon didn't stand a chance with the energy they'd brought from Haverport.

Rory huddled up with her team, sweaty with dirt-covered knees as she listened to Coach's plays for the rest of the game. Despite their massive lead, he wasn't backing down on the intensity. He was determined to give the seniors an excellent last game, and they were all about it. No mercy. It made Rory grin.

Helen led them in their final halftime cheer before breaking the huddle. Rory screamed at the top of her lungs with the rest of them, tears streaming down her cheeks. After a fierce team group hug, Rory let her eyes wander over to the stands on the other side of the field.

Her heart leapt when she saw Melanie bolt up from her seat, cheering loudly. Rory held up her arms and cheered back, so happy to see her friend. She wasn't sure anyone would come to cheer her on, especially because it was a decent drive from home. But there she was, sitting down next to a familiar group, the sight of them making her tear up all over again. Blake sat next to her wearing his Scoops hat, but it was the sight of what Tyler wore that made her keel over with laughter.

Tied at the top of his head was a lime green handkerchief, just like the one she donned at his games.

She shook her head, pretending to throw a football in his direction, which he stood up to catch. He then yelled for Rory to kick ass. She shaped a heart with her hands and held it up, proud of the way the Homecoming King openly swore in front of everyone with no shame.

So okay...maybe they were still best friends. Maybe she was being ridiculous about the whole thing. Her heart swelled at the sight of her friends in the stands, even when she didn't ask them to come.

But her spirits dimmed slightly as she scanned the crowd, searching for the one person who wasn't there. It seemed Gabi couldn't get out of her diner shift. *Standard.*

She'd disappointed her. Again. And Rory just let it happen to her. Again.

She shook it off, bouncing back and forth and forcing thoughts of her mother out of her head. She wouldn't let the disappointment ruin her last game. Under the sun of another warm November day, she was determined to enjoy every moment.

AFTER SCORING two more goals and shaking hands with a defeated-looking team from Avalon, Rory sprinted across the field to hug her friends, forcefully rubbing her sweat all over Blake's face until he screamed for her to get off.

Melanie swung an arm around Rory's shoulders, squeezing tightly. "Has anyone ever told you how incredible you are?"

"Hmmm," she replied, pretending to think about it. "No, please sing my praises."

Blake was still wiping his face. "You're the devil, actually."

Rory cackled and flailed her arms toward him again.

She felt a firm hand slap her back. "Great game, Ry," Tyler said. "You guys ate them alive."

"Thanks, Ty." She grinned up at him. The handkerchief was now around his neck, and he had a tight smile stretched across his face. He looked...nervous.

She frowned. "What?"

"Rory! You were amazing!"

She turned and was surprised to find Zoe standing there, waving at her. She looked...perfect. Her golden hair flowed with the wind alongside the maxi dress she wore, almost like they were paid actors. She looked like an autumn goddess. Rory's uniform, stained with dirt and grass and blood after scraping her knee, seemed even grubbier-looking in comparison.

But Zoe didn't seem to mind the dirt or the grass or the blood as she reached out and pulled Rory into a hug, squeezing her tight. Rory froze, her arms by her side, eyes wide as she looked at Tyler. He curled his lips in to hold back a laugh.

"Um, hi, thank you," Rory mumbled.

Zoe jumped back. "God, sorry! I should have asked if you liked hugs."

"She likes hugs," Blake blurted. "Too much, actually."

Rory gave him the finger.

"Sorry I could only make it for the second half. I was just so excited Tyler asked me to come today," Zoe said. "He talks about you guys a lot...It feels a little like I'm hanging out with celebs right now."

Rory lifted an eyebrow in Tyler's direction. "You talk about us a lot, huh?"

Tyler looked flustered. "Um, only because we all work together, you know?"

"Admit it," Blake sang. "You're obsessed with us."

Melanie squeezed her hands together. "Can't *live* without us."

"Alright, *stop*," Tyler said, looking embarrassed. "Fine, I may talk about you occasionally—"

"Constantly," Zoe interrupted. "I think *obsessed* is an understatement."

"Even more obsessed than his constant need to do bicep curls?" Rory asked, shoving Tyler in the stomach. He feigned being hurt as he clutched his side.

"Oh no, that obsession runs deep," Zoe teased.

Rory chuckled. Zoe really was so *nice*. And surprisingly funny. It was kind of hard to hate her.

She eyed the two of them, taking note of their body language. No holding hands or arms around shoulders or waists. They kept a friendly distance. She wondered if Tyler did that on purpose, if he felt embarrassed to show affection in front of the rest of them. This would be the first girl Tyler *ever* brought into the group. Jay was constantly cycling through women and wasn't afraid to get handsy around the Scoopers whenever the opportunity presented itself. But for Tyler, this was a whole new thing.

"Michaels, let's go!" Helen yelled from across the field. Even after their last game, it seemed Helen was going to squeeze *every* ounce of her last few moments as bossy team captain.

Rory gave her a thumbs-up, watching as Helen's eyes flicked between Tyler and Zoe. She watched as Zoe gave her a shy smile, like extending kindness to someone as bossy as Helen was second nature.

Helen's gaze finally fell on Rory, her eyes narrowing in a glare.

"Seems I am being summoned," Rory said, turning back to the group.

Melanie pulled her into a big hug again. "Proud of you."

Her chest tightened. This was the first time she was seeing Melanie since she'd spent a week in bed. Rory didn't reach out to her once. She felt like the dirt caked at the bottom of her cleats.

"Looks like I'm not the only one who loves hugs," she teased, trying to make light of the situation.

Melanie laughed, and Rory looked over at Tyler, who was smiling down at her. Tyler, whose hand was now interlaced with Zoe's, his thumb stroking back and forth.

She sunk back and thanked her friends again, then sprinted toward her team. Meeting his friends, holding hands...it really shouldn't be a big deal to her. Not when it was her idea they move on.

RORY CAME DOWN the steps wearing white jeans, a navy crop top, and a matching bandana on her head, her mahogany hair silky and running down her back. It was a team tradition to meet for a girls' night after the last game of the year. Which was a not-so-secret code for *massive party*.

She hadn't been sure what would be worse—going home to a very guilty-looking Gabi or to an empty house. Yet when she'd unlocked the door and found the space dark and cold, she'd been somewhat thankful that she could take a little longer in the shower and bathroom getting ready. Most days Gabi rushed in and out of the house between shifts, getting dolled up for her bartending gig, which seemed to require a tighter shirt, a push-up bra, and a lot of eyeliner. Without Gabi hogging the space, she'd been able to take her time.

But now, as she descended the steps and noticed the light was on in the kitchen, she wished she hadn't taken as long upstairs so she could have avoided whatever conversation was about to unfold.

Her mother stood by the table looking as guilty as predicted. Rory went for the coat rack in silence and shrugged on her jean jacket. She lifted her car keys off the hook by the door, then finally, when she couldn't avoid it anymore, walked past Gabi and unplugged her phone from where it was charging on the kitchen counter.

When she slowed, Gabi spoke. "I'm so sorry, sweetie."

A dark rumble escaped Rory's chest as she chuckled and shook her head. It had been a mistake to think that Gabi would show up. To think Gabi would be proud of who her daughter was *now* instead of only focusing on who she wanted her to be in the future.

She knew she should be grateful that her mother was working so hard to prepare for her future. But after years and years of the same story, she felt bitter. Part of her didn't even want the money or to go to college, just to prove a point.

"Please," Gabi pleaded. "Try to understand."

"I've been trying to understand for years," she said coolly. "And yet, it never seems to make sense."

"What doesn't make sense?"

"How a mother can care so little about her daughter."

Gabi looked flustered. "Everything I do is for you."

"No," she said, her blood boiling in her veins. She desperately wanted to scream. "Everything you do is for a version of me that you hope for. Not the version of me that you have."

Her mouth fell open. She stammered, unable to form sentences.

So, Rory did it for her, digging the knife even deeper. "I must be such a disappointment to you. I'm not bookish or going to Yale. I'm never going to be your best friend like Lorelai is to Rory. So maybe you shouldn't have had me at all."

That must have struck a chord, because Gabi's face went stark white at her words. She didn't bother to wait for her response, flinging open the front door and heading for her car.

Wiping away her tears, Rory grabbed her phone and pressed Call on a recent number.

He answered after two rings.

"Hi," she said, her voice hoarse.

"Rory," Jay said. "Baby, what's wrong?"

Chapter Nine

THE WAY HE SAID IT—*BABY*—ALL warm and soothing, had fresh tears pooling in her eyes and words tumbling out of her mouth. Her phone was on speaker on her lap as she drove to the grocery store, where she remained parked in the lot as they continued talking for another half hour.

She did leave out *some* details from her story, like the part about how uneasy she felt about Tyler's relationship with Zoe. But between sniffles and sobs, she told him everything else—about her mom and what she'd found in the attic, about Melanie, about soccer being over and how ill-prepared she felt for her new job at the school yearbook. She touched on what was going on with Tyler and his new girlfriend, including how he brought Zoe to her soccer game that day. Kept it vague, skimmed over the trigger points.

"Damn," Jay said. "I don't think I've ever seen Tyler with a girl. Right? Unless I wasn't paying attention?"

Rory closed her eyes as she rested her head back on the driver's seat. She was supposed to grab some snacks for tonight but was now sufficiently late in delivering them.

Talking to Jay made her feel calmer though, and the last thing she wanted to do was hang up.

Especially after the way he'd called her *baby*.

"No, you're right," she answered. "I've never seen him with a girl."

"Probably because he's always been so obsessed with you," Jay mumbled. "But hey, looks like he's moved on."

Her stomach dropped. She hated that it mattered so much to her. Was there a chance that he was doing it to spite her?

No, he's not like that, she reassured herself. Even if Tyler was different from the others, he was still a guy. Moving from one girl to the next was like a teenage rite of passage...right?

She sighed as she got out of the car, making her way toward the entrance of the store. "What snacks should I get for tonight?"

"Takis, duh," Jay said. "Oooooh, and what about those, like, Reese's snack mix bags?"

"I see college hasn't changed the range of your palette."

"Basically the only thing that hasn't changed." His honesty resonated through the phone's speaker.

Her heart twisted. She'd spent all of this time talking about herself and hadn't even bothered to ask him about college or how *he* was doing. Given his incessant texting and his ability to chat with her for almost an hour on the phone, let alone on a Saturday night, something was definitely off.

"Shouldn't you be out partying?" she asked.

"Overrated," Jay answered.

Her mind drifted to all the times Jay had itched to go to parties over the years, always trying to weasel his way out of closing the shop or sending them rallying messages. "I'm sorry, but that's the least Jay-like thing you have ever said to me."

"Yeah, well, turns out college isn't exactly what I thought it would be."

She wanted to push him, to dig and find out what was really going on with him.

She turned the corner into the snack aisle and found Jess. She wore the all-black Post Road Market employee uniform and was in the middle of restocking chips, looking rather pissed with each bag she threw onto the shelves.

"Oh my god, Jess is here," she whispered into her phone, stepping back so she wouldn't spot her. "Since when does she work at the grocery store?"

"Since always," Jay answered. "She's helping the bakery make cakes."

Rory's mouth fell open. "How did you know about her second job and I didn't?"

"Because, believe it or not, I actually *listen* when my friends talk to me."

"Aww, we're your friends? I thought we were all beneath you," she cooed.

He chuckled. "Not sure if Jess would actually consider me a *friend*, but she did tell me about her off-season gig."

"Well, she's not working on the cakes at the moment. She's currently restocking chips, and not looking too pleased about it." Rory was peeking around the Pringles pyramid, watching Jess aggressively handle the innocent chip bags, which were probably all crumbs at this point.

"Is her face all red like it got when you made her drop that cake?"

"Okay, you know what?" she said, fighting a smile. "That was an honest mistake, and again, it happened *one time.*"

Jay laughed loudly, his voice echoing off what sounded like an empty room. "But the look on Jess's face when her beautiful cake was smeared all over that carpet? Never forget."

Rory shook her head. "Should I talk to her?"

"I'm going to go with no."

Before she could slink away, Jess looked up and caught Rory's eye. She tossed the bag she was holding, pushed her glasses up the bridge of her nose, and crossed her arms.

"She sees me, I better go," she mumbled.

"Tell Mom I said hi," Jay said. He always referred to Jess as his work mom. "And call me later if, you know, you want to?"

Rory's heart broke a little at the vulnerability in his voice. Throughout the past week texting him, she wondered if maybe he was talking to her because she brought him comfort—a piece of home he could easily access with a few taps on a screen. But all of the flirting and the innuendos he sent over text meant something, right? He did just call her *baby*, a first for the two of them.

She had no idea what to think, but after crushing on Jay for so long, Rory was a little too curious not to find out.

"Yeah, okay," she said gently. "I'll call you when I get home."

She hung up the phone as she approached Jess, who was now staring at the bags of chips, her arms still crossed tightly against her black polo.

"You're a long way from the cake aisle," Rory teased.

Jess blew at a blonde strand of hair in front of her face. "If you're just going to mock me, then buzz off."

Her eyes went wide. Jess was *angry* angry. "Why are you restocking the chips?"

"Because we're understaffed, and apparently my

asshole manager thinks this is a better use of my time," Jess explained. "Not like he actually looks at the numbers. If he did, he would see that the cakes are his bestselling items and we should probably double our output. But that would be too smart of a move for that little shit."

Rory couldn't help but chuckle. Jess was always a fireball compared to the rest of them—all business and no play. It's probably why she got along with Calvin so well. The only times she saw Jess let loose was at their annual Haverfest beach bonfire, when she unveiled whatever disgusting ice cream cake combination she made for them to eat. She'd actually seen Jess smile for the first time that past summer, which was saying a lot, given that she'd known her for almost three years.

"That...sucks, I'm sorry. Need any help?"

Jess rolled her eyes. "I don't need a handout, Gilmore."

She tensed. She hated when anyone called her that, but she also didn't want to argue with Jess. She was clearly pissed and wanted nothing to do with her right now. "I—okay, sorry I asked. Just here to get snacks and leave."

"Good," Jess said. She turned back to her box of chips and resumed tossing them onto the shelves.

Rory grabbed a few bags, far from where Jess was stocking to make sure her chips were actually intact, then hesitated before turning to leave. "Um, good to see you, Jess. And Jay said to say hi to his mom."

Jess perked up, looking over at Rory. "Jay? You talked to him?"

Rory shrugged. "Yeah, that was him on the phone actually. We've been talking."

"Like...talking, talking? What happened to Tyler?"

To her shock, Jess seemed invested. Probably wondering

what happened after the Great Scoops Showdown. When everything had gone to shit.

"Tyler has a girlfriend," Rory admitted. "If you picked up a newspaper last week you would have seen her. He's quite literally Haverport royalty now."

"Wow," Jess breathed. "I honestly never thought Tyler would get over you. Seems weird."

"Um—"

"And Jay? Does he like you?" Jess asked. Before Rory could answer, Jess shook her head. "God, forget I asked. I literally do not care about this."

Rory smirked. "Seems like you do a little bit."

"Nope." She was back to restocking her bags. "The opposite actually. Couldn't care less."

Her face fell. She turned to walk toward the checkout.

"Wait, Rory."

She whirled back around, startled to find Jess sauntering across the linoleum floor.

"But if I did care," she said, stopping when her shoes almost touched Rory's, "you could probably talk to me. I know things haven't been...easy."

She blinked. "What do you mean?"

"People talk," Jess explained. "I know your mom took that bartending gig at Wilson's. And that Melanie hasn't been doing well."

Her throat tightened. Okay, maybe she *didn't* want Jess to care. This was crossing the line.

"I'm—fine. Really. Cool as a cucumber." She winced after she said it, feeling like she'd hit an advanced level of awkwardness.

Jess's brows furrowed. "I don't believe you. But fine, forget I said anything." She turned on her heel and walked to her boxes, not bothering to look back in Rory's direction.

Rory bought her snacks, her insides churning. When had Jess *ever* cared about her? It had been obvious that Jess favored Melanie after their summer working together at Scoops. It only took a few months for Jess to ask Melanie to help her with making the ice cream cakes, a job she never trusted the rest of the Scoopers with. Rory tried not to be bitter, not to show how much it stung.

So what changed? And did Rory just screw it all up by pushing her away?

She groaned, resting her head against the steering wheel of her car. She was really good at pushing people away. Maybe *that* was what she should major in if she went to college.

THE FOLLOWING MORNING, Rory poured her coffee to the brim with a loud yawn. She hadn't stayed long at the party, just a couple hours of screaming rowdy chants and singing through their game-day playlist one last time before they all dissolved into a puddle of tears and told each other how much they were going to miss this. Rory didn't drink—she wasn't ready. And thankfully, it meant she got to drive home that night and tuck into her own bed instead of on Kayla's couch or one of the deflated air mattresses on the floor.

As promised, she called Jay when she got home, talking to him for another half hour on speakerphone as she got ready for bed. He kept asking her if she was okay, wanting to know if she was feeling better from before. Despite her conversation with Jess, which still made her feel a little on edge, she did feel better. Even though Jay had his moments of being a complete dickhead, he was also a loyal friend. He stayed on the phone with her until she was in bed and her eyes were drooping.

She took a slurp of her coffee and carefully balanced it as she went out to the back deck, sliding the glass door open and stepping out into the chilly air. Fall had officially made its appearance. The trees were covered in burnt oranges and reds, leaves slowly gliding down and settling on the damp earth in her backyard. She shivered, tucking her knees inside her big sweatshirt as she leaned back in one of their plastic Adirondack chairs. Gabi hadn't woken her to talk through their fight before leaving for her shift, but she did leave half a pot of coffee, which *almost* felt like an apology. While hot coffee would generally be the way to her heart, she knew it wasn't going to work this time. There was a lot more baggage between the two of them that needed settling.

She heard a door swing open and watched as a flurry of pink charged at her. Bea took the stairs two at a time as she climbed up Rory's deck.

"Rory, are you free today? Can you take me to Lacey's?"

"BEA!"

Mrs. Chapman was now standing on the deck next door in a bathrobe, hands on her hips, her hair still tucked in a silky black bonnet.

"Morning, Mrs. Chapman."

"Rory, I'm so sorry. She has clearly lost her manners."

She chuckled, turning to Bea. "What's going on, girlie?"

"I need to go to Lacey's today," Bea rushed out. "They finally restocked their friendship necklaces and all the girls at school are wearing them and I just *have* to have one before they sell out or I'm going to positively die of embarrassment. Do you want that for me, Rory? To die an unexpected death as an adorable sixth grader?"

She couldn't help but laugh at how serious Bea looked after her breathless monologue, which seemed to only frustrate the girl. Bea was already dressed for the day, wearing a pink cable-knit sweater and a matching frilly skirt, her feet tucked into a fuzzy pair of hot pink boots.

"Sure, Bea bear, I'll go."

She squealed, throwing her arms around Rory's neck.

Mrs. Chapman rolled her eyes. "You better buy Ms. Rory some lunch, Bea."

"Oh I will," Bea said, looking elated. "Anything you want, on me."

"Steak dinner?"

"Okay, maybe not that. Something a sixth grader's allowance can afford."

"So...grinders?"

Her eyes sparkled at the mention of her favorite food. Rory knew exactly the way to her heart, it was dangerous. She was pretty sure she was bound to spoil Bea for a long time to come.

AFTER SECURING the necklaces—one of which hung around her neck after some clever convincing—she took Bea over to the deli. They split an Italian grinder with the works: salami, ham, shredded lettuce, tomato, pickled banana peppers, oil, and oregano. Bea chomped away at her half, her hot pink boots swinging happily beneath her.

Rory smiled. "Thanks for lunch, Bea bear."

"Thanks for the chips and the soda," she answered, digging her hand in a large bag of salt and vinegar chips between them. "And for taking me to Lacey's. Mom was moving *so* slowly, and Tyler was being lazy and still sleeping."

"Past ten? You sure it was Tyler?"

She expected Bea to laugh, but she just growled. "He was out late with her again."

Rory tensed. "Oh."

Bea rolled her eyes. "That's all he does these days, it's dumb. I don't like her."

"Hey now, that's not—"

Bea rolled her eyes again. She was such a sassy middle schooler, and Rory loved every minute of it. "Come on, do *you* like her?"

"She's nice."

Bea glared back at her.

"Bea! She's nice!"

"You're lying. I know when you're lying."

Rory shook her head. Unfortunately, Bea *would* know if she was lying. None of them could ever get anything past this girl. Tyler and her always joked that she'd make a great lawyer. In pink, of course. Always in pink.

"I'm not lying about this, she is really nice," she said honestly. "But I don't know her. I don't know if I can trust her yet."

Bea took a silent bite, her little mind thinking it through. "Do you have a boyfriend?"

She coughed, some of her soda almost spilling out of her nose. "Uh, no. I don't."

Bea grumbled, looking back down at her sandwich. "It just doesn't make sense to me," she whispered.

Rory frowned. "What doesn't?"

Bea shook her head. "Nothing, forget it."

They rode in silence back to Misty Bay. Rory offered Bea her phone so she could pick the music, but Bea shook her head, the little one lost in her thoughts. She remained quiet for the rest of the drive until Rory pulled onto their road. Bea sat up straight, lifting her hand.

"Who's that?" Bea pointed.

She pulled into her driveway and parked, then looked where Bea was pointing, up at a tall form leaning against her porch.

Her heart started pounding.

Bea grinned, showing her little crooked teeth. "You sure you don't have a boyfriend?"

He smiled at the sight of her and winked in her direction.

Jay. He was home.

Chapter Ten

Rory jumped out of the car. "What are you doing here?"

Jay Sanchez just kept smiling, that familiar smug look on his face making Rory's heart skip several beats. She forgot how handsome he was. His deeply tanned skin, his toffee-colored eyes, his lean frame. Jay was always slender yet fit, built like the soccer player he was. Soccer was one of the things they had in common, her mind drifting to their afternoons scrimmaging on the beach, the rest of the Scoopers getting mad at them for kicking up so much sand.

Rory couldn't help it as her eyes drifted to his faded Haverport High Varsity Soccer sweatshirt, then to the pair of charcoal joggers on his legs. He even wore his Scoops hat backward on top of his wavy midnight-black hair.

"What do you think?" Jay responded, still smiling at her as she approached, Bea at her heels. "I told you the surprise would be epic."

Bea looked up at Rory with a devilish grin. "Told you."

Rory nudged her. "You be quiet over there."

"You free today?"

Rory looked back at him, still stunned that he was here.

At her house. In that outfit. She felt like she was going to combust.

She looked down at what she was wearing and internally winced. Still in her baggy sweatshirt from that morning, her hair a ratty mess piled high in a bun. At least she had the decency to throw on her favorite pair of light-washed jeans with two artfully ripped cuts at the knees.

"Oh yes, she's free," Bea answered for her. "*Very* free."

Rory glared at Bea, who was looking mighty proud of herself.

"Bea bear, where you been?!"

Rory's heart jumped to her throat at the sound of Tyler's voice from next door. She watched him approach with an amused grin on his face at the sight of her with Rory, matching in their new necklaces. But when his eyes finally caught on the third person in their group, he paused, the grin sliding off his face.

"Jay," he said. His voice sounded less confident. Small, even. "You're here. Why are you not at college?"

"Drove down to see my baby," Jay answered.

Before she could comprehend what was happening, Jay slid an arm around her waist. He tucked his hand underneath her sweatshirt and slipped a finger around a belt loop of her jeans, pulling her closer to him.

She watched Tyler closely, watched his expression turn utterly horrified. His eyes were wide, his lips pressed into a firm line. He was not happy. At all.

It felt...good. She was giving him a piece of his own medicine, and she liked it.

"Your...your baby?" Tyler choked.

"Yeah, well, she was so upset yesterday, and I had no plans today. So, I thought I would come home and surprise her," Jay explained. "Are you surprised, baby?"

Tyler did not look pleased with any of this information —that she was upset, that she called Jay to talk instead of him, that he called her *baby*. He looked down at her, his face etched with hurt.

"Yes," Rory replied shyly. "Yes, very surprised."

"I'm just—I don't—" Tyler stammered.

Jay pressed his mouth into a forced smile as he looked up at Tyler, who had at least four inches on him. Being under six feet never stopped Jay from being the most confident person in the group. He knew he was handsome, and he always used it to his advantage. "Is there a problem?" he asked.

Tyler froze, just staring blankly. For a moment, she wondered if he was going to attack Jay. Her heart pounded in her chest, waiting with bated breath.

But he just shook his head. "No, no problem. Come on, Bea bear, let's go home."

Bea smiled at Rory. "I want a full report when you return, understand?"

She grinned. "Yes, ma'am."

Then Bea pointed to Jay. "And no later than eight thirty, do you hear me?"

Jay barked out a laugh. "Eight thirty? But that's so early!"

"That's thirty minutes before my bedtime, and I expect to hear that update tonight."

"Bea, now," Tyler huffed.

She watched her shuffle behind Tyler, his back hunched and tight as they walked home. He held the door open for his sister before briefly looking over at the two of them. Jay's arm was still protectively around her, his thumb rubbing back and forth on the skin above her jeans. Tyler stared back at Rory, almost like he was pleading with her. *Last chance.*

But she didn't budge, and instead leaned her head against Jay's shoulder. He purred at the gesture.

Tyler shook his head and went inside.

"Well, that was satisfying," Jay murmured into her hair.

She smiled but didn't really have the energy to laugh. It was satisfying at a surface level, but it also left her feeling a little sour.

Jay curled his arm in, holding Rory to his chest so she was facing him. It was the closest they'd ever stood together. She felt like she couldn't breathe.

"Now," he said. She could smell his minty breath. His body was warm against her as cool air breezed by, the rustling of the leaves like a harmony around them. Around this very new, very unpredictable moment. "All the food sucks at school, and I have found myself dreaming about Pop's for a solid month now."

"Dreaming about fish and chips? Kinky."

"Well, it's when I'm not dreaming about other things," Jay teased, winking at her.

She held her breath. Dear god, was this really happening? With the way that Jay held her waist tightly and smiled lazily down at her, it was clear. He wasn't just messing around like he always did. There was something here for him, too.

"I already ate," she confessed. "But I'm happy to steal some of your fries."

"Only if I can call you a seagull," Jay teased.

"I thought you called me *baby*."

"I can't help it," Jay said, his voice so low it rumbled out of him. Like he was confessing his darkest secret. "You've always been my baby."

Even though the line was cheesy, she melted. She smiled up at him, tucking her arms close and placing her hands on his chest. "Well, in that case," she teased, "I get half of your fries."

Jay barked out a laugh, giving her one tight squeeze before letting go. "Get your cute ass in my car."

She did, opening up the passenger door. She noticed a curtain moving at the window next door and looked up, wondering if she would see Tyler standing there, watching them. But she saw no one, just the outside breeze rolling through the open window. She got in, letting Jay reach for her hand as he pulled the car onto the road.

"Okay, I seriously should have just bought you some fries," Jay chaffed. "You're hogging."

"But I'm your *baby*," she taunted, snatching a couple more fries from his Styrofoam container. "With that kind of title, I get to eat from your plate whenever I want."

Jay just chuckled, looking amused. Looking happy.

She took a sip of her Diet Coke, watching him gaze out at the ocean. They had taken the fish and chips to go and now sat on a very cold, very deserted beach. Haverport felt like a different town during the off-season. It was quiet, uncrowded, and peaceful. No summer people filling up the parking lot at the public beaches. No long lines at stores or restaurants. No screaming kids and tired parents who always looked like they wanted to pull their hair out. No traffic down the main drag.

But it also meant no Scoops and no late nights with the people who mattered to her most. Having Jay here felt like home as they sat on a quiet beach at Hillside Park, just the two of them.

He tucked the empty container aside and pulled her close, placing her calves over his thighs as he rubbed a hand up and down her leg. Sitting next to him apparently wasn't good enough. After curling that arm around her back at her house, Jay hadn't stopped touching her. He held her hand in the car. He rubbed her back as they waited for seafood, slowly brushing it up her spine until he reached her neck, drawing circles with his thumb.

It was incredibly intimate for having not yet *defined* what they were. Even more so given that they hadn't kissed. Yet now, with the way Jay was looking at her, she had a feeling that was going to change. Real soon.

Though, something wasn't sitting right with her, and it was getting harder to ignore. Jay finally had the chance to do whatever he wanted, party whenever he wanted, *be* with whomever he wanted, yet he had a plethora of time to chat with her. It felt like an outlet for escape.

She sucked in a breath. "Jay, tell me the truth."

He reached his other arm around her waist, tucking it under her sweatshirt once more. "The truth about what?"

"Tell me what's going on at college," she said. "About how you're really doing."

His eyes went wide. She waited for it, for those pupils to turn onyx, for the fighting to start. That was how it always was with them. Especially when Rory pushed too far for his liking, got too personal. But he was *touching* her, for crying out loud. If he couldn't get vulnerable with her now, then maybe they didn't stand a chance.

But to her surprise, he didn't get mad. He just let out a long breath, looking out at the ocean before them. "College sucks, I hate it."

"But you were so excited about it."

He shrugged. "I know. It's just not living up to my expectations."

"Classes?"

"No, not my classes. Those are fine, I guess."

"Parties?"

"Only been to one, it sucked. Carl throws better ones."

"Okay...friends? Have you met anyone new?"

"Why, want to get rid of me already?"

She pinned him with a *Be serious* look. "Not at all."

"Good," he said, pulling her close. Their noses were touching. He cupped the side of her face with his hand. Her heart was pounding as fast as it did during a soccer game. "Because I'm not going anywhere."

Holy crap. He was really going to kiss her.

Jay pulled back and brushed his thumb against her lips. He let out a shaky breath. "I just thought...I thought college would be different, you know? Nothing's right, and I sort of feel like I'm losing myself. I'm on campus going through all the motions, doing what I need to do, but I don't know...I just feel lost."

She didn't know what to say, but she knew this wasn't something she needed to fix. So she whispered, "I'm sorry," as he tilted his head down to hers again, holding her close.

"You're the only thing that feels normal to me right now," he said. "Does that scare you? Because if it does, we don't have to do this. I don't want to pull you into whatever this is—"

"Jay."

His toffee eyes dimmed as he looked into hers, looking like he was bracing for disappointment.

"It doesn't scare me," she whispered.

He nodded. At that moment, he didn't look like the

confident Jay she'd always known. He looked like a kid. Timid, scared, vulnerable.

She decided to be the confidence he needed and closed the gap between them, pressing her lips to his.

In an instant, his hands were in her hair, loosening her bun as he kissed her. His kiss was hot, urgent. Shivers ran down her spine.

I'm kissing Jay Sanchez. I'm kissing Jay Sanchez.

She wrapped her arms around his back, but it wasn't enough for him. He slid her on his lap, her legs curled up on his side as he held her tightly, his lips warm as he slid his tongue down her throat. He was good at this, *really* good. It kind of pissed her off that they'd waited for so long.

The thought made her pull away. "Why now?"

Jay just pressed in again, kissing her with such ferocity, she felt like she couldn't comprehend it all. But he slowed soon after, dropping a delicate kiss on her neck before whispering in her ear.

"Because I'm an idiot, and I didn't realize what I was missing," he said like a prayer.

She pulled back, looking into those candy-colored eyes again. "Yeah, you are an idiot."

He smiled at her, looking so happy it almost broke her heart. She hated that he was going through so much, and so far away from home. She wanted to give him what felt good, to make his world a little brighter after months of feeling so dark and so alone.

He didn't give her too much time to think as he leaned in again to kiss her, rubbing the small of her back underneath her sweatshirt, his fingertips trimming the back of her sports bra. So she played too, moving her leg to straddle him as she ran her hands through his wavy hair, letting his

Scoops hat fall behind him, loving the rumbling sound that escaped his chest when she did it.

He broke away from her. "I'm sorry for being an idiot."

"Like at the party," Rory added.

Jay exhaled. "I deserved that slap."

"You did," she grumbled, turning her head away from him, her stomach turning at the memory of that horrible night.

She felt his hand trace under her chin, guiding her back to him. "And you were right. I should have never asked you to fake flirt with me to get girls, or put you in a position that made you uncomfortable. Even when I—" He broke off.

Rory cocked an eyebrow, waiting for him to continue.

"I knew how you felt," he admitted. "Or at least, I had a feeling."

Rory covered her face with her hands and groaned. "How?"

Jay pulled them away, holding them in his and tracing her palms with his thumbs. "I guessed. You get adorably red every time you get mad at me. It makes it fun to mess with you a little bit."

She glared. "Even when it means making things really fucking awkward between me and Ty?"

His face fell. "Yeah, that was bad."

"*Really* bad."

"Please," he said, letting go of her hands and wrapping his arms around her waist tightly. "Please forgive me. I've had a lot of time to think about it. I really messed up."

She reached up and ran a hand through his hair, loving the way her touch was making him ease some, his eyes closed, his face relaxed.

She lowered her face to his, her lips close enough to brush against his. Then she smirked. "I'll think about it."

He tightened his grip. "Tease." Then he kissed her again.

She knew he wasn't innocent, that he'd been wrong in the past with the things he'd said. But right now, she didn't want to go back. Just forward. Right now, the only things that mattered were his lips, his hands, and the warmth of his embrace shielding her from the cold ocean breeze.

Chapter Eleven

"Wow," Melanie whispered.

"I know."

"I mean...it just..."

"Doesn't seem real?"

Melanie shook her head as she curled up on the couch, blowing on her coffee. They had the day off for the election, when Haverport High's cafeteria was transformed with voting booths and an absurd number of red, white, and blue flags. Rory could already picture Mr. Clark and his gleaming nightmare-ish smile standing outside of the school, greeting the townies as they exercised their right.

Voting apparently made people hungry though, which meant Haverport Diner was packed and Rory was left with an empty house. Melanie came over as soon as she poured her first cup of coffee, and she'd listened to every little detail about Jay.

"I'm not going to lie...I'm in a bit of shock," Melanie admitted. "I mean, this feels like it came out of nowhere."

She shrugged. "He told me he didn't realize what he was missing until he left."

"Yeah, but still, that feels like such a huge jump," Melanie responded. "So are you guys, like, officially dating now?"

Her heart twisted. It *was* a huge jump, and they didn't have any kind of conversation defining what they meant to each other before Jay drove back to campus. But when he called her later that night, she couldn't find the courage to ask.

"No, we're just...seeing each other, I guess."

Melanie's eyebrows furrowed. "And you're okay with that?"

"For right now, yes," Rory lied. Well, it felt like a half-lie. While she wanted Jay to claim her in that way, she was nervous about what that would mean. "I still don't know what's going on with me next year, and I probably shouldn't hop into some kind of long-distance relationship."

Melanie's eyes went wide like a doe. "Long-distance? Are you planning on moving far?"

"I—" Rory thought about it for a moment. The idea of moving away made her nauseous. Could she actually stomach going away to college?

"Because if you are, we need to discuss. How far do I need to force Calvin to drive so I can see you?"

"Maybe I just won't move then," Rory blurted. "Maybe I'll stay here."

Melanie leaned in, eyes sparkling. "Don't tease me like that."

"Says the girl thinking about going to Yale," she pointed out.

"Yeah, we'll see," Melanie mumbled, taking a sip of her coffee.

Rory's phone dinged. She grabbed it, wondering if it

was Jay—who, she found out, tended to sleep in late each morning—but realized it was Gabi.

GABI

Looks like they double booked at Wilson's tonight, so I'm off the hook! Takeout and Disney?

She sighed. It was an enticing bribe. But she hadn't spoken to Gabi since the weekend, and she wasn't in the mood to do so now. Not when her mind was preoccupied with Jay. Her skin tingled as she thought about his hands on her.

She closed her phone, looking up at her friend. "Wanna go to the movies tonight?"

"Haverport Cinemas? You know, I actually haven't been there yet."

She frowned. "Calvin seriously hasn't taken you to the movies? I told you he's slacking."

"Let's just say we've been busy," Melanie said with a smirk, taking another convenient sip of her coffee.

"Gross."

"Even more gross than you sucking face with *JAY*?!"

She hit her with a pillow, causing some of the coffee in her mug to splash onto the rug as they fell into a fit of giggles.

"Consider a night out at the movies your extended education of Haverport," she said when they settled into the couch. "Tickets on me."

THEY STOOD in line at the cinema, purses stuffed with the snacks and candy they were sneaking in, waiting to buy tickets for *Happy As a Clam*. It was a new animation film that Rory was dying to see, and thankfully, Melanie didn't make fun of her when she suggested it.

"So, are you going to be alone for Thanksgiving?" Melanie asked her.

She smiled at the thought of the holiday season around the corner. "No, believe it or not. Gabi always takes the day off."

Even if she was pissed at her mother, Thanksgiving was the one day a year she *knew* she could look forward to. They never made a traditional meal—just rotisserie chicken, mac and cheese, and ready-to-eat biscuits from Post Road Market that they ate on the couch while binge-watching an entire show. Last year was the entire *The Summer I Turned Pretty* series. They hadn't discussed this year's show yet.

"Do your grandparents fly up?"

"Only for Christmas," she answered. "Gabi really leans into the whole single-parent, have-to-do-this-on-my-own thing."

"Sounds familiar," Melanie quipped.

Rory groaned, thinking about how much their lives mirrored fiction, no matter how much she tried avoiding it. "It's 'cause she's embarrassed, I think. About whatever went down between them."

About how Fred Barry broke her heart.

Or...she assumed so. She wondered what Fred Barry was doing for the holidays. Was he still living in Florida? Probably not, given how Gabi's letter had bounced back. Did he have a new family, kids that he actually *wanted*? Or was he alone, just like them?

"Okay, don't mean to startle you, but the king and queen are here," Melanie whispered.

She whipped her head around right as Tyler and Zoe entered the cinema and approached the line. Tyler's eyes fixed on her, and he frowned.

Good to see you too, bestie.

Zoe greeted them, putting on her best smile. But she could tell it was forced.

"What, um, what movie are you guys seeing?" Zoe asked.

"*Happy As a Clam,*" Melanie answered. "Rory loves her animation."

Rory's face flushed. "I mean, come on, think about the art that's used in these films," she blabbered. "It takes so much thought and patience and creativity to make something like that. How could you not love it?"

She only rambled like that when she was nervous, and right now, between the intense way Tyler was looking at her and Zoe's anxious energy, her heart rate was spiking.

"I think that's what we—" Tyler started.

"No, silly, we're seeing *J'adore,*" Zoe interrupted him. "That new French rom-com?"

Tyler looked like it was news to him. But Zoe didn't back down, staring straight at him, looking flustered.

"Two tickets to *Happy As a Clam,*" said the cashier. Melanie reached for the tickets, thanking him politely.

Instead of reacting, Rory shined her most dazzling smile in their direction, then took her ticket from Melanie's hand. "Enjoy your rom-com."

They walked away from the couple. She could feel Tyler's eyes on her as they stopped at the concession stand to get sodas, but she didn't give him the satisfaction of looking back.

"I need to use the bathroom," Melanie whispered, moving to get up from her seat.

"Don't miss," she teased.

Melanie rolled her eyes. "I'll be right back."

Rory smiled, wiggling into her seat to get comfortable. They were halfway through the film, and she was loving it. The happy little clam was currently not happy, because nothing was going his way. The story was cute, but the artwork was even better. She couldn't help but marvel at every shot. She wished she could have a remote and pause each motion, take in every detail.

Lost in a world of lines, colors, and singing clams, she didn't glance over when Melanie sat back down.

"Do you think they had real people dancing to try to capture these movements, or do you think they drew it all?" Rory asked.

"Are you dating him?" said a deep, not-Melanie-at-all voice.

She spun around to face Tyler, who was now sitting next to her, his bulky frame taking up the entire seat.

"What are you doing here?" she hissed.

"I went to the bathroom and passed by Melanie, so I knew you'd be alone," he said. "Answer me."

She crossed her arms, feeling a bit smug at the way he was looking at her. Oh, he was *angry*. She could practically feel the steam coming out of his ears. "Why do you care?"

"Because he treats you like scum," he said, the volume of his voice causing a few moviegoers around them to turn.

"Be quiet or we're going to get kicked out," she whispered.

"Honestly, Ry, I knew you liked him. I picked up on that. But I really didn't think you would stoop as low as *dating him*."

"We're not dating."

Tyler laughed, but it was a sarcastic *I can't believe I'm hearing this* kind of laugh. "That makes it so much worse."

"Again, why do you care?" she hissed. "Don't you have a queen to attend to?"

Tyler shook his head. "It's not like that."

"What the hell does that mean? Because from what I saw, it *is* like that. Holding hands, taking her to the movies, introducing her to your friends, bringing her over to meet the parents, then up to your room and *closing the curtains*."

"It's not *like* that," he repeated.

"Whatever, Tyler," she said, using his full name. Letting him know that she wasn't messing around, that she was furious with him, too. "I told you I wanted things to go back to what they were, but now you're busy with your girlfriend and you don't give a shit about me anymore."

His face fell. "Is that really what you think?"

"Yes, it is. And you know who has been there for me?"

"Don't say that asshole's name."

"HEY," said a very angry-looking cinema employee who'd appeared out of nowhere. "If you two don't quiet down I'm going to have to kick you out. Final warning."

Melanie returned then, sidestepping to make room for the employee stomping back up the stairs. She noticed who was occupying her seat, and her doe-eyes widened again.

"Get out of her seat," Rory spat.

Tyler shook his head. "You're making a huge mistake."

"Says the guy who's dating the Homecoming Queen to gain popularity."

She knew she would regret those words later. But right now, a sick, twisted part of her wanted him to know how she felt, wanted him to hurt.

He jumped up and shot toward the Exit doors. A tear slowly rolled down her cheek.

Melanie sat down and squeezed her shoulder. "You okay?"

"No," she croaked. "Want to get out of here?"

She nodded, and they swiftly packed up their empty wrappers and watered-down sodas and left.

Rory came home to the sight of Gabi on the couch in her sweats, watching the local news with a pepperoni pizza from Penny's in front of her.

Gabi turned down the volume. "That was a short movie."

She huffed, shrugging off her jacket and tossing it over a kitchen chair. "Yep, it was."

"Hungry?"

She shuffled over hesitantly as Gabi handed her a slice and made room for her to sit. She folded it in half, the grease from the pizza sliding down her hand as she took a big bite.

The screen was flashing with images from today's election results. Mr. Clark won by a landslide, shots of his campaign party flashing on the screen.

"No shock there," Gabi said. "It would have been nice to have someone blue running the town hall for a change, but I guess people still really like him."

"How many years has he been the first selectman?" she asked, watching images of Mr. Clark waving to the cameras, an arm casually wrapped around Mrs. Clark's waist. She noticed the absence of Zoe in that perfect little family shot. It appeared going to the movies with Tyler was more important.

"Almost as long as I've been here, so too long," Gabi answered. "Would love to see some fresh faces up there someday."

"Maybe you?" she said with a smirk.

Gabi snorted. "Yeah right. My expertise in slinging shots and balancing plates will go far with that job."

She shook her head, wondering why Gabi didn't try to do something more with her life. But she'd never been brave enough to ask, and she wasn't in the mood to change that. Her eyes drifted out to the swing set in the backyard, shrouded in darkness.

Gabi clicked the TV off. "We need to talk."

"No, we don't."

"I feel awful, sweetie, and..." She watched as Gabi wavered, not finishing her thought. "Rory, is something wrong?"

Rory frowned. "No, why?"

"Because I'm your mother, and I know what that look means."

She looked down at her mismatched pair of socks, not sure how to respond. So, she didn't.

"Any chance it has to do with whoever is making you giggle on the phone until two, sometimes three in the morning lately?"

She blinked, shifting her gaze up. "You can hear me?"

"Whoever he is, he sure makes you laugh hard," Gabi answered. "You even woke me up one time."

"Crap, I'm sorry."

Gabi smiled. "All good. So...who is he?"

She sighed, studying her chipped rainbow nail polish. Another reminder of how preoccupied she'd been these days.

"Jay," she whispered.

Gabi tapped a finger on her chin. "Isn't that the guy you work with?"

She nodded. "He's off at college now."

"Yet he calls you every night?"

"He's a little lonely and homesick."

"Makes sense," Gabi said. "Are you seeing him then?"

She thought back to their kiss on the beach, his hands on her skin, the feel of his lips branded on her neck. "You could say that."

"And you're being safe?"

She felt her cheeks flush. "We—we haven't—"

Gabi waved her off. "You can tell me when you're ready. As long as you promise me you'll make smart choices."

She softened at that. It was a command, and in any other circumstance, Rory might have come back with a retort to brush her mother off. But, for some odd reason, she liked having Gabi boss her around. It meant she cared, that what was going on in Rory's life right now mattered to her.

"I promise," she answered.

Gabi nodded, staring back at her daughter, her face shifting from concerned parent to guilt in a matter of seconds. A look she knew all too well.

"What?" she asked. "Just spit it out."

"How'd you know something was up?"

"Because I'm your daughter, and I always know when you're about to drop a bomb on me."

Gabi visibly winced. "I—okay. You're not going to like it."

"Tell me."

"I have to work on Thanksgiving and Christmas."

She knew it wasn't biologically possible, but at that moment, she felt her heart fall from her chest and land in her belly, like a shriveled-up, lifeless rock.

Apparently, her facial expression was telling enough, because a millisecond later, Gabi was scooting over and reaching out to grab her hands. Rory yanked them away, standing up from the couch.

Tears were already falling down Gabi's cheeks. "They're paying me triple, sweetie. Between that and the tips, I'll walk home with almost a grand both nights. Maybe more."

She took a long, deep breath to calm herself down, just like Vanessa taught her. "What about Grandma and Grandpa?"

"They booked a cruise," Gabi answered softly. "So I thought—"

"You thought you might as well take advantage of it," she interrupted, finishing the sentence for her. "Unbelievable. First the game, now this."

"Please, sweetie, talk to me."

She threw up her hands. "What's there to say, huh? Actually, how about this. This is what I get for believing for *one second* that you would choose me over money."

"Rory, it is *not* about the money," Gabi said, standing up. "You know it's not."

"Sorry—my *future*," she said, on a rampage. She knew she should bite her tongue, but she'd never been good at that, anyway. So, she just let it all out. "Don't you think I'm going to hate being in college knowing that it ruined any chance of a relationship we might've had? Do you really think I'm going to *like* it when all is said and done?"

That shut her up. Gabi stood there, mouth opening and closing, but no words came out.

"You know what, enjoy your two grand, do what you want with it," she said. "I'm going to bed, and I'll make sure to keep it down tonight."

She stomped up the stairs and slammed her bedroom door before curling into herself, holding a hand to her mouth to muffle the sound of the sobs that ricocheted out of her.

Chapter Twelve

Rory headed for the computer lab after school that Wednesday, clutching a brand-new sketchbook and her own set of colored pencils while harboring a stomachache that wouldn't subside. She knew it was a combination of nerves and crying herself to sleep the night before. She felt ridiculous assuming that the holidays could somehow be protected, that despite the lonely days Rory spent throughout the rest of the year, she could at least look forward to subpar rotisserie chicken and mac and cheese on the couch. The thought of doing those things by herself didn't sound appealing, so she vowed before falling asleep that she would give the yearbook her all.

Her mind drifted to Jay as she took a seat, waiting for the meeting to start. Her logical side knew she had to ask him if they were officially dating. Was that something people did? Or were they simply a couple now? The only other boyfriend she'd had was Nick Vasquez during freshman year. It lasted a couple of months, up until he sat her down and told her he preferred guys instead. She was upset, but not exactly heartbroken, and ultimately felt proud that Nick was honest and open with her. She was friendly with him when he passed her in the halls, always with Phillip in tow, Nick's steady boyfriend of almost two years.

Tyler never liked Nick, which made a bit more sense to Rory after the revelations that came out over the summer. One thing was for sure—jealousy was not a good look on her friend. The way he'd laughed in disbelief when she admitted that she wasn't officially dating Jay. How exasperated he sounded...

She pushed away thoughts of Tyler and the movie theater as the rest of the yearbook staff filed into the lab, taking their seats and drawing their attention to where Penelope stood writing down dates on the whiteboard. They were deadlines, all the little dates for which parts of the yearbook needed to be done before finally submitting for print on May 18.

Penelope capped the dry-erase marker with a smile. "I think these dates speak for themselves, editors. We have a lot of work to do over the next six months to make the best yearbook Haverport High has ever seen."

"Wait a minute," said a gangly-looking sophomore guy at the computer next to Rory. "You have Christmas Eve for our first design deadline. That's technically a holiday."

"Not for everyone in this room," Penelope said firmly. "I meant it when I said this was going to be a hefty commitment, and that means sacrificing some of your time to get the job done. If that scares you," she said, holding up a finger, "the door is that way."

Rory chuckled to herself. Even if Penelope wasn't the most liked person, she couldn't deny it—she'd make a great leader one day. Inclusivity and a balls-to-the-wall approach? She was bound to set this world on fire.

Penelope smiled. "Something funny, lead designer?"

She just kept smiling, lifting up her water bottle in a cheers. "Not at all, editor-in-chief, carry on."

Vanessa was sitting in a chair next to Penelope with a big grin on her face.

She winked back, taking a sip from her bottle. The entire layout needed to be drafted by Christmas Eve. Looked like Rory had holiday plans after all.

Penelope wasn't joking. The yearbook was a time- and energy-sucker.

The first week was a lot of back-and-forth with Vanessa as they settled on their style guide. Rory didn't think choosing colors and fonts would be such a big deal to her, but as she and Vanessa started collaborating on their official "look," she was shocked by how many *opinions* she had about it. The colors mattered. The typefaces mattered. After a week of debating and a lot of forced Jedi/Zen breathing from Vanessa when Rory started panicking about how much they *weren't* doing, they finally landed on a plan they both felt proud of.

The coffee table back at home was covered in colorful sketches. Rory sat on the couch clutching her hair as she gazed at all the different designs.

"Do I have to remind you again?" Vanessa asked, walking over with two mugs.

Rory threw her arms out wide. "How are we ever going to decide which one to go with? There are so many to choose from."

"But only one perfect one," Vanessa replied, plopping down next to Rory and setting the mugs on a side table.

It was Thanksgiving, and Gabi was already gone. She'd lain in bed that morning, planning on wasting the day away watching movies on her laptop, until the doorbell rang just thirty minutes after Gabi left. She shuffled downstairs to find Vanessa at the door, holding two slices of Grampy's blueberry coffee cake.

"How in the world—"

"My uncle works at the bakery," Vanessa started before letting her finish. "Grampy gave us a cake to enjoy today."

Grampy's blueberry coffee cake was coveted in their town. During the summer season, the lines got so long that it sold out daily before nine a.m. It was a terribly kept secret that Grampy set slices aside for the true townies, who all knew that three knocks on his back door would earn you an incognito exchange of brown paper bags. Unless, of course, you were Vanessa's family.

Their exchange this morning was so comical, she was half-inspired to draw a comic out of it.

"Vanessa, it's Thanksgiving. Why are you here?" she'd said when she opened the door.

"Because you said you were going to be alone," Vanessa answered brightly, stepping into the house. "Plus, my little cousins won't stop with the pillow fights, and the constant screaming and noises in the kitchen made my anxious dog pee all over my bedroom rug and...yeah, this introvert is about to explode."

Rory turned on the coffee maker. "You're an introvert?"

"Why else do you think I hole up playing video games after yearbook meetings?"

"Okay, fair."

"Now," she'd said, placing the cake down on the table

and shrugging off her leather jacket. Even when she wasn't in school, Vanessa wore those black cat ears on her head. Rory loved it. "Where are those designs?"

So there they were, plates with leftover crumbs cast aside, rifling through designs. The yearbook was broken into three major sections—club and sports pages, class and faculty picture pages, and the senior section. Right now, they were focusing on the first two, because the senior section was turning out to be a whole feat in itself. Between the superlatives, the special senior events like the picnic and prom, and the tribute pages that parents purchased, the designs were bound to get tricky.

So for now, it was clubs, sports, and class pictures. All of which were already giving Rory a headache.

"It's hard to imagine what the print versions will look like when all we have are minimal sketches," she admitted.

"We could ask the team to draft them up," Vanessa said.

"That feels like a waste of their time."

Vanessa shook her head. "I actually had to do that for the lead designer last year."

"Did you have twenty-six different designs?" She scrubbed a hand down her face, defeated.

"How about we nail down our favorite three and ask editors to get us mock-ups by Monday's meeting?"

Rory frowned. "We're really going to make them work over Thanksgiving weekend?"

Vanessa shrugged. "Time is not a luxury we have."

"You're just as much of a shark as Penelope."

"You know, I'll take that as a compliment."

There was a soft knock on the door.

She tilted her head. Why was her day of wallowing in bed turning out to be a rather busy one? Who *else* could possibly be bothering her today?

Then she remembered who just got into town, and she raced for the door.

Jay stood on her porch and smiled, his chest and shoulders visibly relaxing at the sight of Rory. He didn't waver before he stepped into the house, throwing his arms around her waist and pulling her in for a tight hug. He tucked his face into her neck and brushed his lips against her collarbone. "Missed you, baby."

Vanessa coughed, and then Rory heard papers shuffling over near the coffee table.

She turned around. "Going already?"

Vanessa flushed. "Don't want to get in your way."

"You're not in the way," she said, prying herself from Jay's tight grip. "Jay, this is Vanessa, we've been working on the yearbook together."

Jay grinned at first, but then cocked his head in Vanessa's direction. "You have ears on your head."

Rory swatted him, widening her eyes, but to her surprise, Vanessa smirked at him.

"Thanks, glad they're still there," Vanessa teased back, reaching for her human ears instead of her signature headband, giving them a tug. She shuffled the papers again, trying to pull them into a pile.

"Wait," Rory said, approaching the table again. "Let's narrow down the designs now so we can send them over. By Tuesday. I'm not a monster like you."

Vanessa hesitated, then nodded. "Okay, boss. Which ones?"

"Boss?" Jay said, a grin plastered on his face.

Rory ignored him as she spread the papers out, then pursed her lips in thought. She'd felt lost at which designs she loved or hated before, but now that she was under pressure, it became clear.

She pointed them out. "These. I want to see these."

Vanessa's eyes twinkled. "Done. I'll send these over as soon as I get home."

"Give one of them to Gina," she said. "I want to see how she does. I think we should consider her for the senior pages."

Vanessa nodded. "My thoughts exactly."

After a slightly awkward goodbye, Vanessa took off, leaving her alone with Jay.

He grabbed for Rory the second the door slammed shut. "So, you're the boss, huh?"

"No, not really. Just the lead designer."

"*Just* the lead designer?" Jay teased, bending over to nibble her ear.

She sighed. "This is going to pretty much be my life for the next six months."

"Does that mean you're not working at Scoops this spring?"

"No, I will. Probably only night shifts though," she said. "Why do you ask?"

He shrugged. "Wanted to know if I'll get the chance to makeout with you in The War Room."

She perked up. "Does that mean you'll be coming back to work this summer?"

Jay nodded. "I don't have it in me to make any other plans."

Most of the time, Scoopers who left for college wouldn't come back to work there, either getting better-paying summer jobs or even part-time internships. Rory had naturally assumed Jay would want to find something else. But apparently, she was wrong.

She kissed his cheek. "So if Melanie and Calvin's go-to makeout spot is the bathroom, what's ours?"

"The attic," Jay bantered. "No, even better. *The walk-in.*"

Rory laughed, thinking about what it would be like to makeout inside a literal walk-in fridge. "I'm thinking the attic might be a little more comfortable."

"But think about Calvin's face when he opens up the walk-in to get can of whipped cream and is welcomed with such a lovely surprise."

"You're ruthless."

Jay chuckled, closing the gap between them as he kissed her fervently.

She pulled back slightly before letting him continue. "I haven't heard from you in a few days."

"I know," he whispered. "I've had this...thing on campus. It's sucking up my time."

She frowned. "What kind of thing?"

He nuzzled her nose. "I joined a club."

Rory grinned. "You did? That's awesome!"

"It's no big deal," he said, dismissing her. He cupped the back of her head with one hand and kissed her again, holding her waist tightly with the other as he backed her toward the couch. Jay eased her onto the cushions before lying down himself and pressing his body against hers.

She curled her arms around his waist, pressing her fingertips into his back as he kissed down her neck, pulling the collar of her sweater down so he could continue his trail.

Jay traced his lips back up her neck, closing in to kiss her. But she held up a finger to stop him, making him groan slightly.

"Maybe...maybe we shouldn't," she whispered.

"Oh, I think we should."

She put her hands on his chest. "Jay, come on."

He closed his eyes and groaned again. "Baby, this is

literally all I've been thinking about since the last time I saw you."

"You've only been thinking about having sex with me?"

"No, well, not exactly," he admitted, brushing a hand through his hair. "I haven't stopped thinking about you. Being with you. Kissing you."

She'd wanted this for so long, to have all of Jay's attention on her. But deep in her heart, she didn't want it to be like *this*.

So she thought of a diversion.

"Shit, it's late," she said. "I'm going to miss kickoff."

Jay frowned. "You're seriously going to the game?

It was a Haverport tradition. The varsity and JV football teams always played each other on Thanksgiving, and the winning team enjoyed a Thanksgiving feast on the 50-yard line, courtesy of the coaches. Varsity was clearly going to win this year, and despite their fight, she had yet to miss one of Ty's games.

"Yes," she said. "Plus, all the Scoopers said they were going. You can see them."

"But what has he done for *you*, baby? This seems like a one-sided friendship to me."

The memory of a dark, humid night flashed before her eyes. An arm around her waist, lifting her into a car. A chilled water bottle thrust at her chest. A Jeep speeding down Main Street.

It wasn't one-sided. She knew that.

She just smiled. "Come with me."

He sighed. "Fine. Let's go."

Chapter Thirteen

EVEN IF IT was a picture-perfect fall day for a football game—crisp air, bright blue sky, golden leaves floating in the wind—Rory couldn't shake her nerves as she approached the stands with Jay. He held her hand tightly on their climb up the metal bleachers, shuffling through the crowd to find their friends.

"IS THAT WHO I THINK IT IS?!" Blake screamed.

Jay let go of Rory and held up his hands. "Blakey boy!"

Blake sprinted down the steps toward her and Jay, hauling him into a fierce hug that threw off his balance. The two of them were chattering away as she followed them up to where Blake had been sitting with Zach, Melanie, and Calvin. Melanie caught her eye briefly, her eyebrows raised, before Jay forced her into a hug.

"Missed you, newbie," Jay said to her. He glanced up at Calvin and nodded. "Army boy."

Calvin nodded back, not flinching at the nickname.

Her eyes roamed the group, searching for the missing Scooper. "Where's Jess?"

"Working," Calvin answered. "She got called in at the last minute."

"Why does everyone work on Thanksgiving," she mumbled.

"Yeah, *yearbook editor,* why were you working?" Jay teased her, curling an arm around her waist.

She could *feel* the tension in the group as soon as he did it. Jay just smiled at her before glancing at the rest of them, his chest puffed up, looking mighty proud of himself.

"Did—did I miss something?" Blake asked, his eyes wide like saucers.

Jay kept smiling at them. "Seems my baby has been keeping secrets."

"Baby?!" Blake sputtered. He turned to Melanie, who was tucking a wavy strand of hair behind her ear. "You knew, didn't you?"

"Of course I knew," she said softly.

"Why am I always the last to know," Blake grumbled.

Calvin just crossed his arms, his eyes on Rory. "Huh."

Jay bristled. "Got a problem, army boy?"

"Nope," Calvin said, his eyes still on her. "Just surprised."

But she could sense it—there was something else. Melanie clearly hadn't told him anything about her and Jay, and her friend's loyalty made her heart swell. Calvin, however, looked displeased at this sudden turn of events.

"Wow, look at us," Blake said as they all sat down. "We're all in relationships."

Rory's eyes flicked over to Jay at the use of the big R word, but he seemed unfazed. He just kept smiling at the group.

"For now," Calvin murmured, his voice only loud enough for Rory to hear. He was watching her again as he placed his arm around Melanie's shoulders. Even if he wasn't speaking his mind, she was able to catch the gist of what Calvin was trying to tell her.

He didn't think whatever this was between her and Jay would last.

She shook her head and turned away. Then, she tightened the green bandana on her head with nervous hands and tried to avoid the way it gnawed at her during the rest of the game.

Jay was due at his abuelita's for dinner before the game finished, so he kissed her goodbye and left after the third quarter. Which was how Rory ended up in Calvin's truck with Melanie after watching Tyler and his team devour a turkey with their bare hands on the 50-yard line.

"Are you *sure* you don't want to come back with us to Sandy Cove?" Melanie asked as they pulled up to Misty Bay. "The Fletchers and Calvin's grandma are coming over as well, we're going to have a lot of food. And jam."

Rory shook her head, avoiding Calvin's gaze. His judgment toward her was reverberating off of him, and she needed out of his presence. Even if the idea of going back to Melanie's cottage was way more enticing than stepping foot in her sad, empty house.

"Thanks, but I have a lot of work to do," she replied. She would start to tackle the senior pages, maybe nail down a few design concepts, before flicking on *Sleeping Beauty* and heating up her leftover Thai takeout.

She reached for the door handle.

"Why are you with him?" Calvin asked abruptly.

Rory whipped her head around and glared at him. "Um, because I like him?"

"Even after all the ways he's hurt you and said horrible things about you?"

Melanie, sitting between the two of them, shook her head. "I haven't told him anything, I promise."

"She didn't need to," Calvin added. "I've seen enough at Scoops to know he treats you like dirt."

"He's working on it," she responded through gritted teeth. "He's trying to be better."

"And is that really what you want?" Calvin asked. "Don't you want to be with someone who treated you well from the beginning?"

Her face felt hot as she squinted her eyes. "He's in a relationship."

To her surprise, Calvin chuckled. "Come on, Rory, do you really think his feelings for you changed that quickly?"

"Calvin," Melanie interjected harshly. "Leave her alone."

He paused as if considering, then sighed, tilting his head back on his seat. "Okay, fine, I'm sorry."

She didn't bother looking back at either of them as she slammed the truck door, storming up to the house. As she secured the lock, that sickening feeling crawled up her belly again. She paced the room, angry at how invasive Calvin had been. Why, when he insinuated that she should be with Tyler, did she not tell him that she didn't like Tyler like that?

She dropped to the couch, shoved her face in her hands, and swore.

Rory was standing by the microwave waiting for her Thai food to heat up, staring out at nothing in particular as rain softly pattered against the window.

A fierce knock on the glass made her jump. She swiveled to find a slightly damp Tyler standing there, arms crossed, looking down at his shoes.

She slid open the back door. "Yes?"

"You here alone?"

She gestured toward the cold, lonely house. "Clearly."

"Gabi's working?"

"Unfortunately," she grumbled, making room for Tyler to enter.

Tyler brushed the rain off himself, then offered her a look filled with sympathy. "I'm sorry, Ry."

She shrugged, crossing her arms. "Why are you here?"

"Because my mom wanted to know if you'd like to come over for dinner."

The microwave beeped.

"I, um, I'll be good," she responded.

"Let me guess...leftover Thai."

She grinned. "You know me so well."

Tyler chuckled, but it didn't last long, his eyes and face growing darker as he gazed down at her. "I saw you. With him."

She pulled the warm plate from the microwave, fanning her hand over the food as they stood there in silence, not saying a word.

"Why won't you talk to me about this?" he pleaded.

She set her plate on the counter. "Ty, have you seen

yourself lately? All you do is get mad and yell at me. Remember the movie theater?"

"Yeah, because I care about you, Rory," he admitted, stepping closer to her. "I don't want to see you get hurt."

Her heart began hammering in her chest. "Why?" she stammered. "Why do you care so much when you have a girlfriend?"

"Because—because—dang it," he muttered, rubbing his hands on his face. "Because we're best friends."

"Are we? Because it sure doesn't feel that way."

"You *told* me you wanted this, Ry," he said, his wet sneakers squeaking as he stepped closer to her, his face earnest. "You said you wanted things to go back to normal. I'm trying to do that."

"Nothing feels normal," she whispered.

"You're right about that," he said, his face even closer to hers now. "Especially if you're with *him*."

He spun around and left the house. Rory's heart was beating at the speed of light, blood pulsing through her veins. She was so mad at him, so angry he'd moved on and left her behind.

Before she could even think about what she was doing, she followed him out into the rain. His fists were clenched by his sides as he continued home despite hearing her door slam open.

So she kicked off her sneaker and raised it, forcing all of her anger into her throw and watched it land right between his shoulder blades.

Tyler stopped, his back straightening. He slowly turned toward her, his eyes wide with shock.

"You're an idiot," she said.

She half expected him to leave her there and keep

going, back to his perfect life with his perfect family dinner and his perfect new girlfriend.

But he didn't.

He came rushing forward and closed the distance between them, wrapping his strong arms around her waist and lifting her up. For a brief moment, he just stared into her eyes, longing and anguish etched on his face. It was still there. He still cared for her.

She nodded, letting him know she understood. That she saw him, every bit of him. And that she was okay with whatever he was about to do next.

So, he leaned in, and he *finally* kissed her.

She'd kissed boys before, had even kissed the one boy she'd always had a crush on. But never in her life had a kiss caused what felt like an electrical shock to course through her entire body. Kissing Tyler was like turning on a switch. Everything was darkness before, and now, it all made sense.

She threw her arms around him and kissed him back, his soft lips rolling against hers, his hands holding her tightly to him, grasping this wild, perfect moment. Even as the rain picked up, her hair getting soaked, she wrapped her legs around his torso and tilted her head, deepening the kiss. He moved a hand to the back of her thigh, the other still firm at the small of her back, holding her steady. Just like he always did.

Then it hit her, what they were doing. How wrong it was, yet how right it all felt.

She broke away. "Tyler, we should—"

"Mm-mm," he mumbled, shaking his head as he pressed his lips to hers again. So she let it happen, melting into him, savoring the taste of his tongue, the breath they shared.

When they finally slowed, she nipped at his bottom lip before pulling away and staring into his eyes. He pressed his forehead against hers and sighed, droplets of rain sliding down his cheeks. He was still holding her.

"You're really strong enough to keep me lifted like this?"

"If I put you down then it's over," he whispered. "I don't want it to be over."

Butterflies danced around in her stomach. She felt her cheeks flush. "I—well, at some point my food will get cold."

"That's what microwaves are for."

She smiled, shaking her head at him. "Tyler..."

He groaned, letting her down gently but shielding her from the rain.

"Sooo," she said softly. "What now?"

"I have no idea," he whispered, stroking her cheek with the back of his hand.

"You're still with Zoe."

His hand froze. "And you're with Jay." She felt his muscles stiffen when he said the name.

"Do we...break it off with them?"

"I..." He trailed off. Then, to her absolute dismay, Tyler let her go and stepped away, running a hand through his hair. "I can't."

She felt like she'd been hit with a hammer. "What do you mean you can't?"

"I can't break it off with her, Ry."

She glared at him. "Why?"

"It's hard to explain."

She crossed her arms, in complete disbelief that he was doing this to her. "Is it because I'm not as popular as her? Will I ruin your royalty status?"

"You can't honestly think it's about that."

"Fine, then is it because I'm not blonde and pretty?" she asked, not hiding the venom in her tone.

"Ry, don't," he said, reaching for her. "You're the most stunning person I've—"

"Stop," she said, holding up a hand. She pushed him away, losing her balance from the slick grass beneath her and almost toppling over. He tried to steady her, but she twisted out of his grasp. "If you're not going to break it off with her, then I don't want to hear it."

"P-please, I—" he stuttered. "I need you to trust me."

"And what? Secretly date you so you can keep this weird high school royalty facade you've got going on?" She stormed away from him, grabbing her sneaker as she went.

Tears rolled down his cheeks when she spared him a final glance. "Ry, I don't want to hurt you. I don't—"

"You already have, Tyler," she said coldly.

She stepped into the house, throwing her wet sneaker at the bookshelf across the room, watching a few books crumble to the floor. Just like her heart.

Chapter Fourteen

She couldn't stomach her food, let alone being in the house by herself after that. She grabbed her keys and left, pulling out of the driveway with no clear destination in mind.

She'd kissed both of them. In one day.

Kissing her boyfriend...or whatever Jay was...made sense. But kissing the boy-next-door who'd been her best friend for a decade? That wasn't supposed to happen, and yet here she was. And her heart was broken because of it.

Rory pulled into the parking lot of the grocery store, parked her car in a dark corner, and screamed at the top of her lungs. How *dare* he do this to her. If Calvin hadn't put all these ideas in her head, she probably wouldn't be here right now. She would have kept her cool and not chased him out the door. She would have stayed woefully oblivious to what it felt like to kiss Tyler Chapman, what it was like having his hands on her, listening to the satisfied murmur climb up his throat.

She hopped out of the car and slammed the door. She needed to talk to someone, but going to Melanie's wasn't an option right now. If she did, she would probably end up punching Calvin in the throat for instigating the living hell her day had turned into.

Rory stepped into Post Road Market, pulling her hood over her head so no one would recognize her. Not like she would run into too many people though—the place was virtually empty. Everyone was likely home enjoying Thanksgiving dinner. But she was here...and on the hunt for the one other person she could count on to be scowling somewhere.

This time, she wasn't stocking shelves. She found Jess at the bakery, piping frosting on a purple cake, her eyebrows knitted tightly together in concentration, a pair of massive headphones perched on her head.

Rory stepped into Jess's line of sight and waved her arms. Jess looked up from the cake and pulled her headphones from her ears. She narrowed her eyes. "What are you doing here?"

"Spending my pathetic Thanksgiving at the Post Road Market, you?"

Her face softened, but only slightly. "You look like shit."

Rory wiped at a wet strand of hair sticking to her face. "Thanks, you're too kind."

Jess quickly finished piping her cake, then slid it into the glass display case between them before washing her hands. "You eat yet?"

She shook her head, watching Jess as she removed her denim apron and hung it up on a hook next to the bakery's entrance. She tipped her head in Rory's direction, cueing her to follow as they weaved through the store. Jess started grabbing random items off shelves, then pointed to a fridge stocked with drinks. "Pick something out."

She obeyed, grabbing a lemonade and then following

her to an empty table next to the bakery. They sat, Jess placing her items in front of them—pasta salad, wings, rolls, and two slices of chocolate cake.

"Happy Thanksgiving," Jess mumbled, handing Rory a fork.

She smirked. "Such a lovely way to spend it."

Jess shoved a forkful of pasta salad in her mouth. "Trust me, I'd rather be here than anywhere else."

Rory took a timid bite of a wing, realizing she didn't know anything about Jess besides the fact that she lived with her boyfriend and that she was 22, the oldest out of all the Scoopers.

"Gabi working?" Jess asked.

"Yup."

Jess nodded, the two of them eating in silence for a beat. She wasn't big on words, and the stillness made Rory massively uncomfortable. She soon realized that Jess was probably giving her the space to talk.

She sighed. "I kissed him."

"Jay?"

"Well, I guess, yeah," she replied. "And...and Tyler."

Jess froze mid-bite, staring at her. "Wow."

She sucked in a breath. "That's all you got?"

Jess looked back down at the food, taking another bite.

Rory couldn't bear the excruciating silence. "Please say something," she whispered.

"I don't have much context to work with here, Gilmore."

"Don't call me that."

Jess put down her fork, leaning back against her chair and crossing her arms. "Alright, fine. Only if you tell me what's going on."

So she explained everything. From making up with

Tyler earlier that month to him dating Zoe and her being with Jay, then the constant fighting...and the eventual kiss in her backyard.

To her surprise, Jess actually chuckled, a small smirk curling up her right cheek as she opened up one of the cake containers. "Sounds complicated."

"Complicated is an understatement," Rory grumbled.

"But I'm kind of curious...why come to me? Why not Melanie?"

She huffed. "Calvin."

Jess hummed, as if in agreement with Rory's decision to stay away. "He giving you shit?"

"Kind of," she explained. "He basically thinks Jay and I won't last."

"And after tonight, do you think he's wrong?"

She rolled her eyes before placing her forehead on the table. "No," she admitted.

"You have to break off whatever this is with him."

"But I've wanted this...wanted *him* for so long," she whispered.

"Clearly it's not what you want, though."

She heaved out a sigh, everything feeling heavy. Nothing made sense. Maybe she was just doomed to that kind of fate—pining for something she couldn't have. Waiting for the people around her to choose her instead of something—or someone—else.

Her thoughts drifted to her father. She wondered for the hundredth time how Fred Barry was spending his Thanksgiving. Was she cursed to always have poor relationships because of him? Because she'd become accustomed to longing for things out of reach?

And if so, was this whole thing with Tyler just a trick of

the mind? Did she actually like him, or was she just afraid of losing him?

"Now this is a very sad excuse for a Thanksgiving meal," said an amused voice next to them.

Rory looked up to find Kevin standing there. His shoulder-length honey-brown hair was pulled back into a bun, and the beginning of some sort of tattoo was peeking out from the neckline of his sweatshirt. She didn't really know Kevin that well, other than the fact that he owned the bike shop in town and was friends with Calvin.

She watched Jess roll her eyes. "What do you want?"

"I just missed your sunshiny disposition, my dear Jessica," Kevin replied, a playful grin on his face.

Jess looked ruffled at Kevin's use of her full name and the way he was goading her.

"Why aren't you in Vermont with all the other Birkenstock-wearing, Bernie Sanders–worshiping hippies?" Jess asked him.

"You mean my family? So kind of you to think of them," he said, a big grin still plastered on his face as he crossed his arms. "Unfortunately, I couldn't make the drive up to Burlington this year. I committed to making one of the floats for the Festival of Lights, and I'm a bit in over my head."

"Sounds about right," Jess jabbed.

Kevin chuckled, looking over at Rory. "She has so much faith in me."

She was loving the way Kevin razzed her friend, and how much feistiness she gave back.

"You say yes and overcommit way too often," Jess said bluntly. "And you're losing money because of it."

"But it's for charity!"

She crossed her arms. "And how much of your own money have you sunk into this project?"

Kevin frowned. "You sound just like Calvin."

"He *is* in business school now; you should listen to him."

Kevin kept on smiling, putting his hands on his hips. "Please tell me how this conversation went from your sad Thanksgiving dinner to my terrible business decisions."

Rory pointed to Jess. "Blame her."

Kevin looked amused, but if she wasn't mistaken, she caught a gleam of sadness in his expression before he asked Jess his next question. "Why aren't you with him?"

Jess shrugged, eyes back on her cake as she pierced it with her fork. "He's with them tonight."

"And he really didn't take you?"

Jess glared at him, her expression looking like a silent plea for him to shut his mouth. The two of them held eye contact for an unnerving moment until Kevin eventually caved.

"Well, ladies, enjoy your dinner," he said, heading deeper into the market.

Rory watched as Jess silently ate her cake, avoiding her eyes.

"Jess," she said eventually. "What were you guys talking about?"

"None of your damn business," she growled.

"You told me I could come to you with all of my crap. I could be that for you...if you need it."

Jess glared up at her. "I don't need it."

"Was he talking about your boyfriend? Who is he with?"

"Buzz off, Rory. I'm not here to talk about my shit life. Just yours."

She whistled. "Wow, you are *mad*."

Jess started collecting the containers and forks before them.

"Jess," Rory pleaded, watching as she stood and threw away the trash. "I'm sorry. I shouldn't have pried."

Jess turned around, pointing a shaking finger in her direction. "Listen, kid. I told you I would be here for you, and for some freaking odd reason, I'm okay with it. But my life is off-limits. You got it?"

She just nodded, remaining in her seat as Jess escaped behind the bakery counter.

Chapter Fifteen

EVEN THOUGH EVERYTHING else in her life felt like a mess, at least Rory knew that things at the yearbook were going well for her. She was a few weeks into her new role as lead designer and had found her groove, spending her afternoons finalizing design concepts, approving spreads, assigning editors to different designs, and drawing the pages for the senior section. At the rate she and Vanessa were going, they would reach their first deadline for Penelope a week before Christmas Eve.

Rory sat at a computer next to Gina that following Thursday, giving her final thoughts on a spread concept for the senior page, when Vanessa and Penelope approached them.

"So, we have a slight problem," Penelope admitted.

Rory frowned. "What?"

"The printers just told us that they won't have enough time to finish the books for the start of senior week, so we may have to push up the final deadline."

"That sounds bigger than a *slight* problem," Gina quipped.

Rory ran a hand through her hair. "When is our new deadline?"

"April 30th," Vanessa whispered, her words an apology.

Gina's mouth fell open.

"That's...but that's..." Rory stuttered. "That's the day after prom."

"It's the latest I could push them," Penelope explained. "We need prom pictures—obviously—so we'll get those inserted as soon as Sean sends them over."

Gina scowled. "Sean is going to have to work at prom?"

"We may *all* have to work the night of prom."

The room went dead silent at that.

Rory stood up and roved her eyes over the computer lab. "No, we won't. Don't worry," she said, holding up her hands to reassure everyone. "I will handle the last-minute spreads, and all of you going to prom can enjoy it your time without thinking about this. Okay?"

There were some murmurs and nods, the staff swiftly returning to their screens as they executed Rory's designs.

Rory turned back to Penelope and Vanessa. "I'm happy to leave prom early, or hell, skip the whole damn thing," she said. "But I won't take that away from them, okay?"

Penelope raised an eyebrow. "Commendable leadership, Michaels."

Vanessa's eyes gleamed. "I'll join you. We'll pull an all-nighter."

Rory winked. "It's a date. Now, if you'll excuse me, I need to use the little girl's room."

She held her head high until she was completely out of sight, then heaved a large sigh, leaning against a cold locker in the hallway. She closed her eyes, wondering what the night of prom was going to be like. The only reason she wanted to go in the first place was to be with the other Scoopers. But having to watch Tyler dance with Zoe all night, secretly knowing the way his soft lips felt on hers?

"Rory?"

She blinked her eyes open and found Zoe standing in front of her. She was wearing Tyler's letterman jacket, which looked bulky and awkward on her slim build.

"Everything okay?" Zoe asked.

"No," Rory admitted. "Just...prom."

"Worrying about prom already?"

She shrugged, crossing her arms. "You have to worry about everything when you're on the yearbook committee."

"Oh, that's right, Tyler told me you were doing that. That's so cool," Zoe said, her words coming out quickly. She was nervous.

Rory felt a chill rush down her spine. Was Zoe acting nervous around her because she knew about the kiss?

"Hey, um," Zoe started. "This—this is awkward, but—"

Shit. Shit. Shit. She clenched her teeth, held her breath, and braced herself.

"Will you be at the game?"

She froze for a moment. "The...game?"

"Yeah, the state championship?" Zoe continued slowly, giving Rory a funny look now. "I know things with you and Tyler are...weird right now..."

What the hell does that mean? Rory thought.

"...but I know it would mean so much to him if you came. You're, like, his favorite person in the whole world."

She coughed, suddenly feeling *very* uncomfortable. "And...you aren't?"

"God no," she said, and to Rory's bewilderment, she smiled. "I mean, sure, he cares about me, but if you're not there, it will crush him."

Her body melted just thinking about the kind of effect she had on Tyler. "Is he nervous?" she asked softly.

"Very," Zoe admitted. "But he's too proud to come talk to you after some fight you had at the movie theater?"

Rory exhaled. *She doesn't know about the kiss.*

And why would she? That would be incredibly odd for a boyfriend to tell his girlfriend. *Hey, Zoe? I kissed Rory, but it meant nothing. I still want to be with you. Carry on.*

"Please tell me you'll be there," Zoe pleaded.

"I've never missed a game."

"I know, I just..." Zoe hesitated. "I just know how much he needs this to go well, and you seem to be the only thing that truly calms him. I needed to make sure."

She registered the concern chiseled all over Zoe's beautiful, dewy, pimple-free face.

"Promise me?"

She couldn't help but smirk at Zoe's determination and gall to approach *another girl* and plead for her to come watch *her* boyfriend play football. What a weird, weird world she was living in.

"Okay, Zoe, I promise."

"Thank you!"

Zoe threw her arms around Rory's shoulders, then instantly let go. "Sorry, are we officially hugging friends? Blake said you love hugs..."

"Hugs are fine."

"Good," Zoe said. "See you Saturday!"

She watched her walk away, her mind spinning. She leaned against the locker and slid to the floor, resting in a crouched position before pulling out her phone and typing.

RORY

SOS. Emergency sleepover.

She typed back instantly.

MELANIE

I'll bring the ice cream.

RORY PACED BACK and forth in the living room. They'd reached the point of the emergency sleepover where it was time to share secrets—bowls of half eaten strawberry ice cream on the coffee table, comfy sweats and fuzzy socks on, hair tied up in ponytails, credits rolling on the TV after watching *One Hundred and One Dalmatians*, candles burning on end tables.

And Rory had one big, fat secret to share.

"You're officially making me nervous," Melanie said, eyeing Rory. "Spill. Now."

She wrung her hands. "I had the Thanksgiving from hell."

Melanie hummed. "Me too."

She stopped, blinking at her friend. "Crap, Mel, I—"

"You first," her friend said, holding out a hand in a plea for Rory to continue.

She sat down on the couch, tucking a leg underneath her. "Mel, really, my problems are dumb compared to—"

"Rory, please, for me? Let's talk about you."

Feeling antsy, she bolted back up and paced again. "I did something stupid, Mel. Like, really, *really* stupid."

Melanie raised her brow. "I doubt it. You are the furthest thing from stupid."

"I do not deserve you," she grumbled. She paused, facing Melanie full on. "Okay...I-I kissed Tyler."

Melanie covered her mouth and let out some kind of exasperated sound that was half laugh, half pure shock.

Rory sat back down, covering her face with her hands. "Stupid, right?"

"Oh my god. Where? How? When?"

"Backyard. Late at night. He was being all broody about Jay again, and we were fighting, and he stormed out, and...I chased after him."

"And the kiss?" she cooed.

"Probably the hottest thing I've ever experienced in my life."

Melanie screamed, laying down on the throw pillows and placing her hands across her heart. "I'm going to combust from cuteness."

"But you're missing the *emergency* part of this conversation, which is the fact that I'm technically seeing someone else," she rationalized. "And so is he."

Melanie sat back up. "Did you guys talk about it?"

"Briefly? He...told me he couldn't break it off with her." Her voice croaked as she said it.

Melanie tapped a finger to her lips. "Something weird is going on here. There's no way he wouldn't choose you."

"Well, he didn't," Rory growled. "So he's still seeing her and I guess I'm still seeing Jay, and I don't even know what's going on with him...you see? I'm a mess!"

Melanie reached for Rory's face and guided her down to her lap, then stroked her mahogany hair. "You're not a mess, you just have two hot boys very into you."

"Does Calvin know you think they're hot? Because he might lose his mind."

The sound of Melanie's cackle reverberating off the walls made her smile.

She closed her eyes. "Do you think I'm horrible? For cheating on Jay?"

Melanie's hands kept brushing through her hair. "Is it cheating if you're not actually dating him? Sounds like you guys haven't even had that talk yet."

She sat up, facing her. "I just figured we were. Why are boys so confusing?"

"Maybe it's time to ask him." Melanie shrugged. "If that's what you want, of course."

She groaned, laying back on her friend's lap. "I don't know what I want."

They sat in silence, the movie puttering out on the TV.

"Tell me about your Thanksgiving, Mel."

"It was pretty horrible," her friend mumbled. "Thanksgiving hasn't felt normal for a while, though."

"Do you miss him?"

"Yes. Every minute of every day."

Melanie didn't say more, so Rory didn't push. She flicked on the next movie on her list, the two of them watching in comfortable silence.

Rory escaped up to her room and clicked the door shut. She stared at her phone and took a deep breath.

Just do it, she told herself.

She hadn't heard much from Jay again this week. His texts were sparse and short, but she had chosen to take it as a good sign. She hoped this club was working out for him.

But she knew she couldn't avoid this conversation any longer. She tapped his contact name and hit Call, then held it up to her ear and listened as the phone rang. It eventually went to voicemail.

Rory cursed and covered her face with her hands as she thought through the conversation she knew she needed to have.

Before she could think through a solid plan, her phone rang. She grabbed it and answered.

"Hi," she mumbled.

"Hi, sorry, sorry," Jay said on the other line. He sounded out of breath. "I'm late for a meeting. This campus is so damn big."

"A meeting at ten at night?"

"Yeah, it's insane." Jay chuckled. "Everything okay?"

"Um, well, not really."

The sound of whipping wind slowed on the other line. "What's wrong?" he asked.

She shook her head. "Nothing. You're busy, I don't want to hold you up."

"Just tell me."

She squeezed her eyes shut and took a deep breath first. "Jay, what are we?"

"What do you mean *what are we?*" he snapped.

"Like, are we...in a relationship? Are you my boyfriend?"

The silence was damning, but Rory waited for him to respond.

"I...didn't think we had to put a label on it," Jay replied. "We're just having fun."

She concentrated on her nails and tried to keep her voice as calm as possible. "Are you seeing other people?"

"Uh, I—"

"Like, have you hooked up with anyone else?"

"Define hook up."

His answer already said it all, but she continued anyway. "Have you kissed anyone else since our conversation on the beach?"

"Rory..."

"I won't be mad," she answered honestly.

"Why? Have *you* kissed anyone?"

"Yes." The word came out before she could stop herself. But after it did, she felt relieved. She sighed, settled down on her bed, and listened to him snigger on the other line.

"Damn, I honestly wasn't expecting that," Jay replied. "I was mentally preparing to get an earful."

"Because you thought I would be mad that you're hooking up with other people?"

"Well, yeah. I like fooling around with you, but I don't know, things on campus have started to feel different, and you and I haven't..."

She understood. "So you figured you would find someone else who would bang you."

He exhaled. "I haven't *banged* anyone, but I've kissed a few people."

Rory curled into the fetal position, resting her phone on her ear. "So we're just...hooking up."

"Does that make you mad?"

"No. I guess after we talked on the beach and you said all of those things, I thought—"

"That I wanted a relationship," he said, cutting her off.

"Maybe," she murmured.

"I told you, though. I told you I wasn't sure what this was, and I gave you an out."

"I know you did."

They remained silent, the sound of howling wind picking back up on the other line, signaling he was on the move again.

"Who'd you kiss?" he asked.

She bristled. "You don't know him."

"Oh come *on*. The Port is small, there's no way I don't know him. Who is it?"

"I'm not telling you," she replied, her tone terse. "Just like I won't ask about who you've kissed."

Jay snorted. "Fine, that's fair."

She heard a door creak open on his end, and then the howling wind ceased.

"So..." Rory started. She wasn't sure where to go from here.

"Listen, Rory, I don't think I can make it to the game," Jay replied. "This thing came up on campus that I really don't want to miss."

She tucked her knees into her sweatshirt, settling into the warmth of her bed. "Okay."

"But I'll see you next week when I'm home, yeah?"

"Sure, yeah, okay."

"Alright, baby, see you then."

Rory placed her phone on her nightstand as she mentally played through the conversation again. He was fine with her kissing someone else—even though he had no idea *who*—and she gave him the go-ahead to do whatever he wanted, as well. All of it felt sticky and complicated, and she wasn't sure how much more of it she could take.

Chapter Sixteen

The game was held on neutral turf, giving neither Haverport nor Westford the home-field advantage. The temperatures were now low enough that Rory had to reach deep into her closet for her down jacket that morning. She wrapped her navy-and-white scarf around her face, the green bandana tied tightly to her head. Her stomach was knotted all morning, thinking about how Tyler was doing. There was so much riding on this game for their town, and she wondered if scouts would be there to watch him play. She was thankful that Blake and Zach didn't say much when she picked them up, the three of them remaining in comfortable silence as they drove the thirty minutes to the stadium.

The parking lot was packed, but Rory was able to squeeze into a spot close to the exit. The nervous energy was palpable as they walked toward the stands, the north side already covered in a sea of navy and white, while the south side donned black and yellow.

They paused for a moment at the bottom of the stands. Blake shivered, causing Zach to reach an arm around him and tuck Blake into his jacket, his hand playing with Blake's red curls. Rory rolled her eyes at the dramatics.

"This could be you, you know," Blake teased. "But you didn't force him to come."

"He had a thing," Rory replied. She ignored his gaze and turned to find Melanie.

They eventually found her and Calvin, and the five of them squeezed onto a bench. Rory gave Melanie a hug, her eyes darting to Calvin's face. To her surprise, he smiled at her, his features soft and relaxed. She pulled away from her friend's grasp, too stunned to smile back.

Does he know? she wondered.

The crowd roared as the Haverport team jogged onto the field, the cheerleaders at their heels, jumping up and down with new sparkly pom-poms glistening under the bright autumn sun. Zoe was at the front of the helm, her hair curled and tied into that signature cheerleader ponytail, a small corsage tied around her wrist. Another Haverport tradition for the senior cheerleaders—wearing flowers with the team colors on their wrists for the last game of the year.

Rory scanned the jerseys, finding number 17. Instead of jumping up and down and hyping his team up like he always did, Tyler was pacing back and forth, his gait taut and nervous. Rory glanced around the stands to see if she could find the Chapmans, but before she could eye them, the whistle was blown, the captains shook hands, and the boys lined up for kickoff.

She watched as Tyler clicked on his helmet as he walked by the cheerleaders. Zoe held out a fist to him and he bumped it like they were pals, which seemed strange. But she instantly forgot it as she watched him scan the stands, his gaze landing in her direction. She was too far to actually see his features, but he'd definitely found her green bandana. His chest visibly expanded, and then he was jogging up the field, ready for the game to begin.

THE TEAMS WERE neck-and-neck by halftime. Even though Tyler was able to escape their grasp and score a touchdown, Westford's defense was strong as steel. Walker and Tyler worked together seamlessly, keeping up team spirits and executing each play flawlessly. But it couldn't stop the clever strategy of their competing team, the score at a stubborn seven to seven when the halftime buzzer went off.

Rory snuck away from the group to use the bathroom. Her nerves were running rampant, every facet of her body tense as she wondered how Tyler was doing right now, how he and his team were feeling in the locker room during their pep talk.

She stood in a line that snaked out of the bathroom building when she saw Tyler's father walk by with a man she'd never seen before. Mr. Chapman didn't notice Rory as he got on the line for the snack stand, the two men talking just loud enough for her to hear.

"Well, we appreciate you coming out to watch our boy," Mr. Chapman said.

"He's a solid player," the man responded. "I'm surprised no one has snatched him up yet."

Her spine zipped up when she realized what was going on. *A scout.* This had to be the reason why Tyler was nervous for today's game, despite it being the state championship and all.

"I can't guarantee anything, but I will advocate hard for him," the man continued. "And maybe we'll see you in the stadium next year."

Mr. Chapman grinned. "Thank you. He's wanted this for a long time. Although it will be weird to have him so far away if all goes to plan."

So...far away?

Rory felt like someone was wringing her insides dry. Her vision blurred as she sucked in small, short breaths, realizing what Mr. Chapman was saying.

Tyler would leave her. He would go off to college to play football, and he wouldn't need Rory or Scoops or any of them anymore.

She stepped out of the line and walked around the bathrooms so no one would see her spiral.

He would have no need for her after graduation. Tyler would leave, and they would probably grow distant, the days of playing football and soccer in their backyards slowly fading into lost, forgotten memories. Maybe that's why he didn't want to be with her, why he wouldn't break it off with Zoe. The pain of leaving would be too great, so why go through it at all?

Rory's panic switched to anger. Anger that he was going to leave her behind. Anger that he didn't want to take a chance on her despite their history. Anger that he didn't even tell her about this, about the scout and what was happening at this game and his next steps toward college. He was pulling away from her, and he hadn't even left yet.

She tore off the green handkerchief tied to her head and walked out the gates, chucking it in the trash without looking back.

RORY WAS VEERING off the highway, taking the exit toward Haverport, when Melanie called her. She answered, turning on the speakerphone. "Yes?"

"Rory, where are you?"

"I had to leave," she grumbled. "Hard to explain."

"Okay, well, uh..." Melanie stuttered. "S-something happened."

She tightened the grip on her steering wheel. "What happened?"

"I-I don't—" Melanie couldn't get the words out. Was she crying?

There were muffled sounds, words exchanged in whispers that Rory couldn't make out, before the phone was given to someone else.

"He's injured," Calvin said, his voice calm.

She felt her heart stop. Her vision went blurry and, in an instant, she was pulling off the road, throwing her car into park. "Wh-what happened?"

"One of Westford's defensemen tackled him from behind after he made a catch. They think it's something to do with his leg or knee. He's still on the ground, not moving."

Panic rose in her chest. *On the ground. Not moving.*

"They're rushing onto the field with a stretcher," she heard Melanie say distantly.

"Where are you?" Calvin asked pointedly.

"Not there," she whispered, more to herself than anyone else.

She could feel the tension through the phone as Calvin

remained silent. There were nervous murmurs around him on the phone, a few people yelling in the distance. "Why?" he finally asked.

Rory wasn't sure why she said it, especially to Calvin, but she was tired of fighting the truth. "Because he doesn't need me anymore. He'll leave me, just like everyone else."

She heard Calvin sigh over the phone, like he was calculating the exact words to say next. She waited impatiently for his reply, regretting her words instantly. She felt too exposed.

She heard shuffling on the other end of the phone, the sounds of Calvin descending the stands and stepping away from the crowd so he could say what he needed to in private. For the briefest moment, she felt thankful for him.

"No matter the distance, I don't think he could ever leave you," Calvin replied slowly. "I don't know exactly what's going on between the two of you, but I do know that you will always be his family. Because that's what you've been to him since the moment you first met. And true family never leaves."

Rory was now crying on the side of the road, her face in her hands. "No one sticks around for me, Calvin. I don't know what it's like to have a real family."

"But you do," he countered. "Just because Scoops is closed right now doesn't mean you don't have us. You basically told my girlfriend the same thing when she moved here last summer, and the same goes for you. We will always stick together. No matter how messy life gets. Understand?"

She was openly sobbing now, all her emotions flooding over. Calvin didn't hang up, didn't even say anything until Rory was finished, just being with her on the phone. Staying with her, like a family was supposed to.

"Thanks," she murmured, wiping away tears and snot with the sleeve of her sweatshirt.

"Promise me something?"

She let out a shaky breath. "What?"

"Talk to Melanie about Tyler. She's honestly your biggest fan. She would do anything for you."

He must not know then. Melanie didn't tell him a thing. She truly did not deserve her.

Rory wiped her nose with her sweatshirt sleeve. "Calvin—"

"I know she's going through a lot," he interrupted. "But she is a hell of a lot stronger than she looks. She lost her brother, Rory. She doesn't want to lose her sister, too."

She was crying again. "What am I supposed to do right now?"

"Go home. Wait for him. Talk to him and be honest. What do you have to lose?"

Everything, she thought. Because she finally realized that Tyler was everything to her. He always had been.

She grumbled a thank-you to Calvin and hung up the phone, taking a few calming breaths before driving back to Misty Bay. She didn't bother turning on any lights when she walked through the door. She sat down on the couch and watched the Chapman house through the window, waiting for them to get home.

It was sometime past midnight when she drifted off to sleep, both houses still blanketed in darkness.

"Sweetie?"

Rory felt herself being gently shaken awake, a warm

hand steady on her shoulder. She blinked her eyes open, the kitchen light now turned on. She glanced at the clock on the microwave. It was 1:26 in the morning.

She bolted upright, glancing next door. Their car was parked out front. She looked up to Tyler's room, noticing his lamp was on.

"Rory, sweetie, what's going on?" Gabi asked. "Why aren't you in bed?"

She stood up abruptly, heading for the back door. "Tyler, he was hurt at the game. I have to go see if he's okay."

"It's one in the morning," Gabi said, chasing after her daughter. "That's probably not wise—no, Rory—"

Rory didn't obey as she slid the door open, racing down the steps and over to the Chapman house. She found Mrs. Chapman in the kitchen, one arm hugging her stomach, the other clutching her cell phone to her ear.

Rory knocked on the window, and Mrs. Chapman smiled slightly, telling whoever was on the phone to hold on as she slid open the door. "His father is putting him in bed."

"Is he okay?" Rory asked through tears. "Can he walk?"

"Not right now, no," Mrs. Chapman explained. "But the doctors said he didn't break anything. It sounds like some kind of nasty sprain."

"Can I see him?" She knew it was a long shot, but she was desperate. She couldn't fathom the idea of him hurt.

Mrs. Chapman placed her hands on Rory's shoulders, rubbing her thumbs back and forth reassuringly. "It's probably not a good idea right now. He's in really rough shape."

Rory couldn't see Mrs. Chapman through the tears pooling in her eyes. She caught the familiar scent of Gabi's lavender hand lotion as she hooked an arm through Rory's and thanked Mrs. Chapman. Rory didn't fight Gabi as she led her home and guided her up the stairs to her room, tucking her into bed like she used to.

Rory sat up as soon as Gabi closed the door, looking out her window to Tyler's room, and watched as Mr. Chapman flicked off his bedside lamp. She dug for her phone in her sweatshirt pocket and dialed his number.

One ring. Two rings. Three.

Her heart pounded in her chest. *Just answer. Please answer.*

"Ry?"

His voice was hoarse. He was crying.

"Ty, I'm so sorry," she blubbered. "What's going on? Are you okay?"

"No, I'm not okay. We lost. Everything is ruined. And... and you weren't there."

"Yes, I was," she whispered. "I was, I was."

"But not when I needed you," he stammered. "I was on the grass and I looked up in the stands and I...I couldn't *find* you."

"I know," she cried, her words thick in her throat. "I'm sorry. I screwed up. I shouldn't have left."

He was now sobbing into the phone, sounding more broken than ever. She wished she could crawl into bed with him and hold him close, tell him how sorry she was, how she knew she'd screwed up, that she wanted to make everything better for him.

"Please, I'm-I'm the worst," she admitted. "I was selfish and hurt. I should have been there for you."

His crying slowed for a moment. "I can't do this right now. I-I need to sleep."

"Okay," she breathed. "Goodn—"

He hung up before she could finish.

She could only sit there staring at her phone screen,

feeling like she had so much more she needed to say. To tell him how she truly felt.

Because somehow, softly, like a gentle fall breeze rushing through golden leaves, she'd fallen for her best friend.

Chapter Seventeen

TYLER DIDN'T SHOW up at all the following week at school. Not seeing him in person was eating at Rory from the inside out. After their phone call, he ignored her texts and kept denying her calls. By day three, she stopped Zoe in the hall, feeling all kinds of shame that she had to find out how her best friend was doing through his girlfriend.

Zoe was gracious and said he still wasn't well, but that she was delivering his schoolwork to him each day so he didn't fall behind. "He won't see me either," she admitted to Rory. "I've only seen his mom."

Her anxiety with each passing day swelled to an all-time high, and it didn't help that Jay was officially home for his winter break and wanted to hook up with Rory—constantly. She'd tried distancing herself from him, saying she was busy with yearbook meetings or that she had homework that needed to be finished. But that didn't stop him from finding opportunities to surprise her, waiting by her car when she was delirious from looking at spreads for hours in a dark computer lab, or knocking on her door far too late on a weeknight. He'd wrap her in his arms and kiss her deeply.

It was the Thursday after the game, and Jay was pulling her down onto the couch. His hands were roaming to places they hadn't yet, and it made her nervous.

She stopped him. "Jay, come on."

He groaned. "Rory, baby, I want you. Don't you get that?"

"I know," she whispered.

Rory tried pushing off those new feelings for her best friend. Tyler had cut her out of his life, and the idea of telling him how she felt would only make him leaving for college that much worse. So, she distracted herself with yearbook and school assignments and Jay's hands and mouth, hoping that those feelings would eventually drift away.

Jay traced a finger down her neck. "Don't you want me, too?"

Before she could answer, the lock on the door clicked. Jay bolted upright and fixed himself, flinging his arm over Rory innocently. She just sat there in a daze, looking at the microwave clock. It was 9:32 at night. Why was her mother getting home so early?

Gabi stepped into the house, eyeing her and Jay suspiciously as she closed the door behind her. "Well hello, I didn't expect company this late at night."

Jay jumped up, holding out his hand. "Jay Sanchez. I'm sorry for coming around unannounced."

Gabi eyed Rory before shaking Jay's hand. "It's alright. But if you don't mind—"

"I'm gone," he said, grabbing his jacket from the kitchen chair and looking back at Rory. "See you Saturday?"

She nodded, her heart twisting in her chest thinking

about being at the Festival of Lights with the Scoopers...but probably without Tyler. He was radio silent in their group chat as they made plans to meet up and watch the parade together.

Gabi took a seat on the couch, her eyes still on Rory. "Please tell me I didn't interrupt something."

"You did," Rory admitted with a heavy sigh. "But honestly, it's okay."

"Trouble in paradise?"

"Just...trouble seeing it as paradise?"

"Ah," Gabi said, flicking off her sneakers. "Do you still like him?"

Tears pricked her eyes. She glanced away so she wouldn't notice. She really didn't want to explain all of this to her mother. It wasn't like she'd ever be around to help her with any of it.

Her silence must have spoken for itself, because Gabi let out a long breath before continuing. "I know you hate that I'm not home much, but I'm here whenever you're ready to talk to me."

"What if you don't like what I have to say?"

"Impossible, sweetie."

No, it's not, she told herself. Gabi would flip if she knew what she was really up to...like learning the true identity of her father, even though every attempt to find him always came to a dead end.

She sniffled and discreetly wiped away her tears.

"Rory, have you applied for schools yet?"

She froze, her body going cold. With the craziness of joining yearbook and everything going on with Tyler and Jay, she'd let the deadlines for applying to colleges conveniently slip by. The idea of actually submitting an application made her nauseous. What she really wanted was to take a year off, figure out what she wanted to do with her life. But she was afraid to admit that truth. She'd spent years watching her mother come home looking exhausted night after night.

"Um, yes," she lied. "I have."

Gabi beamed, jostling Rory's arm. "This is great news! Where? Tell me everything. Maybe we could schedule some college visits this spring."

Rory frowned. "You'll take off of work?"

"Of course! We'll have a road trip, doesn't that sound fun?"

No, she thought. But Gabi looked so happy. She didn't want to squash it. "I applied for UCONN."

"Of course, a good safety school," she said. "Where else?"

She wanted to balk at her mother's use of the term "safety school." At this point, Rory would be thankful if UCONN even let her in. She wasn't exactly known for being a brainiac.

She quickly racked her mind thinking of the other schools her teammates talked about applying for, listing them off. "Quinnipiac and...Northeastern."

"Northeastern! Wow, Boston. That would be such a fun place to visit."

Rory nodded, desperate to change the subject. "Why are you home so early?"

"Wilson's asked if I would work the stand at the festival tomorrow," Gabi said, her voice almost giddy with excitement. "I said yes, but only if I could go home early and hang out with my daughter."

A smile bloomed on Rory's face. "Really?"

"Really," she said. "Now, where are you on your Disney list?"

She snatched her phone and pulled up the list. "*The Jungle Book*. I was also going to throw a frozen pizza in the oven."

"Screw that, I ordered from Penny's already. Is the buffalo chicken pizza still your favorite, or am I about to embarrass myself?"

It technically wasn't her favorite anymore, but she didn't care. After the week from hell—and the big fat lie she just cooked up—Rory was happy to finally have one thing go right. "Yeah, it is."

RORY SHUFFLED down the hall that Friday, feeling every ounce of dread in her chest. Tyler wasn't at school—again—and he still wasn't talking to her. Jay was also being cryptic in his texts, and she wondered if it had anything to do with her not agreeing to go all the way with him yet. Jay said he wanted to change, but what if all of this was a ruse to get in Rory's pants? Just like he did with all the other girls she watched parade through his life.

The scent of roses and vanilla distracted her as she opened up her locker, coming from a tall, concerned-looking blonde who settled next to her.

Rory grabbed her coat and closed her locker. "Still no word from him?"

Zoe shook her head. "I've never seen him this sad. I-I don't know what to do."

She shoved her coat in the crook of her arm. "Yeah well, you can't go wrong with food when it comes to Tyler. That's always the way to his heart."

"I'll keep that in mind," Zoe replied, her face still full of concern. "Hey, do you, um, have a minute?"

Rory felt the familiar tightening in her chest. "I have to meet with Vanessa about yearbook stuff—"

"Seriously, it will only take a minute."

Rory huffed. "Fine, what's up?"

"Not here."

Rory followed her down the hall and into the girls' bathroom. They casually checked their hair and makeup, waiting for other girls to leave, before Zoe turned to her. "Okay, I need to tell you something, and it's going to sound really freaking strange."

"Uhhhh, okay?"

Zoe took a deep breath, running a hand through her hair nervously before staring back at Rory. "So, you know I'm dating Tyler."

Rory frowned. "No shit."

"Okay so what if...what if I told you that it wasn't actually real?"

She didn't respond, just stared at the girl, flabbergasted.

Zoe continued. "I know it sounds insane."

"Wait, you're not actually dating him?" Rory blurted. The room was starting to spin.

"Correct."

She felt anger bubbling up in her chest. "Okay, and does he know that? Are you just playing him? Because I swear to god, Zoe, if you are—"

Zoe placed her hands on Rory's shoulders. "He's in on it, don't worry. I would never do that to him."

"I'm-I'm so confused."

"I know...everything," she says. "I know that you guys kissed, that he's in—"

"Stop," Rory said, wrenching out of Zoe's grasp.

"I know how he feels for you, Rory."

"Okay, so then tell me why he hasn't done anything about it?" she demanded. "If he does like me, then why is he still keeping up this facade with you? Why haven't you broken things off?"

"I've told him that we should," Zoe admitted. "Ever since he kissed you, I told him to go for it. But he hasn't. He says he doesn't want to break our...deal."

"And what is your deal?"

Zoe pressed her lips into a firm line. Apparently knowing the "deal" was going too far.

"If you're not going to tell me what's really going on, then what was the point in telling me at all?"

"Because I don't want you to give up on him. I wanted you to know the truth."

She was crying now. "Am I supposed to thank you?"

"No, I'm sorry, Rory. If I knew when we started things, I would have never done this to you."

Rory scoffed, crossing her arms. "Yeah right. Let me guess, this is just some scheme to keep up with your Haverport High royalty status. Probably to make that asshole Walker jealous or something."

Zoe's face darkened. "Fine, make your assumptions about me. But I'm telling you right now that whatever you're thinking is probably false. I just wanted you to know the truth, even though Tyler will hate me for it. Because we're friends."

Rory couldn't help herself—she laughed. "We're friends?"

Zoe just gave her an icy stare. "Not anymore," she answered, and then stormed out of the bathroom.

Chapter Eighteen

NOT REALLY DATING.

Rory blasted music in her car on the way to Scoops the next night, but no volume could drown out the sound of Zoe's words that played over and over in her head.

Part of it made a lot of sense; Tyler's relationship with Zoe *was* really strange. But in any romance book or movie where the characters fake dated, the goal was usually to make someone else jealous—something Rory hated to admit had worked on her. Yet now that it had been made clear they were on the same page with their feelings, Tyler still hadn't broken off the ruse. Whenever this trope played out in fiction, it always ended with the fake daters winding up in a relationship. It made her sick to even think it, but maybe the reason why Tyler hadn't broken things off with Zoe—even after Zoe told him to *go for it*—was because he was developing feelings for Zoe as well.

She slammed her car door, ignoring Melanie's concerned look at the outburst. Jay was standing a few feet away from Calvin, like being in his proximity would scar him. He moved swiftly once she approached, curling an arm around her waist. Calvin gave her a curt nod, not bothering to say a word to her as he pulled Melanie in and kissed the top of her head before leading them down Main Street to find Blake and Zach.

Losing the state championship certainly didn't slow down Haverport when it came to its annual holiday festival. In fact, if anything, the loss spurred the town to celebrate even more, like they were trying to compensate for how close they'd come to winning State for the first time. Main Street was converted into a winter wonderland. Streams of garland twined around lampposts with big red bows. Wreaths were tied to shop doors, twinkly lights glistening in windows. Many of the shops and restaurants set up booths right outside for easier access, selling steaming mugs of hot chocolate, candy canes, fluffy winter scarves, and colorful streamers tied to the tips of sparkling wands.

"Where'd they say to meet them?" Melanie asked.

"Outside of the cafe," Calvin responded, pointing to Seabreeze Café just down the road. "Blake said they're selling white chocolate peppermint mochas again."

"Oooo, tell him to get me one," Melanie cheered.

"Headband, it's almost eight o'clock at night, you don't need more caffeine."

Melanie slapped him playfully. "When has that ever stopped me before?"

"Yeah, army boy, let your girlfriend have caffeine. And sugar," said Jay. "Stop being such a hard-ass."

Calvin didn't react. He just smiled, pulling Melanie closer to him as he planted a kiss on her forehead. "Then it's a good thing I already told him to grab you one. My girlfriend can have whatever she wants."

"Good, because for a second there, I thought I was going to have to beat you up," Rory quipped.

"I'd pay to watch that," Melanie teased.

They finally reached the cafe, finding Blake and Zach huddled together holding a tray with six massive lattes to go.

Rory and Melanie squealed, planting sloppy kisses on Blake's cheeks as they took their coffees, Zach laughing at Blake's embarrassment as he handed a latte to Jay. When he held out the last one to Calvin, a slim hand shot out and took the cup out of Zach's grasp.

Rory's body stiffened as she watched Jess take a sip of the latte, a smug look on her face as she eyed Blake's boyfriend. "Zach, you're new to the group, so let me fill you in," Jess said. "Calvin doesn't like joy or fun things. Sugary coffee falls into that category."

To Rory's surprise, Calvin laughed, his eyebrows raised as he shoved Jess slightly. "Funny coming from *you*."

Jess just chuckled, a real smile blooming on her face. It was odd seeing Jess like this. She was pretty sure she could count on one hand the times she'd actually seen Jess happy.

Jess took another sip of her drink, eyeing her and Jay. His arm was still looped around her waist, his thumb running back and forth over the skin underneath her sweater. She gave her a feeble smile, but Jess just nodded. Relief washed over her, and she felt thankful for this unexpected little group of hers. This family, as Calvin elegantly put it.

They shuffled their way through the crowds, finding an empty pocket of sidewalk where they could settle in and wait for the parade. Blake was rehashing some kind of crazy story with Jay from that summer, the group laughing and teasing one another, but Rory remained silent. She couldn't help but search the crowds, wondering if Tyler would show up. The Festival of Lights was his favorite. She'd joined the Chapmans over the years to watch the parade, standing too close to the street with Tyler as they caught candy tossed from the different colorful floats, the two of them competing for the biggest pile by the end of the night. Their tradition shifted to hanging with the Scoops crew during the parade, but he'd yet to show, yet to respond to any of them in the group text.

She needed to talk to him. Needed to confront him about what Zoe had confessed.

Not really dating.

The crowd cheered as Haverport High's band marched down the streets, their light-strewn instruments making their horns shine like beacons in the night. The colorful floats soon followed, covered with more twinkling lights and more sparkly garlands, the scent of evergreen misting through the air as festive trucks strapped with trees and wreaths drove through.

Jess groaned. Rory looked over and saw her shaking her head, her face in her hands.

"It's so over the top," Jess grumbled.

Rory looked out and saw the float parading down the street; a truck that had been transformed into a colossal sled, with lights and silver bells intricately trimming the edges. Around it were smaller sleds lined with Christmas lights attached to bikes as riders cruised down the road, all dressed as elves. Sitting at the center of the float was Haverport's fire chief, Ed Nickels, dressed in a Santa suit and waving, his jolly laugh booming across the crowd. And next to him, dressed like Rudolph the Red-Nosed Reindeer, was Kevin. He wore a long-sleeved brown shirt and matching khaki pants, with a bright red flickering nose on his face. His hair was even long enough to tie into two buns at the top of his head to look like small antlers. He held out a large silver bucket, collecting money that townies tossed in for charity.

Calvin covered his mouth with his hand, trying not to laugh as Jess punched his arm. "Did you even try to stop him?"

"You know how he gets," Calvin replied. "When he sets his mind to something, there's literally nothing that will stop him."

Jess sighed, turning back toward the float. "How much money did he sink into this?"

"I don't think you want the answer to that. He finally let me look at his books."

Jess turned around, eyebrow raised. "And?"

Calvin let out a lengthy breath. "It's not looking good."

"How bad?"

"He's not pulling in enough business in the summer to make up for the off-season," Calvin admitted. "If something doesn't change, the bike shop will be closed by next fall."

Rory caught Jess's frown, the way her forehead creased as she processed this information. Jess glanced up at Rory briefly, her face flushed. Rory knew that whatever was going on wasn't her business—she'd made that much clear the other night at the market. She smiled shyly and looked away, noticing two figures now approaching the group.

"So, are we still sneaking into Scoops tonight for some ice cream, or...?"

Rory stood there, stunned as the Scoopers cheered for Tyler's surprise appearance. Zoe was with him, her arm linked with his. He was limping slightly, but on the move, a black brace clinging tightly to his knee over his jeans.

She remained quiet as Tyler filled everyone in on how he was doing. All about his knee and his recovery, but not a blip was spoken about football or losing the game. They knew him well enough not to bring it up.

Tyler kept sneaking glances at Rory, eyeing the way Jay

held her possessively against him, but not saying a single word in her direction. At least Zoe had the courtesy to smile and say hi to her, even though she knew how pissed she likely still was.

Rory now noticed the way Zoe's hand looked stiff on his arm, and how everything about the two of them felt clinical and practiced. *How did I not notice it before?* she wondered.

Tyler's eyes were still on her. She wondered if he knew what Zoe had confessed to her, wondered what was going on in that head of his.

As the parade dwindled down and crowds moved, a familiar group of football players approached the Scoopers. Walker wobbled slightly at their helm, undeniably tipsy from whatever was in the flask he was not-so-discreetly hiding in his letterman jacket.

"Yo, Chapman," Walker said loudly, slapping a hand on Tyler's back that made him wince. "You good, man?"

"Been better," he mumbled. "I'm sorry about the end of the game."

"Yeah, well, if you hadn't blown up your knee, we'd probably be champions," he said.

Tyler's face darkened but he didn't budge. He looked down at his shoes.

Rory was seething. She pulled herself out of Jay's grasp and walked right up to Walker. "Yeah, well, *maybe* if you guys didn't suck without Tyler, he wouldn't have to carry your asses to victory."

"Woah, woah, Michaels, calm down," Walker protested, holding his hands up in a show of innocence.

She felt her blood go hot as she stepped closer to Walker, invading his space. She could smell the cheap vodka on his breath. "Don't ever tell me to calm down. You know I'm right, and you're too much of a coward to admit it."

She felt a hand on her shoulder. "Ry," Tyler said softly.

"I'm not saying you're wrong, Michaels," Walker admitted. "What would you like me to say? That he's the man because he's the best football player Haverport has ever seen and he's dating the hottest chick in school?"

"Yes," Rory replied curtly. She flicked her eyes over to Zoe, curious to see her reaction at hearing Walker's *hottest chick in school* comment. Zoe didn't seem pleased, her arms crossed tightly against her chest as she glared at him.

Walker inhaled dramatically, turning to Tyler, who stopped him. "Don't, dude. It's fine," he said. "Go sober up before someone catches you. The last thing you need is to lose your scholarship."

Rory couldn't believe how kind Tyler was being. Walker simply smiled and looked over at Zoe. "That's probably why you're dating him and not me, right? Stand-up guy and all."

"Exactly why," Zoe sneered. "Goodbye, Walker."

The Scoopers all remained silent as Walker stepped away with his group, his eyes lingering on Zoe as he left.

Tyler's hand was still on Rory's shoulder. She looked into his eyes briefly, but before she could read his expression, Jay was pulling her out of Tyler's grasp. "So," Jay said behind her, both arms wrapped tightly around her waist. "Ice cream?"

The rest of the Scoopers confirmed, making their way toward the shop. Tyler hesitated, his eyes locked with Jay's in a standoff. Rory felt like she was going to melt from the anger radiating off them. But Tyler soon cut his gaze, looping an arm with Zoe's again as he turned from Rory, following the group up the street.

Jay didn't budge, resting his chin on her shoulder. "You good, baby?"

"Um...I don't know."

"Because you went all wild animal for a moment."

"He just..." She heaved a sigh. "Walker makes me so mad sometimes."

"He's clearly jealous that Tyler's with Zoe," Jay responded. "Which, is it just me, or is that relationship kind of weird? Maybe she *should* date Walker."

Rory hated the way her heart fluttered at the thought of Zoe breaking things off with Tyler. But then the thought of that lovely blonde angel being with *Walker* made her head spin. Was that why Tyler was fake dating Zoe? To protect her from assholes like Walker?

She pulled herself out of his grasp. "Come on, let's catch up with them."

"ARE you sure you don't want to come to the diner and hang out tonight?" Gabi asked. "They'll have roast beef and sweet potato casserole and cheesy broccoli."

Rory smiled, shaking her head. "Tempting, but I'm sure."

Gabi sighed. "Fine. Come on by if you change your mind, okay?"

She nodded, watching Gabi leave for her shift. Rory sat on the couch, still in her pajamas, wrapping paper scattered across the floor. As promised, Gabi woke her up at the crack of dawn with coffee, pancakes, and presents under the tree, all so Rory could have some semblance of a normal Christmas before she had to leave for her shift at eight.

They even FaceTimed her grandparents, but their reception cut out as they cruised across the Caribbean, looking sunburnt and blissfully happy.

Despite being as busy as she was, Gabi nailed it with her presents this year. Ten bottles of nail polish for Rory's signature rainbow nails and a fancy new sketchbook with a set of pencils. "Your one from the dollar store is looking ratty," Gabi said. "An artist needs the right set of tools."

Rory got her a new set of inserts for her sneakers, which had Gabi cackling as she made fun of her mom for getting older. She also got her a new case for her headphones that clipped on her keys (Gabi was constantly losing them), and as a joke, a bright red thong. "Come on, none of the other bartenders catching your eye?" Rory teased. Gabi flicked Rory's arm and told her to watch it, but not before a smile sneaked across her lips.

It wasn't like everything was fixed between the two of them, but after their night of eating buffalo chicken pizza and staying up far too late watching two movies from her Disney list, things felt marginally better. So much so that Rory found herself letting go of the Fred Barry mystery.

Her phone started buzzing from inside the couch cushions where it must've slipped during gift-unwrapping. Rory fished for it, expecting it to be Jay calling her to wish her a Merry Christmas. She hadn't heard from him at all since the Festival of Lights. She figured he'd been busy with his family, and truthfully was okay with the distance. Having space to think didn't feel like such a bad thing.

But it wasn't Jay. When she saw who was calling, she rushed to answer, fumbling with her phone as she held it up to her cheek. "Hello?"

"*Joyeux Noël, mon amour,*" Bea said on the other line. "You won't believe what I got."

She chuckled, remembering how Tyler told her that Bea was taking French this year, and how she loved sneaking it into any and every conversation. "*Bonjour*, princess. Do tell."

"Bea, who is that?!" She heard Tyler's deep voice in the background. Then some wrestling and laughter as Tyler pulled the phone out of Bea's grasp.

"Sorry about that," Tyler said, and her heart pounded in her chest at the sound of his voice. "We clearly need to have a conversation about *boundaries*."

"Since when do we have boundaries with Rory?" Bea protested next to him. "Tell her to come over here."

Tyler just chuckled, and then, to Rory's surprise, he did. "Get over here."

She felt panicked. Things were still so unsettled between the two of them. So much they needed to talk about...so much she needed to say to him. "Um, I'm still in my pajamas, and—"

"So are we," Tyler said.

Rory turned around, looking through the window above the couch. Tyler was looking out from his own living room window next door, Bea beside him. She wore a silky pink matching pajama set, and Tyler was still in his sweats, his durag tied to his head.

Her heart stuttered at the sight of him. "I'm not sure if I—"

"Look," he explained, a smile blooming on his face. "Mom made way too much gumbo, as per usual, and she's about to pull some beignets out of the fryer."

Rory moaned, her stomach growling even though she just downed a mountain of chocolate chip pancakes.

"You should not be alone today," Tyler said adamantly. "Now, get over here and I'll let you put as much powdered sugar as you want on your beignet without judging you, and we can even watch whatever Disney movie is next on that list of yours."

"And make friendship bracelets!" Bea yelled, holding up a plastic case of beads to show Rory what she got for Christmas.

Rory grinned. "Alright, fine, you relentless piece of crap," she said. "I'm coming."

RORY REMAINED in her pajamas the rest of the day—a festive pair of Christmas flannel pants and her favorite Haverport sweatshirt that was fraying at the seams. She kicked her feet up on the ottoman in front of the Chapman's couch and rubbed her belly as she let out a satisfied sigh, her stomach bursting from the all-day New Orleans–inspired feast—beignets, shrimp and grits, gumbo, chive biscuits, and bananas foster that Mrs. Chapman let her flambé despite Tyler's utter terror. True to his word, he did not judge her for the amount of powdered sugar she put on her beignets, but he didn't hold back his laughter when she ended up coughing from the overload, some of the sugar shooting out of her nose.

Despite her full stomach, she didn't object as Mrs. Chapman came around with spiced hot chocolates, each mug overflowing with pillowy homemade whipped cream and cinnamon sprinkled on top. She handed one to her and Tyler. "None for you, Mom?" he asked.

"Honey, I am beat, I need to go to bed."

"It was all so delicious, Mrs. Chapman. Thank you," Rory said.

"Anytime, sweet thing. Do you want me to take Bea up with me?" She pointed down to Bea, who was now curled up and sleeping between her and Tyler. Bea's arms were covered in the friendship bracelets they'd made together, a few stacked up Rory's wrists as well.

Rory just smiled, brushing a hand over Bea's warm cheek. "Nah, let her sleep."

"You're a saint, child," Mrs. Chapman teased. She looked over at Tyler. "Not too late, okay?"

"Yes, ma'am."

The two of them sat there watching the Scat Cat sing his iconic "Everybody Wants to Be a Cat" and listening to Mr. Chapman snore softly in the recliner next to the couch.

Rory felt Tyler's gaze on her, and heat rose in her cheeks. It was easy being around him and his family, a blissful distraction from what was brewing. But now with the house silent, the lights from the tree and the television illuminating the room, she sensed the mood shifting.

She checked her phone again, trying to escape the pull she felt toward him. But her screen was blank. Still no word from Jay.

"Hey, look. Snow," Tyler whispered.

She glanced out the back door and noticed flurries trickling down, sticking to the porch. "Wow, I honestly don't think I've ever seen it snow on Christmas."

"Want to go outside?"

She nodded, lifting Bea's head gently and placing a pillow under it. She picked up her mug, watching Tyler sit up, his face twisted in pain as he stretched out his leg.

"Don't," he said, pointing at her. "Your face says it all."

She frowned. "When my best friend is in pain, yeah, I'm going to be concerned."

"Rory, I'm fine," he said. "But if you insist, you can carry my hot chocolate so I can unlock the door."

She followed his instructions, then followed Tyler as he hobbled outside into the darkness, featherlight snowflakes dancing under the moonlight. She shivered from the cold, but Tyler was already one step ahead of her, wrapping a blanket around her shoulders. He laid another blanket on the deck and motioned for her to sit, holding the railing as he lowered himself down next to her with a hefty grunt.

He took his mug from her. "You going to share some of this blanket or nah?"

She nodded, and Tyler lifted a corner and cuddled underneath it. They were now sitting so close his body heat warmed up their little cocoon. She could barely breathe.

"Thanks for inviting me over today," she whispered.

"You know you don't need to wait for an invite, Ry," he responded. "But I know things have been...weird between us. And I'm sorry for that. I screwed up."

Her eyebrows furrowed. "What are you talking about? *I* screwed up."

He shook his head. "I was so angry at myself for losing the game, and you were an easy target. I shouldn't have blamed you for anything."

"It shouldn't have been all on you to win that game, Tyler."

"I know," he exhaled. "We were so close. And if I'd just—"

"*Hey*, look at me."

He did, his eyes briefly scanning her lips before meeting her gaze. She ignored the butterflies fluttering in her stomach. "You still had an awesome season, even broke school records. You should feel proud of that."

He didn't respond, but his bashful smile warmed her down to her toes. She took a sip of her hot chocolate and stared up at the snow, a few flakes landing in her hair. Her mind was racing as she tried thinking through the right way to say what she needed to say, to tell him the truth about what she knew.

Before she laced together the right words, she felt his warm hand on her chin, turning it toward his face. "You have whipped cream on your nose."

He wiped it off with his thumb but didn't immediately move his hand, still cupping her chin. His face was so close, his breath on her lips, the smell of spiced chocolate swirling between them. Her words melted away as she let his warmth seep into her. She wanted him to close the gap, to taste his lips again.

The back door slid open with an abrupt slam, causing the two of them to jump, dribbles of hot chocolate and whipped cream spilling onto their laps.

"It's SNOWING!" Bea screamed, running out onto the lawn, the cuffs of her pajama pants getting soaked as she twirled.

Car lights beamed from Rory's driveway, stealing the moment's perfect darkness. She glanced in a panic to see who it was, wondering if it was Jay surprising her. But she relaxed when she saw Gabi stepping from the car, holding a box of leftover pie.

"I should, um—" she stammered.

"Yeah, okay."

She stepped away, mumbling to him about thanking his mom again before hastily heading back home. Once she was inside, she shuffled away from the windows and leaned against the wall.

"I'm getting comfy and then we're going to eat this

entire pumpkin pie," Gabi said cheerfully as she made her way up the stairs, oblivious to Rory's anxious state.

Rory was frozen to the wall, trying to get control of herself. Those few moments with Tyler were the most exhilarating she'd had since she kissed him last month. She'd never felt that way about Jay. He was a good kisser, but he never left her breathless. Tyler didn't even *kiss* her tonight and it had her pulse skyrocketing.

She reached for her phone, opening up her last text with Jay. Without giving herself a moment to overthink it, she started typing.

RORY

This isn't working anymore. I'm sorry.

She hit Send, then turned off her phone.

Second Semester

Chapter Nineteen

Rory shook her head as she typed back, exasperated. When she turned her phone on the day after Christmas, she still had no response from him. It took Jay two more days to finally say something.

She choked out another laugh.

JAY

> Are you trying to force me into a
> relationship?

RORY

> No, I'm giving you an out.

Rory watched the gray bubbles as Jay typed, then erased, then kept typing. She didn't wait for him to respond and instead kept going.

RORY

> You have clearly been busy with stuff at school, and I'm happy for you. But I need something more. I'm not a hookup kind of girl. I don't deserve to come in second place.

It took Jay several minutes to respond.

JAY

> Who's the guy?

She scoffed, then turned off her phone again. *Yes.* It was also partly about him. But after mulling over their conversation throughout winter break, she realized it was so much more than that. For a while, Rory *had* felt like Jay was choosing her, that she was his *baby* and all of that. But the last few weeks since he'd showed up on her doorstep, he'd become distant, and when he was around her, all he wanted was to get physical. Something else was going on, and she didn't feel like accepting crumbs.

Even if what she wanted was never going to be available to her. Not if Tyler and Zoe were going to keep up this whole *fake dating* thing.

So, she did the only thing she could fathom handling at the moment—her work for the yearbook. Thankfully there was still so much to do, and now that she was taking classes so she could execute her designs on the computer instead of waiting for someone else to do it, she was able to bury herself in her tasks.

She didn't see much of Tyler after Christmas—he was busy with rehab every day after school, trying to get his knee back into playing shape—but that didn't stop him from trying to reach out to her. She wanted to respond, but every time she went to type something back, her heart hurt thinking about the day he would finally be okay to play again. It meant him moving to college and leaving her behind. So she ignored his attempts, keeping her head down and doing nothing but work, work, work.

January came and went. February shaped up to be a blustery, cold bitch, and not just because of the weather. Valentine's Day at Haverport High was always next level, the halls covered in pink and purple hearts. Secret admirers sent candy grams to their lovers—a cruel joke of a fundraiser hosted by the drama club. Rory couldn't help but notice the obnoxious number of candy grams Zoe received throughout the day. Despite her best attempts at trying to avoid him, she couldn't stop her mind from wondering why he was going so overboard with this fake relationship when he'd been staring at her lips on Christmas, looking like he wanted them on his?

None of it made sense. So she stayed glued to her computer screen, her mind focused on page spreads and not on her heartbreak.

When the ice on the ground finally started to thaw and tiny buds on trees began to bloom, the yearbook was officially designed. Every spread was ready for real words to occupy the placeholder text, for photographs to replace stock images, and for final submissions of senior photos and tribute pages to be placed in the back—pages paid for by parents who wanted to embarrass their child with baby pictures for everyone to keep for the rest of their lives.

Rory sat with her legs propped up on the desk, ankles crossed, and sipped on a Dr. Pepper as Penelope scrolled through each spread, giving Vanessa notes for any changes she deemed necessary. Thankfully, there weren't many.

Penelope leaned back in her chair after scrolling to the last page of the yearbook, clicking her pen. "This is really good, guys. The designs are so out there and fun. I think people are going to be shocked."

"Because it's not boring and minimalistic?" Rory bantered.

"Let's go with classy," Penelope said in a valiant effort to try and defend previous book designs. "But yeah...exactly."

"It was all Rory," Vanessa said, beaming.

"Shut your mouth," Rory said, nudging Vanessa. "You made all of those final calls. None of this would have been possible without you."

Vanessa winked. "We make a good team."

"Now I guess it's my turn to pull some late nights." Penelope sighed. "We've got some editors working on the text that I'll need to copy edit, and then approve all of the photography. Gina, what's our status on the senior submissions?"

Gina poked her head out from behind her computer. "I've got sixty-five percent of senior headshots submitted, and we still need to fill ten tribute pages."

"Ten?" Penelope squeaked. "Wasn't the deadline for those two weeks ago?"

Gina nodded somberly. Penelope groaned.

"What if we offered parents to purchase quarter pages?" Rory asked.

"For a quarter of the price?" Penelope asked.

Rory nodded. "I'm going to be honest with you, the prices to purchase a page or even a half page in the yearbook is pretty steep. My mom looked at it and actually laughed."

"Oh," Penelope said, her face glazed over as she thought it through.

"*But,*" Rory continued, "if we offered a way for parents to purchase a smaller spot that's a little more affordable, we'd fill those pages quicker."

Vanessa shrugged. "Worth a shot, and I do like the idea of making things more affordable."

Penelope nodded. Case closed. "Done. Gina, will you draft an email to go out to the senior parents and send it to me? I'll give it a quick look over and get it out tonight."

"On it, boss!"

Penelope turned to Rory. "You know, Michaels, you're probably the most unexpected person to be on this team, and yet you've turned out to be the most vital."

She smiled at that. Even if the words were coming from someone like Penelope, it was still satisfying. It made her feel like she was actually needed. It made her feel less alone.

Her phone jingled in her pocket as the yearbook staff packed up for the night. Rory saw it was Melanie and immediately answered, walking away in search of privacy. "Mel, hi, my god I've missed you."

"I'm sorry," Melanie said on the other line. "It's been... kind of awful lately."

"I can't imagine," Rory whispered, feeling like a horrible human again for not trying to visit Melanie during an even more terrible season of grief. It had been over two weeks since she saw her friend face-to-face. Calvin was probably disappointed in her. "And you should never apologize for this, okay?"

"Okay," Melanie responded. "I do have a very, um, odd request though. Are you free tonight?"

"Yes, of course," Rory said, not even sure if she was, but she didn't care. "What's the plan? Rob a bank? Steal Grampy's blueberry coffee cake recipe?"

Melanie laughed, the lightness of her friend's voice filling her with hope. "While I would love to steal that heavenly recipe, there's something else I'm going to need you for tonight."

"What's going on?"

Melanie let out a heavy, loaded sigh. "Leila has an art exhibit opening tonight at Baybrook. And...apparently it's all about Duncan."

Rory was stunned into silence, processing this information for a moment. Leila was Duncan's girlfriend from last summer. They broke up right before he died, but she could still hear Leila's wails from the funeral ringing in her ears. She shook her head, brushing away the horrid memory. "You...want to go with me? Not your parents? Calvin?"

"No, I just—can't with them. And Calvin has class."

"Lazy," she teased, hoping to get another laugh out of Melanie. She did. "Yes, of course I'll go with you, Mrs. Ass Hat. I'll come pick you up now."

Rory squeezed Melanie's hand. "You sure about this?"

Melanie nodded, looking out at Baybrook School of Fine Arts from where they sat in the parking lot. Even though it was small, the campus was like a work of art in itself—a few ornate marble buildings circled a quad, with a gorgeous three-tiered water fountain at the center. Even the lights were artfully placed around campus, showcasing each building's interesting angles. The gallery banquet hall was lit as students and guests streamed in and out.

Rory stepped out of the car. "Is this all for her?"

"No. She told me it's for her sculpture class, so it features all the students taking it."

"You talked to her?"

Melanie nodded. "She called me last night."

Rory stopped her friend, placing her hands on Melanie's shoulders. "Again, are you sure about this?"

"I'm kind of curious," Melanie whispered. "Aren't you?"

"I mean, obviously," she answered. "I just want what's best for you."

Melanie looped an arm through Rory's. "Just be here with me, okay?"

She nodded, a lump rising in her throat.

She'd become what Melanie needed—starting with a steady arm for her friend to lean on as they walked through the doors of Baybrook. The different sculptures were incredible—some of them welded or carved into figures that were recognizable, like people or animals or plants. Others were a bit more abstract, pieces collected together to represent ideas and concepts, like political divide or famine or heartbreak. Rory picked up a program for the event and flipped through it, scanning the different descriptions for each piece. Every single one of them was inspiring. She could have spent hours in that hall gazing at the sculptures, taking them in.

But she wasn't there for herself, she was there for Melanie, who was leading her toward a section in the back. A charcoal-colored curtain covered the doorway of this exhibit, and unlike other sculptures that had plaques with intricate explanations for each piece, this plaque only had one word.

grief

All written in lowercase letters. Like the artist didn't have the energy to capitalize the title, as if grief had consumed them to their core.

She felt shivers down her spine, afraid of what Melanie was about to experience.

She tightened her grip on Rory's arm. "Don't ask me again. We're doing this."

"Okay," Rory whispered. "I've got you every step of the way."

Melanie peeled back the curtain, the two of them stepping in before being blanketed once again in darkness. But not complete darkness—the room had enough lighting set ingeniously at different points to accentuate the pieces within. The sculptures around the room were black and solid, but with the lights, she could almost picture them as wistful puffs of smoke. Her eyes were glued instantly to the center of the room. A spotlight was fixed on a slim white stand, a beacon of pureness in a room covered in dark. And placed at the center of the stand was a tiny sculpture. A sandcastle.

Melanie cried softly as Rory wrapped her in her arms. The sandcastle was a symbol of hope, a memory of goodness when grief consumed your being. It was like taking her friend's inner core and putting it on display. Rory was nauseated by it. But...she was also impressed.

"Mel?" whispered a soft voice at the curtain.

Rory and Melanie broke away, looking at Leila, who

was standing at the curtain. She was wearing a floor-length black dress, her blonde hair wild like the wind, her hazel eyes glistening with tears.

Melanie gave Leila a shy smile. "The sandcastle..."

"He said building them with you was always his favorite part about being in Haverport," Leila said. "I...I hope you're not mad."

"I'm not," Melanie breathed. "It's beautiful, Leila."

Leila nodded her head. "Take all the time you need."

Rory peeked past Leila's head before she closed the curtain, noticing there was a line forming to get into her exhibit. But it seemed Leila was watching guard, not letting anyone else in until Melanie was finished.

Rory gave her friend one more fierce hug. "Calvin was right."

"He always is," Melanie grumbled. "But about what?"

Rory wiped a tear from her cheek. "That you, Melanie, are strong. I would have never been able to do this."

Her friend shrugged, toying with the pink seashell dangling from a chain around her neck. "If I didn't have friends like you, I wouldn't either."

They both cried at that, holding each other close, staring off at the tiny sandcastle. From that moment on, she vowed to be the kind of friend Melanie deserved. Because friendships like this were hard to come by, and she was going to hold on to it with everything she had.

Rory left Melanie with Leila so the two could talk about the exhibit, giving her one last chance to make a lap around the banquet hall. She stopped in front of the display titled

We Found Love in a Hopeless Place. The sculpture was simply a garbage pail with scraps of bulging out the top and scattered across the floor.

"So where do you think love is if it's just garbage?" said a middle-aged man next to her.

Rory glanced at the guy to make sure he wasn't being a creep, but he kept a respectable distance. Combed gray hair, a trimmed beard, and a tweed jacket. Definitely an academic type.

She scanned the sculpture again. A mix of items were scattered haphazardly—torn-up bags from an online shopping spree, a box that once held a Kindle, sticker wrappers, broken pens and pencils, empty coffee bags, shoe boxes, old phones with cracked screens. It felt like the garbage had a theme.

"Maybe because it's all supposed to represent love that was found," she said without really thinking. "The things we find that bring us joy. The things we love when life feels a little hopeless."

The man smiled at Rory, then held out a hand. "Roger Farrow."

She shook it. "Rory Michaels."

"Pleasure to meet you, Ms. Michaels," Mr. Farrow said. "Come to visit a friend's exhibit tonight?"

She pointed to the charcoal curtain, to where Leila and Melanie still huddled closely. "Leila's exhibit is kind of about my friend."

"Ah yes, grief," Mr. Farrow said, like the concept was familiar. "The students fought over using that room, but Ms. Collins was the right call, I think."

He must be the professor, Rory thought. "It needed that cloak and dagger effect," she admitted. "The sculptures wouldn't have felt the same without the darkness and the placement of the lights."

Mr. Farrow smiled at Rory's again, thoughtfully this time. "Ms. Michaels, are you a college student?"

"High school senior. Not sure if I'm going to college, to be quite honest."

"And why is that?"

She stared at the trash, surprised she was admitting this *to a stranger*. "Because why waste the money if I don't know what I want to study?"

"But you like art."

She looked up at Mr. Farrow. "Well...yeah, I guess."

"It sounds like you *do* have something you're interested in."

Why was this man being so...invasive? "No offense, professor, but art school doesn't exactly help you with getting a job in the real world."

"Do you really believe that?"

A little twinkle in his eye danced as he waited for her response. "It's not exactly known for it," she said.

Mr. Farrow reached into the inside of his jacket, pulling out a notebook. It wasn't the kind of notebook she would imagine a professor in a tweed jacket to have on hand, though. Actually, it looked like something she would carry in her own backpack. The cover was an abstract painting with bold colors and gold, glittering letters that read *I AM A HOT MESS*.

"Five years ago, a talented painter at our school started a canvas series to reflect the crippling anxiety attacks she'd experienced her entire life," Mr. Farrow explained. "One of her tactics to feel settled from her anxiety was to simply write out her unedited thoughts in a notebook. But she complained about how neat the notebooks were—she wanted something as messy as she felt in those moments. And so she decided to combine the two, using her paintings to create her business, Hot Mess Notes. She has dozens of designs and sells hundreds of notebooks every day.

"Is she the next Van Gough? No, but that was never the goal. The goal was not only to reach people through her art, but also offer it in a way that makes sense in the world we live in.

"Now tell me, Ms. Michaels, in what ways have you experienced art in our world? And do you think it is still a necessity?"

Her mind immediately drifted to *Happy As a Clam* and the exquisite animation she obsessed over. Then to the yearbook, and how the art they'd been working on for months would live on as history for the rest of her classmates' lives.

Mr. Farrow reached into another pocket and pulled out a business card, interrupting her roaming thoughts. "If you decide, Ms. Michaels, that maybe this world *does* need more artists, I would love to see your work. Give my office a ring and we can set up an appointment."

Rory thanked him, watching him walk off before glancing down at his business card.

He wasn't just a professor. Roger Farrow was the *dean of the school*.

Chapter Twenty

Rory was sitting on her front porch staring at the business card in one hand, a hot cup of tea in the other, as an early spring rainstorm breezed past. She still wasn't sure what to make of Dean Farrow's offer. It had been almost a week since he handed her that card, and she had yet to make a decision whether she should call him or not. The only "work" she had to show him was her spreads from the yearbook, and even that felt like a stretch.

But...could she see herself at an art school like Baybrook? While she wished she could deny it, the answer was *yes*. Being around other artists who actually enjoyed sharing their ideas and interpretations, debating artistic choices of famous works around them, being on a smaller campus that focused on craft rather than taking required classes she didn't care about...it seemed a little too good to be true.

Yet she knew it was far more complicated than that. She couldn't just apply to art school and go. Gabi had been working to save for college, and she was still under the impression that Rory had applied. She had a feeling as soon as she told her that she wanted to go to a small art school instead, it would crush her.

Plus, it was close to home. Did she really want to stay in Haverport? Baybrook didn't have dorms, and it would probably be cheaper for her to stay here. But would Gabi even let her after that kind of disappointment? Would she have to get an apartment, and another job to pay her bills?

Her mind was racing through all of the complicated details when she saw Tyler's Jeep pull into his driveway next door. He glanced over at her from inside the car, the rain coming down hard now. Her face flushed, thinking about the last time they were in the rain together.

He raised an eyebrow at her—*a challenge*. Would she let him approach her? Would she finally talk to him?

She nodded, motioning for him to join her. He scrambled out of the car and almost tripped over himself as he jogged over to the porch. She noticed the way he was trying to contain the smile on his face.

Rory shoved the card into her pocket. "Look at you jogging over here. It's like you have a whole new leg!"

Tyler grinned, bending slightly. "I can jump, too. Want to see?"

"Don't hurt yoursel—"

He jumped on her porch, causing the wood underneath to rattle from his strength. They both laughed as Tyler took a seat next to her, swinging an arm around her shoulders and giving her a tight squeeze. The comforting familiarity made her heart patter in her chest.

"So does this mean you can play again?" she asked.

"It does," Tyler answered. "My PT says I still need to take it easy this spring, though."

And after the summer? Rory thought. Did this mean he was planning on playing this fall? The two of them had yet to talk about college and what was happening after gradua-tion. She sighed, her mind drifting again to the card burning a hole in her pocket.

"Hey...can I get your opinion on something?" she asked.

"Always, Ry."

She pulled the card out and held it up to him. He took it, holding on to it like it was precious.

"How'd you get this?" he asked once he'd read it.

"I went with Melanie to Leila's exhibit for her sculpture class last week, and I spoke with the dean for a few minutes."

"And he just...handed you his card?"

"Yeah. I guess he liked what I had to say. He asked me to call him to make an appointment so he can see my work."

"Do you have work to show him?"

"I could bring some of my yearbook spreads, maybe some of my sketches," she responded. "It's not much, but I don't know, is it worth a shot?"

Tyler sat there in silence, staring at the thick paper card. Rory realized she was holding her breath and let it out slowly, nervous all of a sudden. Was he going to tell her that it was a bad idea? That she should go to a real college and forget it altogether?

But he didn't shut her down. Instead, he turned his dark chocolate eyes to hers and said, "I think this is incredible."

She felt her face heat. "R-really?"

"Absolutely," he nodded. "And I think it makes a lot of sense."

"Why?"

He gave her a *You have to be joking me* look, which made her laugh. "Ry, you've been making me watch Disney movies on repeat since I moved to Haverport. Your room is like a freaking art exhibit, and you're never afraid to wear what you want or try something new, like with the year-book. You would kill it at a place like Baybrook."

She sniffled, realizing there were tears on her cheeks. She didn't bother wiping them away. "But Gabi...what do I do? How do I tell her?"

Tyler brought his hand up and wiped away her tears. "I don't know, Ry. It won't be easy. But I think you'll always regret it if you don't try."

She placed her head on his shoulder. She smiled, remembering when they'd sat like this on Christmas during a snowstorm, the almost-kiss.

"Ry?"

"Mmm?"

"Why have you been ignoring me?"

She stiffened. "I've...had a lot going on. Finishing up the yearbook."

"I know, I get that. But it's been weeks since I've heard from you. It feels like I messed up or something. Is it because we...?"

Kissed? Rory finished his question in her head as she sat up, looking at Ty. His eyes were insistent as he scanned her face, as if her ignoring him was eating him alive.

"Zoe told me the truth."

She could see the wheels turning in his eyes, calculating his careful response. "What did she say?"

"That you guys aren't really dating, that it's all fake."

Tyler looked away for a moment. "Is that all she said?"

"Well...yeah. She wouldn't tell me why, which makes all of this so much more confusing."

He didn't say anything, just kept looking over her shoulder.

"Please tell me the truth, Ty," she pleaded.

She watched his shoulders sag, the expression on his

face softening as he finally looked back down at her. He grabbed her hand and leaned in, his thumb brushing back and forth over her knuckles. "Back in November after the Homecoming game, Zoe's dad invited me to dinner. He said that a player like myself should be playing college football, and he had a connection through a friend at the University of North Texas."

Her body went rigid. "T-Texas?"

He nodded. "So I went to the dinner, and it went really well. But he kept making these comments about how nice of a young man I was, that I should take his daughter out, and all that. So, that night, Zoe and I made a pact. We would pretend to date until graduation."

She was silent for a moment. "That night when you had Zoe over, you closed the curtains—"

Tyler cut her off. "We were doing homework. That's all we do together. I have straight As for the first time in my life."

Her shoulders relaxed, but it still didn't make any sense. "But...why would Zoe want to do this? I mean, I know she's like, stupidly nice...but that feels like a really, *really* big favor."

"It was...mutually beneficial," Tyler explained.

Rory's mind immediately went to the Festival of Lights. "Walker?"

Tyler hesitated, like he was about to tell her. Then he just shook his head. "Ry, I'm sorry, I can't. That's her thing to share, when she's ready."

She was frustrated by his answer, but then her mind drifted back to what he'd told her. *Texas.* "You're moving. Like, *really* far away."

He lifted a hand to her face, brushing his thumb against her cheek. "I don't know yet. I still haven't heard."

She clamped her eyelids shut, letting her tears fall, the crackle of thunder dulling the sound of her sobs as Tyler pulled her close, rubbing his hand up and down her arm.

"I can't lose you," she admitted.

"You won't, Ry, I promise."

"I don't have much of a family."

"We'll always be family. And I don't think you could get rid of Bea if you tried."

She laughed and wrapped her arms around Tyler's waist.

"Plus," he said, his voice hoarse. He sounded like he was crying, too. "You have him. Jay."

She looked up at Tyler, and sure enough, tears filled his eyes. Her heart melted, knowing how much he cared for her. How much she was going to miss him. "I broke things off with him," she confessed.

He stiffened. "What?"

"I ended things," she admitted. "On Christmas."

"When on Christmas?"

"After...after we, um...after I went home."

Tyler looked out at the storm, his eyebrows knitted together.

"Ty...Ty, say something."

"I have to go."

She let his hand go, watching him stand up and walk down the porch steps. She stood up as well. "What...are you mad at me?"

He froze, not looking back at her, the rain ricocheting off his shoulders. "No."

She growled, frustrated. "Then what is it? Ty, my thing with Jay was...stupid. Then I kissed you and everything changed. I couldn't be with him like that anymore."

He didn't move, so she took that as a sign to move closer

to him, not caring that she was now getting soaked as well. "Ty, look at me."

Slowly, he did, his body still rigid like he was trying to restrain himself.

You'll always regret it if you don't try. He said those words to her just moments ago, so she decided to take his advice. She'd call Roger Farrow tomorrow. She would tell Gabi, no matter how much it would hurt her mother, because deep down, she knew what she needed to do next with her life. And she desperately wanted Tyler to be a part of it—and not just as her best friend. As the person she wanted by her side through it all. So she would try right now, because she knew she would regret it for her entire life if she didn't.

"I'm falling for you," she admitted, her voice shaky but sure. "And I want to be with you."

He squeezed his eyes shut, tilting his head up to the stormy clouds. She couldn't tell if he was still crying or not, his face wet from the rain still coming down.

"But if you...if you don't want to be with me, you need to tell me, Ty," she said, her voice choppy. "Please, I can't keep waiting around, hoping that you'll choose me, too."

He looked back into her eyes, and for an excruciating moment, he just stared at her, the thunder booming in the distance. She took a step back, knowing what was coming, that he was going to shatter the heart she just handed him into a million pieces. But he reached for her instead, cupping her face with both hands, pulling her close to him.

"You are the person I've always desired most, since the day I met you," he confessed. "Not being able to talk to you these past few weeks has been excruciating, because I want to share everything with you. I wanted to tell you how my recovery was going and wanted to vent to you when Bea spent an entire week only speaking in French. I wanted to watch Disney movies with you when my brain was feeling too fried from homework, watch your sad attempt at playing football in the backyard, or even just approach you in the hall when I was having a rough day. You are the person I share my deepest secrets with, the person who knows all of my flaws."

She waited for it, waited for him to say he was ending this thing with Zoe and wanted to be with her. That he would choose her, too.

But he didn't. He didn't pull her close or brush his lips against hers. He just looked at her with sad eyes. "But I'm going to leave for school, and that will break your heart. I can't do that to you, Ry. You deserve better."

Before she could respond, he let go of her and jogged back to his house, not looking back as he closed the door, the sound of the lock similar to the crack that just reverberated through her heart.

RORY HAD WANTED to wallow in bed the rest of the night, but her mind was plagued by Tyler's words, how he so easily told her what she meant to him, yet in the same breath turned her down. His confession ran like a ticker tape in her mind, and she needed something to ease her thoughts. Something to hope for.

So she opened her laptop and sent an email.

Now, days later, she was sitting in a tufted leather chair that she was pretty sure was about to swallow her whole.

Roger Farrow placed the printed sheets on his desk and

leaned back in his own chair. "Ms. Michaels, I'm really glad you called."

Rory shifted uncomfortably in her seat, pulling at the hem of her skirt. She hadn't been sure what you wore when you visited the dean of a college, so she settled for a navy skirt and a sage green button-up cardigan with a pair of loafers. She crossed her legs as she squeezed her hands together, trying to calm herself. "You like them?"

"Yes, these are clever. I think your classmates will enjoy having such a unique yearbook to look back on."

"That was our goal," Rory said, beaming with pride. She was anxious to see what the final result would be, but that would come after adding all of the prom pictures, and prom wasn't for another month and a half.

"Tell me, Ms. Michaels. If you were to attend Baybrook, what kind of art would you want to focus on?"

She took a moment to think it through, staring out the window to their left, watching students walk through the small courtyard. What classes would excite her the most? "I've always loved design and animation," she admitted, looking back at him. "Maybe digital art of some kind."

He nodded. "Based on your work, I feel a graphic design major would be something you could thrive in."

She felt her body soar at the sound of it. *Something you could thrive in.* She never really thrived in school, always coasted by, her grades just good enough to pass. But *thrive?* She never imagined that for herself.

The dean leaned against his desk, folding his hands together in front of him. "I do have to be frank with you. We want our students to have a well-rounded education in the arts. All students are required to take a variety of core classes. You saw the results of the sculpture program, and students are also required to take classes in drawing, painting, and illustration. Many of the students coming in have ample experience with this type of art."

She felt flattened by this after soaring high above. "Does this mean I won't be accepted?"

"No, that's not what I'm saying," he replied. "The graphic design program is still really new for Baybrook, and as you can see, we're actively recruiting to find students who don't just apply for our core fine arts programs. I think you would be perfect for the graphic design program, but I just wanted you to know that it's going to be a lot of work. It may feel like you're having to catch up."

She twisted her hands in her lap, wondering if it would be worth it. Would going to a normal college be easier? Or was she just afraid of doing things that felt too hard?

"If my opinion matters at all to you, pardon my boldness when I say that you'd have no trouble being admitted to our program," he continued. "And based on our discussion at the exhibit, I have a feeling you will succeed at whatever you set your mind to here."

She looked into Dean Farrow's eyes, noticing the way they twinkled with excitement, just like they did at the exhibit. This man was passionate about his students and their success.

"Why did you approach me at the exhibit?" she asked.

He smiled, leaning back in his chair again as he crossed his arms. "It's part of the grading process. I help out the professors at every exhibit by talking with guests to hear about their interpretations of the art around them, and those comments are taken into consideration for final assessments."

"But isn't the purpose of art to have different interpretations and opinions, to have discourse with one another?

What if someone's interpretation doesn't match the artist's purpose?"

He grinned. "We don't look for correct interpretations. If a piece isn't sparking that kind of intellectual discussion, we bring that to the artist and ask what could have been done differently. With the way you were taking in *We Found Love in a Hopeless Place*, I had a feeling I was in for a good discussion.

"This right here, Ms. Michaels," he continued, pointing between them. "This level of deeper thinking is what we look for in our students. You may not have all of the skills, but you strike me as someone with curiosity and drive. That's why I'm confident you will succeed."

She liked the idea of succeeding, of being a student with ideas and thoughts that really mattered, where getting good grades wasn't all about getting the right answer. At some point she'd stopped fidgeting. It felt like everything was clicking into place, her mind finally at ease from the anxious energy her chat with Tyler had sparked. She asked for an application.

RORY WAS STILL up when Gabi arrived home later that night. Her laptop was open, papers scattered across the table as she collected files of her work to submit with her application. Not like she really needed to; Roger Farrow already had printed copies of her spreads. But she did it anyway, at least for admissions to have everything on hand.

Gabi walked around the table and opened up the freezer, grabbing a carton of ice cream. "What do we have here? Late-night homework sesh?"

She hesitated, wondering if she should close her laptop and hide the application she was working on. But at some point, Gabi would find out the truth, so she decided it was now or never.

Rory twisted in her chair, looking at Gabi as she pulled down a bowl from the cupboard. "It's a college application."

The bowl almost clattered to the ground, but Gabi caught it quickly, sliding it on the counter as she swiveled to face her. "An application? I thought you already applied to schools."

She exhaled. She did consider applying to the schools she listed to her mother that past fall. But every time she sat down to do it, she froze, anxiety building up in her chest as she slammed her laptop shut. Filling out the application for Baybrook didn't make her feel that way. It actually made her feel giddy, her heart ripe with possibility.

"Did you not get into those schools?" Gabi asked.

You'll always regret it if you don't try.

She stood up, hands clutched to the back of the chair. "I'm applying for art school."

Gabi cocked her head, looking flabbergasted. "Art school? Like, through a university or—"

"No," she interrupted. "I'm applying to the Baybrook School of Fine Arts. I met with the dean today, and he thinks I would do well."

"Bu-but," Gabi stuttered. "Why would you not want to go to a university? And does the art school even give out degrees?"

"Yes, it would be a BFA, and I'm looking to focus on graphic design," she explained. "I don't want to go to a university."

"Why not?" Gabi pleaded. "Don't you want to go to

college football games and join a sorority and live in a dorm and have late nights at the library with your friends?"

"Not really," she admitted, her voice timid. "Also, do I really look like the sorority type?"

Gabi rolled her eyes. "You're getting away from my point. Don't you want the true college experience?"

She shook her head.

"I think you need to consider it." Gabi harrumphed. "Where else did you get in? We can visit some of them, I'll take time off."

She felt her stomach churn, knowing how easily her mother was ready to take time off when it came to her college education.

She sucked in a breath and confessed. "I didn't apply to other schools."

Gabi's eyes went wide, her eyebrows raised so high on her head they were hidden behind her wavy blonde bangs. "So when you told me you applied to UCONN and Quinnipiac and Northeastern—"

"I was lying. I didn't apply to those places. Didn't apply anywhere."

Gabi let out a high-pitched laugh that sounded more like a screech. Rory watched as her mother paced back and forth, her face purple with anger. "I can't believe you, kid. Why would you lie to me like this?"

"Because college is all you care about," Rory said. "But I wasn't ready for it. I didn't want to disappoint you."

"But it's all we've been working toward," Gabi pleaded.

"No, it's all *you've* been working toward," she said, her voice crackly as hot tears pooled down her cheeks. "You've been so hyper-focused on me going to school that you couldn't even pay attention to the fact that I didn't want to go in the first place."

"Now what? I'll just waste all of my hard-earned money so you can go to an *art school* and starve after graduation?"

"I won't starve. The dean said—"

"I don't care what the dean said, he just wants your money," Gabi spat. "If you decide to go, I will not give you a single penny. You can have your college money next year when you've been accepted to a *real* school."

Gabi left her melting ice cream in the bowl on the table and stormed off, slamming her bedroom door shut.

Even after the fight, after knowing that she may not even be able to afford Baybrook, Rory sat back down at the table and with teary eyes, she clicked Submit.

Chapter Twenty-One

I T W A S three days after the fight, and Gabi was radio silent. She hadn't spoken to Rory, didn't even bother *looking* in Rory's direction as she got ready for work each morning and left. Rory made sure to be tucked away in her room by the time Gabi got home in the evenings. She'd expected her to be mad, but she never imagined she'd completely shut her out.

While she anxiously awaited to hear back from Baybrook, she found herself searching for Fred Barry again. She searched through any records she could find online about the Barry family in Orlando. She found a house, which looked like it was sold in 2006—the same year she was born. Newspaper clippings didn't help much either, just a few mentions of Fred Barry making the all-state team, or his parents (which she couldn't fathom might actually be her *grandparents*) mentioned as donors for different charity events and auctions. But one morning as she sipped on her coffee, she found a quote from her potential grandmother in a small note about a Christmas charity auction that had her pause.

"The armoire is the exact kind of piece I've been looking to add to the collection at our Rhode Island beach house. How lovely that the money will all go to charity."

Rory clicked open a new tab, her fingers flying over the keyboard as she searched for a Fred Barry in Rhode Island.

Sure enough, there was one.

His online presence was still pretty obscure, but she did find a mention of him in a local paper, attached to his work at a construction company that renovated heritage houses along the shore. She clicked out of the article and scrolled, creepily finding an address to an estate attached to the Barry name. It was still under their ownership.

Was it really them? Why get excited about it if she wasn't even sure if this was the man she was looking for?

Still curious, she looked up the distance between Haverport and the Barry estate. It was a 43-minute drive.

Forty. Three. Minutes. While she wasn't a hundred percent certain it was *him*, she couldn't deny the coincidence. And if she was right, it would mean he'd lived less than an hour away her entire life. What in the world happened for Fred to limit his contact to regular child support payments and nothing more?

Her phone rang, causing her to jump out of her desk chair. She grabbed it with shaking hands, noticing Melanie's name on the screen.

"H-hi," Rory answered.

"Hi yourself," Melanie said. "Everything okay?"

"Yes, why?"

"You're, um, ten minutes late picking me up."

"Right, shit, sorry," Rory said, flinging her backpack over her shoulder. She forgot she'd promised to drive Melanie to school this week. Calvin usually did, but he had finals and had to focus on his studying. "Lost track of time."

"I mean if we're *skipping* school, I'm down, I just need to know," Melanie teased.

She hopped in her car, putting her phone in the holder and tapping the speakerphone option. "Skipping school, Melanie Albertson? What would Yale think?"

"Doesn't matter now," Melanie said firmly. "Because I already got in."

Rory froze, her hands on the steering wheel. "Wait, seriously?"

"Yeah...but I haven't told my parents yet."

"I feel like this is the kind of conversation that requires lattes on the beach."

Melanie chuckled. "Do we have time?"

"Well, no," Rory said, turning the keys in the ignition. "But it's senior year. Think they won't let us graduate if we're a little late?"

"If they don't, at least we'll be stuck here together."

Rory grinned. "Sounds perfect to me."

HILLSIDE PARK WAS STILL PRETTY empty, but in just a few months, it would be packed. Despite how much she hated it when the summer people descended and made everything in the Port far too crowded, Rory was excited for the season to begin. With Scoops finally opening back up in four days, the Scoopers were meeting that afternoon for the first staff meeting of the year.

They climbed out of her car into an empty parking lot, a sheet of fog rolling up from the ocean and breezing through

Rory's hair. She shivered, taking a big sip of her latte to keep warm as she leaned against the hood of her car. Melanie did the same, tucking her cardigan tight around her waist with one hand, her own latte in the other.

Rory turned to Melanie, propping a leg up on the hood. "Alright, spill, Mel."

Melanie sighed. "I found out I got in two days ago."

"And you're not excited about it."

Melanie grimaced. "That obvious?"

"Well, yeah," Rory said, shrugging. "You told me last summer you'd been working your ass off trying to get into Yale."

Her friend sighed, looking out toward the ocean. "I hope my parents won't be as perceptive when I tell them. I'm afraid to admit to them how I feel."

"And how *do* you feel?"

Silence lingered, but it wasn't uncomfortable. Rory took a sip of her latte, leaving space for her friend, and let herself wonder if the high school was calling her mother to let her know she was late for class. *Good*, she thought. It would give Gabi an excuse to finally talk to her. Plus, this little escape gave her more one-on-one time with her friend at the beach.

"The idea of going to college scares me," Melanie finally answered. "I just...don't think I can be around the parties and the drinking and—" She broke off, letting out a shudder. She fidgeted with the blue elastic headband in her hair, and the action seemed to steady her. "Being here, in Haverport, it makes me feel settled. I have my...moments. But things generally feel okay. And when I think about going to Yale, nothing feels right."

"What made it feel right before?"

"I honestly thought it would make my parents happy, but after this summer, after..." Tears welled in her eyes as she took another shaky breath. "I realized I was living my life playing defense, doing whatever it took to be the good kid because they had their hands full with Duncan. I wanted them to feel proud."

Rory scooched closer to Melanie and ran a hand through her friend's hair. "That makes sense, Mel. But now...you're feeling like it doesn't make sense anymore, after...everything."

Melanie nodded. "I've realized that it's not worth trying to live up to others' expectations. I mean, look at Calvin. He's going for what he wants, no matter what people think of him."

"And he's a bit annoying about it, if I'm being honest."

Melanie's bright laughter rang through the empty lot, almost like it would lift the fog they were sitting in. "I want to be the same, Rory. I want to just go for something that feels right. Even though I'm not exactly sure what that is."

Rory sighed, looking down at the frayed edges of her shirtsleeve, realizing how much Melanie's little speech was also speaking to her heart. Going to Baybrook would mean living on her own terms, not the expectations Gabi had set for her. Gabi didn't even consider what she would want; her mother only assumed and went for it, working as hard as she could to make it happen. Did that make her a horrible daughter if she chose *herself* instead of her mother's dream?

"Okay, enough," Melanie said, swiping at the tears in her eyes. "Your turn."

Rory scoffed. "You already know about Baybrook."

"*Yessss*, but you haven't exactly been filling me in on what's going on with Jay."

"Oh."

"I know I've been MIA, but I still expect updates," Melanie said. "Are you still seeing him? Are things official?"

Rory stammered. "Um, well, things aren't *anything*, actually. We broke things off. *I* broke things off. With him."

Melanie's eyes went wide. "Did something happen again with Tyler?"

Rory drained the last bit of her latte, then squeezed her empty cup and tossed it into the trash can next to the beach entrance. Her stomach churned as she thought about what to say next. She was probably the only one who knew Tyler and Zoe were fake dating, about Mr. Clark's football connection. But she didn't know the *other* part of their agreement, and she didn't feel it was her place to talk about it.

What would she say instead? That every time she thought about Tyler moving to Texas, she felt like her chest was caving in? That Tyler confessed his true feelings for Rory but was now pushing her away in an attempt to protect her heart?

Stupid, selfless, nice Tyler. She wished that for once in his life he would be selfish and kiss her face already.

She sighed, turning to Melanie. No, she wouldn't reveal this to her. Not yet. She still had so much to work out in her head.

"Jay is going through some stuff, and he kept closing off," Rory admitted. Not exactly a lie, but not the full truth. "Things...fizzled out, I guess."

"Are you sad?"

To her surprise, she shook her head. "No. I think it's for the best."

Melanie linked an arm through hers, the two of them sitting there staring out at the ocean, the fog beginning to lift around them. Rory leaned a head on Melanie's shoulder, feeling thankful that she had a girlfriend she could rely on in what could sometimes be a suffocating town.

She would tell her everything else about Tyler. Soon. Just...not yet.

RORY PULLED into the Scoops lot later that afternoon and parked next to Tyler's Jeep. She rushed into The War Room, knowing she was a few minutes late, but it didn't seem to matter. They were waiting on Jess too.

"You're late," Calvin announced.

"Thank you, Captain Obvious," Rory deadpanned. "I'm not the only one."

"We will start without her," Ron said. "Okay, team, take a seat wherever you can. We'll be here for a little while."

The Scoopers shuffled around The War Room, finding places to sit. Rory's eyes flicked to Tyler, but he didn't notice as he flipped over the empty garbage bin and sat down.

She sighed, scanning the room, and thought about Jay. It felt strange not having him at the first Scoops meeting of the year; being away at college was enough of an excuse to miss it. She did miss him, missed his fuller-than-life presence, the way he made her laugh. But what she said earlier to Melanie still rang true. Breaking things off with him felt right, and even if she missed him as a friend, she didn't miss anything more than that.

She hopped onto the cabinet next to Melanie as Jess flung open the back door, looking frazzled. She still had on her Post Road Market uniform, a smear of pink frosting on her shirt.

"I can be here for a half hour, but that's it," Jess

announced, grabbing a folding chair from the back. "Let's make this speedy."

"You know it's never speedy with Ron," Blake quipped.

Calvin glared at him, a clear warning to keep his mouth shut.

"I think we'll start with the biggest news," Ron said. "It feels bittersweet to announce that this will be my last summer as the manager of Scoops."

The room went dead silent, the drips from the sink the only sound Rory could make out.

"Don't worry, I'm not going anywhere," Ron continued. "I am still staying on as owner, but after this summer, I will be handing all managerial roles over to Calvin."

The Scoopers sighed in relief, then followed with a few whoops and cheers. Tyler reached over and slapped Calvin on the back.

"You guys know he's been working in this type of role here for a while, but he'll have his degree by next summer and it was always our goal to have him take over officially," Ron said.

"Does this mean we're done experimenting with horrible flavors?" Jess asked unapologetically.

The Scoopers snickered at that, remembering Ron's choice to bring in the Blue Bombshell ice cream last summer that, in Rory's opinion, tasted like feet.

Ron frowned, but Calvin gripped his shoulder and answered for him. "Maybe not at first, but I won't stop reaching out to and experimenting with local suppliers and vendors. It helps to drum up business from customers outside of town if they know their favorite flavor is being served somewhere else."

"Just make sure it tastes good," Jess mumbled. Calvin kicked her foot.

"Speaking of new flavors..." Ron started.

They all groaned, but listened as Ron explained what he was adding to the menu this year—some sort of almond butter flavor with amaretto that sounded repulsive. As the Scoopers listened to Jess pleading with Ron not to add a new flavor, Rory's eyes strayed over to Tyler again. For a brief moment, he returned her gaze, their eyes locking across the room. He gave her a bashful smile, and his confession in the rain washed over her again.

It was killing her.

He broke their gaze, and she wondered if she imagined the entire thing. Focusing again on Jess, Ron, and Calvin, she bounced from person to person as they debated about the ROI of bringing in a horrible new flavor for the summer...whatever that meant. She didn't manage to get his attention again, and a half hour later, Jess was flying out the door as Ron was calling the meeting to an end. By the time she made it outside after everyone, Tyler's Jeep was already gone.

Chapter Twenty-Two

THE NEXT MORNING, Rory and Melanie found Blake waiting by their lockers. His arms were crossed and his shoulders were tense as he scanned the halls.

When he saw them, he rolled his eyes. "Finally, took you guys long enough."

"Aww, missed me, Blakey boy?" Rory asked, shooing him aside so she could get to her locker.

Blake frowned. "Have you been on Instagram yet?"

Her brow furrowed. "Um, no...why?"

Blake's gaze shifted between her and Melanie, looking apprehensive.

"Blake," she insisted, hands on her hips. "Spill, now."

"Okay, but don't shoot the messenger."

She promised, watching as Blake tapped to the app on his phone and handed it to Rory. Melanie leaned in next to her as the two of them examined the picture that had Blake all anxious.

It was a picture posted by Jay. He hadn't posted a single thing on his Instagram since moving to UCONN—he told Rory he was done with social media and wanted nothing to do with it. So chances were the fact that he was posting now was meant to be a jab at her.

The picture looked like it was taken at a party. He was leaning against a windowsill, his arm wrapped around some girl with long blonde hair, his hand low on her waist. She was whispering something in his ear, and his eyes were bright.

Melanie rubbed her arm in comfort. But to her shock, Rory didn't feel like she needed it at all. A year ago, this kind of image would have made her spiral. She would have felt angry and jealous. She would have stood there and compared herself to that girl, finding all the flaws in herself and wondering why she couldn't be someone Jay liked.

But now, all she felt was relief. Jay was at a party. He was meeting people at UCONN. She didn't have a right to know anymore, but she hoped he was feeling better about being there.

"Rory?" Blake asked, his voice coated in nervous energy.

She just smiled, handing Blake his phone. "Good for him. I'm happy he's happy."

Blake's jaw fell open, but he quickly snapped it shut when Melanie glared at him. "Um, I, well...wasn't expecting that."

Rory shrugged, opening up her locker. "I broke things off with him, remember?"

"Which, honestly, I don't get," Blake said. "I mean, you've been, like, in love with him—"

"Not in love," Rory said flatly.

"Okay, then let's go with obsessed. You've been obsessed with him for as long as I've known you."

"Well, obsessions can change," she explained slowly, grinning. "People can change."

Melanie squeezed Rory's arm again.

A commotion down the hall stopped their conversation. A handful of people burst out in applause, whooping and hollering at whatever was happening. The three of them followed.

Rory grabbed Blake's and Melanie's hands as they squeezed through the crowd into the cafeteria. Everyone was looking up at a massive banner hanging from an open window at one of the science labs on the second floor, trailing all the way down to the first floor. It was white, and in bold navy letters, the banner said:

Will the queen dance with the king one last time?

And there, standing in front of the banner, was Tyler. He was dressed in a pressed suit wearing his Homecoming King crown, holding a bouquet of white roses.

Rory watched in horror as everyone began cheering and chanting Zoe's name, waiting for her to emerge from the crowd. She held her breath when Zoe finally popped into view, the students going absolutely wild as she approached Tyler. She wore a big smile on her face, mirroring the gooey look he was giving her.

For two people who were apparently "fake dating," they were *very* good at it.

Maybe because the feelings aren't fake at all, Rory thought sadly.

Zoe said something to Tyler and nodded. He wrapped his arms around her and lifted her up as the crowd went berserk at his absurd promposal.

Rory couldn't help it as tears streamed down her cheeks. It was like watching some kind of cruel nightmare.

"Now I get it," Blake mumbled.

She turned around, looking at him. He was looking back at her with remorse, his face full of understanding.

Her eyes flicked to Melanie, who also was looking at Rory with that same kind of sorrow.

Melanie reached for her arm, but Rory shrugged her off, backing away from the both of them. "No, you don't. You get nothing."

She sprinted away, not turning at Melanie's calls to wait up. She ran down the halls and out the front entrance of the school, heading for her car.

Nothing made sense anymore. Her mother hated her. Tyler didn't want to be with her. She wasn't sure where she would be come September. She didn't even have a date for prom.

She turned on the ignition and peeled out of the student lot.

Rory didn't think about where she was going until she parked her car.

Even though she knew where Jess lived, she'd never been to her place before. Her apartment building was tucked down a side street near Hillside Park, not close enough to be walking distance to Scoops, but close enough to the beach. Rory doubted Jess ever went, though. She didn't seem like the beach-going type.

She pulled her car into the parking lot of the complex, on the lookout for Jess's white car. She found it parked in front of an apartment door that looked bare, which was starkly different to the others—doors with potted plants and patio furniture and cheery doormats. But not Jess's place. Her apartment didn't have a doormat or any decor. Almost as if this wasn't important to her. Somewhere temporary.

Rory stepped up to the door, holding her fist up. Only then, she heard loud yelling and cursing. And crying.

"How the FUCK are we going to afford that, Charlie?" Jess screamed, her voice cracking as she said it. "We barely have the money to pay rent!"

"Jess, for shit's sake, it's FINE!" he yelled back. "I put it on my credit card."

"Jesus fucking christ," Jess roared. "Which card did you put it on?"

"Jess..."

"WHICH CARD?!"

"Jess, someone is standing outside."

Rory froze, silence enveloping them. She heard thumping and then Jess was there, throwing the door open. Her face was splotchy and red, tears streaking her cheeks, her glasses gone. Rory watched as her eyes went wide before she squinted them into thin lines, her glare anything but welcoming. "What are you doing here?"

"I-I just—"

"Leave now."

"Jess, is everything—"

"NOW, RORY."

Rory nodded, shuffling backward and stumbling down the front step. "Yes, I'm-I'm sorry."

Jess responded with a slammed door. The yelling started up again, but Rory didn't stick around to listen, jogging over to her car and hopping in. She was breathing heavy, her chest tight with worry for her friend. Could she consider Jess her friend? Yes, she was a Scooper, she was practically family. And yet, Jess constantly pushed them away. What did she have to hide?

She reached for her phone, looking at the time. It was almost nine in the morning, which meant her second class was about to begin. The idea of going back to school for the day seemed like hell. She knew she was being reckless, but it wasn't like she was going to college in the fall if her mother had anything to say about it. So...what did she have to lose?

She cleared her mind and plugged in an address on her phone, putting the navigation on speaker.

Her phone let her know that her next destination was forty-three minutes away.

SHE KNEW IT WAS A TERRIBLE, terrible idea.

Rory veered off at an exit in Rhode Island, the navigation on her phone leading her closer to the beach.

Gabi was *definitely* getting some kind of notification about Rory skipping class. Her mother never said anything about Rory arriving late to school with Melanie. But skipping an entire day? That would get her talking again.

Especially when she found out where Rory was headed.

Her phone led her down a few winding roads. Rory watched as the houses around her got bigger and bigger, turning from single family homes to gargantuan mansions. The people in this town certainly had a lot of money. The Barrys must also be loaded.

She turned onto a tiny street, following a smooth path that led to a pair of towering wrought-iron doors, blocking the way to the colossal estate on the other side. It was like something you'd see in a period drama, tucked into the countryside of Ireland or England—not Rhode Island. The estate could fit ten houses the size of hers in Misty Bay. Maybe more.

The camera at the top corner of the gate kicked into gear, the lens whirring to focus on Rory in her car.

"Can I help you?" asked a gruff voice from the intercom system next to her.

She looked up, noticing that there wasn't any kind of camera system for her to see whoever was talking on the other line. It sounded like a man though. Was it Fred? Could that be her father?

She cleared her throat, taking the chance anyway. "I'm Rory Michaels."

Her response was followed by soul-sucking silence. But she stood her ground, her eyes still on that camera.

It felt like an eternity passed before she finally got a response.

"Stay there."

The intercom system cut off. She wondered if maybe the person would open up the iron gates, letting her drive through. But after a few moments, she watched as a tall figure exited the front entrance of the estate, now taking the paved path toward her.

She stepped out of her car, leaning against the hood as she waited. Her pulse quickened, but she tried keeping her cool and looking relaxed.

When the man made it to the gates, she finally knew who her father was. After looking through all the photos she could find of him in her mother's secret memory box, she would be able to recognize those sea-foam green eyes anywhere. The same ones she saw in the mirror every day.

Fred Barry. Her father. It really was him. And he was nothing like the perfect father she'd pictured in her head.

His eyes were similar, but everything else about him was different. His face was covered in scruff, his build bulkier. He wore a flannel, jeans, and work boots.

And despite his happiness in that photo on the football field, in that moment, he looked everything but. There was no welcoming smile or running hug, like what she always dreamed. Instead, he looked *peeved.*

"Did she send you?" he asked roughly.

"Excuse me?"

"You heard me," he sneered. "Did she send you?"

"You mean my mother?"

"Who else would I be talking about?"

Rory's mouth fell open. He couldn't even say Gabi's name.

"No," she finally responded. "She has no idea I'm here."

He huffed, looking away. "How'd you find me?"

"Google."

He shook his head, looking irritated. "Fucking technology."

You'll always regret it if you don't try.

She took a deep breath, bracing for whatever was to come. "The day I was born, she wrote you a letter. It was sent back."

"We left Orlando," he explained. "And when that letter ended up here, I had it sent back."

Her face felt tight, and she could sense tears coming on. She tried holding them in. The last thing she wanted was to cry in front of this resentful, haunted man. "Why?"

"Because this wasn't how it was supposed to go," he said bluntly. "We had a plan, and she ruined it."

"R-ruined it?"

"We were going to go to college, find a house in Orlando, get married," he explained. "The kid thing wasn't supposed to happen until after that."

Tears now streaked her cheeks. "But she ruined it."

He kept going, completely oblivious to the girl standing

in front of him with tears in her eyes. No sadness or guilt. Just anger. "I begged her to choose me instead, to go with our plan. But she refused."

Her ears were ringing now at the truth that was finally being revealed. Fred Barry wanted her mother to terminate the pregnancy. She didn't.

"So you broke up with her."

"I told her I wouldn't let anything ruin my life. I left town."

Rory was shaking. Hurt, abandonment, loneliness...she couldn't pinpoint the emotions she felt with so many roiling inside of her. Anger felt too mild of a word to describe the burning rage in her belly. She was downright irate. That this man not only decided he didn't want her, but he'd tried forcing Gabi to do something she didn't want to do with her body. All for the sake of their "happily ever after."

Right then, she was mighty proud of her mother for standing up for herself, and for choosing a different end to her story. A different kind of happily ever after.

Instead of throwing a fit, Rory calmly stood up straight, looking this horrific man up and down. "By the looks of it, you didn't need me around for your life to be ruined."

She got in her car and left, not bothering to look at the man who was fuming on the other side of the gates he'd refused to let her through. She sped through the streets to the highway, flying back to Haverport.

Chapter Twenty-Three

HER FIRST THOUGHT was to stop at the diner. She wanted to confront Gabi, tell her what she knew: that her father lived less than an hour away, that she'd met him, and that she finally knew the extent of the sacrifices she'd made for her. Even if that meant Gabi would be pissed she wasn't in school, even if Rory had applied to Baybrook against her wishes, this moment felt bigger than all of that. She just needed to see her. If she was about to be grounded for eternity, well, so be it.

Her conversation with Fred Barry had her thoughts swirling. She refused to refer to him as her father anymore—that man didn't deserve the honor. Despite how mad she was though, Rory was shocked by how much relief she felt following the interaction. She no longer had to wonder about who her father was, or what it would be like to have him in her life. Fred Barry was a deadbeat, a man so bitter and hateful she was glad he hadn't stuck around.

Her phone pinged with a text.

VANESSA

U ok? Didn't see u in English.

Rory stopped at a red light two blocks from the diner. She snatched her phone and typed back.

RORY

Yep, doc appt

She responded straightaway.

VANESSA

So ur coming to the review?

Rory groaned, resting her head back on her seat. She'd forgotten about the yearbook review. It was their last big push after Penelope's final copy edit. It was supposed to be a long one—Penelope even promised dinner would be provided for the entire staff. Typically their editor-in-chief was stingy with the club budget, given their funds were far from stellar to begin with.

A horn honked behind Rory's car, making her jump. She quickly sped off, driving right past the diner before turning on Boston Ave.

She would have to deal with the wrath of Gabi later.

"THIS PAGE HAS IT, TOO," Rory said firmly, pointing to the spread.

Penelope growled. "Seriously, Michaels, you're killing me."

"She's only doing her job," Vanessa said softly.

"Yes, but this is just being nitpicky," Penelope snipped,

tossing her leftover crust on a paper plate. "I had to edit the copy, remember? The text is fine."

"But you don't think it looks weird?" Rory said, pointing to the way the blurb on the page looked uneven. "Especially with an orphan here at the end."

"Goddamn orphans," Sean mumbled. "We're going to be here all night."

Rory clicked to the next spread and pointed to another singular word at the end of a paragraph, the "orphan" that stood out like a sore thumb. She heard the entire staff groan, a few soft mumbles of disbelief. Rory glanced at the clock above the computer lab door—9:37. It had been the longest day of her life, and seeing how they were only three quarters of the way through approving the yearbook spreads, it was far from over. They hadn't even reached the senior section yet.

She sighed, looking over at Penelope, who had her face in her hands. "Okay, how about this. Given that the way the text looks on each page seems to be an issue, we'll divide pages to each staff editor to fix right now, and we"—she pointed to Penelope, Vanessa, and Sean—"can approve the rest of the spreads for the book."

She heard staff editors sigh with relief, a few *thank gods* murmured among them as Penelope assigned pages for each editor to fix. As the team dispersed, Rory joined the other leaders around Penelope's computer.

"Before we dive in, just want to triple check that we're all good for prom night," Penelope said. "Sean, I reserved a ticket for you so you don't have to pay since you're technically working all night. Just find me when you check in."

Sean's cheeks went pink. "Any chance we can make that two tickets?"

Penelope raised a brow, causing Vanessa to giggle to herself.

"I—well," he said, stuttering slightly under Penelope's razor-sharp gaze. "I have someone who offered to help me and I—"

"The senior pages are orphan-free," Gina interrupted, sliding next to Rory with a mischievous grin on her face. "Also, he's lying, he asked me to go with him."

Sean's face went from pink to red as Penelope rolled her eyes. "Will you actually be helping him, or will you serve as a distraction?" she asked Gina.

Gina winked. "Both."

"That's my girl," Rory said, high-fiving her teammate.

"Alright fine, as long as you get the photos in by the end of the night, I don't care," Penelope said. "Vee, how are things looking with the printers?"

Gina leaned in closer to Rory as Vanessa began briefing Penelope about print proofs and shipment dates. "Hey, have you talked to Helen lately?"

She cocked her head. "No, Helen and I never really hang outside of soccer stuff."

"Gotcha," Gina said, chewing her lip in concentration.

Rory frowned. "Is everything alright?"

Gina looked around the group to make sure no one was listening before turning her attention back to Rory. "So apparently she turned down her scholarship to play at Northeastern."

Her eyes went wide. "You're kidding."

"Yeah, and her parents are, like, furious."

"Where does she plan on going?"

"She told me she's going to Barnard instead."

"Do they even have a team?"

Gina shrugged. "Yeah, through Colombia. But she said she's not playing at all."

She shook her head, completely baffled. "That makes no sense. She hasn't shut up about wanting to play college soccer since I met her in middle school."

"Right? It doesn't make sense to me, either. I'm wondering what's behind it—"

"Hey," Penelope snapped (her fingers literally *snapping* in front of Rory's face). "Did you hear me?"

"Um, no?" she said, flustered. "Sorry."

"I asked if you and Vanessa are still good to work on the spreads after prom."

Prom. Images of Tyler and Zoe this morning flashed before her eyes, the way the school cheered for them. The idea of having to watch that all night, of having to somehow find a date that wasn't Tyler...it made her want to scream. It made her not want to go. At all.

"More than good," answered Rory, shining a bright smile in Penelope's direction. "I'm actually not going, so I can get them done earlier."

Penelope inhaled sharply. "Not...going?"

"Oh, thank god, I don't want to go either," Vanessa said, her shoulders relaxing as she admitted her truth. She stood up and linked her arm with Rory's. "I'll come hang at your place. Maybe I'll even get my *mamá* to make us empanadas for dinner."

Rory's heart warmed as she smiled at her friend, relief flooding every crevice of her being. "That sounds perfect. And tell your mother I want her to adopt me."

"Alright, enough of this, we're getting sidetracked," Penelope said, looking like she was ready to pull her hair out. "If we don't finish approving these spreads in the next hour, I'm going to lose my mind."

"Wait, you haven't already?" Rory teased.

They all laughed, including Penelope, who then gave Rory the finger.

Before turning her attention back to the screen, she felt her phone buzz in her pocket.

GABI

We need to sit down and talk

Crap, Rory thought as she read the text from Gabi. She'd snuck into the school after the last period, heading straight for the computer lab, trying to lie low so no one would see her. The school had probably reached out to Gabi about her absence. Or worse...her father reached out.

Before she could respond, Gabi already sent her another message.

GABI

I'm off Sunday night from the pub

Rory exhaled. It wasn't going to be tonight. Gabi was giving her a few days to think. She typed back quickly.

RORY

Sunday is Mel's birthday. After?

GABI

Fine, after

Rory sent back a thumbs-up emoji before shoving her phone in her pocket.

Vanessa leaned toward her. "Everything good?" she whispered.

She smiled. "Seriously, does your mom want to adopt me?"

RORY OPENED the back door at Scoops the next evening and froze. Tyler was in his uniform, signing in, twirling his Scoops hat with his other hand before fitting it on his head.

"What are you doing here?" she asked.

Tyler frowned. "Someone looks disappointed."

"Well...yes," she said, her chest tightening. She wasn't sure if *disappointed* was the word she would go for to describe this moment. Caught off guard was more like it. Maybe even winded...especially with the way his turquoise Scoops shirt fitted tightly to his shoulders. "I was...I was supposed to be working with Mel," she stuttered.

"Calvin called me in, said Mel needed the day," he replied, his expression blank.

She twisted her hands, knowing what that meant. Tomorrow was Melanie's birthday, her first one she would celebrate without her twin brother. Her friend probably wasn't doing well.

She didn't realize Tyler had walked up to her, his massive frame hovering over her like a shield. "She'll be okay, Ry."

Rory nodded, not really believing it. But she didn't say anything as she shuffled around him and got ready for her shift, not daring to return his gaze.

It was just one shift. They'd had dozens together before, so it really wouldn't be a big deal. She would let herself get lost in scooping flavors, blending up milkshakes, and decorating sundaes. If they stayed busy, her mind would be distracted. And before she knew it, her shift would be over.

She stepped out of the bathroom as thunder boomed

outside. The sky had gone from dusty blue to charcoal gray, the skies ominous as lightning cracked through the clouds and rain started pounding on the windows.

"Looks like we're not getting good tips today," Tyler grumbled. He glanced over at her, his dark chocolate eyes roaming her face like he was trying to get a read on what she was thinking.

She felt panic rise in her chest as she whipped her head in a different direction. She didn't want to spend her shift sitting here, staring at him. It sounded like a special hell designed just for her.

"Scoops customers are crazy," she babbled. "They came during a hurricane once; a thunderstorm won't stop them."

"Yeah but—"

"Until then, we'll clean," Rory said, shoving a rag and one of the buckets of soapy water toward him.

Tyler frowned. "This place is already spotless."

"Then we fill candies or fudges or make waffle cones," Rory said, feeling flustered. "Last thing I need is for Calvin to come in here and think we're slacking."

"I—but—"

She walked away before he could complain, turning on the Bluetooth speaker and blasting music to drown out the nervous thumping of her heart, doing anything she could think of to keep her hands busy.

After they filled the spoon containers and the cones and the napkin dispensers, polished the stainless-steel appliances, even vacuumed under the machines to get rogue candies, and mopped all the floors, they still had two hours left of their shift. Only a handful of customers braved the storm for a scoop, licking their ice cream cones in their cars as rain came down hard, leaving their tip jars depressingly bare. So now they stood there, leaning on counters at opposite ends of the shop, letting the storm sounds slice through the awkward silence between them.

"I didn't see you in school yesterday," Tyler muttered.

"Sick."

"You feeling better?"

She huffed. "No."

He looked confused. "Then why are you working?"

"Not the kind of sick that's contagious," she explained carefully.

"Then what kind of sick?"

She sucked in a breath, already regretting the words coming out of her mouth. "The kind of nausea you get when you watch the most absurd promposal in Haverport history."

Ty looked hurt. "It wasn't *that* absurd."

Rory rubbed the sweat from her palms on her khaki shorts. "Yes, it was."

"Ry..." he said, taking a step toward her.

She couldn't deal with this, couldn't deal with the way he was looking at her and having to talk about prom and how much she *wanted* him.

So instead, she changed the subject. "I found him."

Tyler frowned. "Who?"

She turned her face from him, looking out through the foggy windows. "My father. I found him."

"Wait...*what?*"

"I found out who he was from Gabi's old yearbook, and I tracked him down," she explained. "I met him yesterday."

Tyler closed the distance between them, placing one of his massive hands on her shoulder. "How'd it go?"

She shook her head, her breath catching. She wished she hadn't spent so much time daydreaming about a man who wasn't even worth the sticky old chocolate sauce smeared on the bottom of her sneaker. "There's a reason Gabi never wanted me to meet him."

"That bad, huh?"

Rory just nodded.

"I'm so sorry, Ry."

She couldn't help concentrating on the path of Tyler's thumb stroking up her shoulder and down to her collarbone. She also couldn't help how her eyes drooped to his lips, then to his shirt, the tightness around his shoulders and biceps making her mind go fuzzy. She heard him take a deep breath as he crowded her. A breeze rolled through the screen of the front window, the smell of fresh rain on pavement filling her nose, goosebumps flecking her skin. His face was so close she almost felt like she could smell the spiced cinnamon from their hot chocolate on Christmas, or the autumn leaves covering the backyard when he first kissed her. When her entire world changed.

She finally dared to look up at him, his eyes also drawn to her lips. He moved his hands slowly, gracing them up her neck and cradling the back of her head, her Scoops hat falling back onto the counter behind her as he drew her closer to him.

But then he stopped, his eyes still on her lips, so close they could almost brush.

"Kiss me, Ty," she pleaded.

He massaged his hands in her hair, her ponytail coming loose.

"I want to, Ry," he said. "So bad."

"Then why don't you?"

"Because if we do this, if *I* do this, I would never be able to forgive myself."

"For breaking my heart?"

He nodded, leaning down as he placed his forehead against hers.

Rory traced her hands up his side, placing them on his chest. "Ty, not being with you...I think it's already breaking my heart."

His grip tightened. "Every day I'm not with you causes me pain down to my bones. But then I think about leaving you, and I just...long-distance is hard. I don't want to make things harder for you."

Rory huffed. "Stop being so honorable, Chapman, and kiss me already."

"If I do, I don't think I'll be able to stop."

She smirked, nudging his nose. "Fine by me."

"Rory..."

Pounding on the window outside made them jump. Tyler dropped his hands and whipped his head around, making room for Rory to see the unhappy customer.

But it wasn't a customer on the other side of the window, completely drenched.

It was Jay.

Chapter Twenty-Four

"CRAP," Rory muttered, pushing herself off the counter.

He quickly grabbed her hand before she could walk any farther. "Wait, Rory."

She glanced back at him, feeling panicked.

"Do you want me to handle this?"

The metal doorknob in the back turned, the door swinging open.

"No," she breathed. "This was going to happen eventually."

She heard the door slam shut, and he entered The War Room. Rory rounded the corner, Tyler following closely behind, as she watched Jay pick up his stack of new Scoops shirts before checking the schedule for the week pinned to the corkboard.

"So this is the guy, huh?" he asked, not glancing at her once. "I should have known."

"Jay—"

"Does Calvin know the two of you are playing tonsil hockey during a shift?"

She glared at him, on the verge of reminding him how

he loved the idea of making out with her during a shift. "We weren't kissing."

"Looked pretty damn close to it from where I was standing." Jay's mouth twisted into a smirk. An evil one, the kind you would expect from someone who was in the mood for chaos. He still didn't bother looking in Rory's direction, but instead, looked up at Tyler. "Still got a girlfriend?"

"That's none of your business," Tyler said coolly.

Jay chuckled, shaking his head. "So that's a yes."

She took a step toward him. "Jay—"

He reared back. His eyes finally locked on hers, and she could see it—the unadulterated rage. "So much for not deserving to come in 'second place,'" he started, holding his hand up in mock quotations. "Tell me, does it get you off chasing guys who don't want you in return?"

Before she could respond to that blow, Tyler stepped around her and with one arm slammed Jay up against the wall, causing the corkboard to rattle as the stack of shirts in his hand tumbled to the floor. Jay didn't even seem fazed by the brute force of Tyler's hold on him, his forearm holding Jay's chest to the wall like a thumbtack.

"Do not speak that way to her again," Tyler said, his voice calm despite his aggressive hold.

Jay simply laughed. "Or what? You'll beat me up? Please do. I would *love* to show off a black eye from your royal fist."

Tyler shoved him slightly again, tightening his arm against Jay's chest. Jay's feet were barely touching the ground, his whole body practically dangling underneath Tyler's arm. Yet Jay kept on grinning as if this entire interaction was amusing to him.

"GUYS," she screamed. "Enough!"

Tyler loosened his hold. Jay slid back to the ground, still with a shit-eating grin on his face.

"Damn, Rory, that's quite a tight leash you have on him," Jay sneered. "Too bad he's dating someone else."

Tyler's hands curled into fists as Jay chuckled, reaching down to grab his pile of shirts. He took three steps toward the back door before turning to face them again, his mouth still pressed into a forced grin. "See you at the party tomorrow, Rory," he said. Then, before he turned, he dipped into a deep bow. "Your Royal Highness."

They remained standing there as Jay left, the door slamming again from his departure.

Tyler turned to face her, his eyes softening. "Ry..."

Before she could respond, the back door swung open again. They both flinched, but this time it was just Blake stepping inside with Jess for the night shift. Rory didn't look in their direction, nor did she return Tyler's gaze as he whispered to her, pleading for her as she quickly signed out and walked out of the shop, not bothering to shield herself from the pelting rain.

THE RAIN WAS UNRELENTING as she drove past Hillside Park and into the beach communities, turning her car onto the dirt road of Sandy Cove. She pulled into the seashell driveway of cottage five, parking next to Calvin's truck.

Something inside her snapped when she stepped out of Scoops. She was tired...tired of trying to fight it all. Tired of trying to be okay with everything changing so quickly around her. She wondered if life was meant to feel like this —always in motion, always walking through a revolving door, facing one challenge after the next. Was it impossible for things to ever feel solid under her feet? For things in her life to feel like a calm morning breeze instead of a constant raging storm?

She'd immediately thought of the person in her life who had become a constant in this mess of a year, and without even calling, simply drove to Melanie's house.

Rory stepped up the porch steps, sopping wet. She knew it was probably selfish to bombard Melanie right now. But before she could talk herself out of it, Melanie's words came back to her. Reminding her that having friends like her was the reason she was able to be strong through it all.

Rory needed a strong friend, too.

Melanie's parents greeted her with hugs and a warm towel, whispering to her that she was upstairs in her room. Nodding, she climbed the creaky stairs before knocking on the door and pushing it open slowly.

Calvin glanced up at her, his arm tightly around Melanie who was curled up sleeping, her head on his chest.

"If it's a bad time, I can come back," Rory whispered.

Calvin shook his head. "No, she'll be glad you're here." He rubbed Melanie's shoulders, whispering something to her that Rory couldn't hear. She woke up at the sound, her eyes blinking open. Lines from Calvin's shirt were indented on her face, her eyes sleepy, but she smiled when she saw Rory in the doorway.

Without having to say anything, Melanie could somehow read Rory's expression. She slipped out of Calvin's grasp, turning to him. "I love you, but leave."

Calvin smiled in response, kissing the top of Melanie's head before standing up. He walked up to Rory, and she was stupefied when he placed a hand on her shoulder and whispered, "I'm glad you're here, too."

He slinked past her and tiptoed down the stairs, the sound of him talking to Melanie's parents muffled as she closed the door.

Melanie held out her arms to Rory, and instantly, Rory was crying. Still in her wet uniform, she curled up, her chest heaving as Melanie held her, brushing her hair away from her face and holding her close. They remained there in their embrace for a while, until Rory's sobs finally slowed.

"Is it Tyler?" Melanie asked.

Rory just nodded. "He's going to move, Mel. Really, really far away."

"Football?"

"Yeah," she answered, wiping her runny nose with her sleeve.

"Did something new happen with him?"

She sighed. "Y-yes."

"Tell me everything. Leave nothing out."

So, Rory did. From cuddling under the blanket on Christmas to their confessions in the rain a few weeks ago. Then tonight at Scoops when he almost kissed her, held her, looked at her like she was the only thing that mattered in the world. Then how Jay barged in, and the way Tyler protected her from him, the pain she saw in his eyes.

When she was finished, she looked up at Melanie, who, annoyingly enough, was trying to hold back a smile curling up her lips.

Rory glared. "Stop that right now."

"I...what? I'm not doing anything."

She flicked Melanie off, which made her friend chuckle.

"Do you think he has a thing for rain?" Melanie teased, pointing to the wrathful thunderstorm out the window. "Or maybe precipitation in general? Because snow got him going, too."

"Oh my god," she said, rolling her eyes. Melanie was belting out a laugh now.

Rory poked her friend in the side before lying back down and hugging Melanie's waist. "None of it matters, though. Everyone is going to leave."

"Not me," she whispered.

She perked up, looking up at her friend. "No Yale?"

Melanie nodded. "No Yale. After our conversation the other day, I knew right away that I wasn't meant to follow this dream anymore. It's time to follow a different one."

Rory grasped her hands. "And what's your new dream?"

Her friend smiled. "I want to help other kids like me. Like Duncan. Families struggling with addiction. I want others to know they are loved and seen, and that they are never alone."

She rubbed at her arm. "That just gave me chills, Mel. I can feel it. It's what you're meant to do."

Melanie squeezed Rory's hands.

"So...what's next?" Rory asked. "Are you going to college?"

"I'm enrolling as a commuter student at UCONN," Melanie explained. "I'll be living at home."

She exhaled, closing her eyes and leaning her head back in relief. "Oh thank god."

"You're stuck with me, Gilmore."

"I hate you."

Melanie chuckled. "Anything from Baybrook yet?"

She shook her head.

"You'll get in," Melanie reassured her. "They would be fools not to accept you."

She stared at her friend in awe. "Mel...you want to know why you're going to be incredible at helping others?"

Melanie rolled her eyes. "Why?"

"Because you're so fucking nice," she said. "I mean you're literally in the middle of grieving and your selfish friend comes over to cry about her boy problems and you...just...listened to me."

"Is that why you didn't tell me about Tyler? Or when you broke things off with Jay?"

Rory sucked in a breath.

"Why do you keep pushing me away?"

She sat up, brushing the snot dribbling down her nose with the back of her hand. "Because I felt like my crap was meaningless compared to all the stuff you were going through. It seemed silly compared to...um—"

"Losing a brother?"

She cast her eyes down and nodded.

Melanie paused, her arms still tight around Rory. "Isn't that what friendship is about, though? I spent so much of my life trying to hide the pain, not letting anyone in. And then I came here and met people like you and Calvin and...I realized that friendship is so much more than going to football games or eating gross ice cream cakes on the beach. True friends are the kind who sit in the hard places with you, carry grief with you, hold you when you cry, make you feel welcome and seen and loved. You've been that for me, Rory...since the day I met you. And I know you want to sit here and think that your problems are silly or not as important as mine, but that's just not true. They matter to me because you matter to me. And I want to sit in the hard places with you and remind you that I choose to be here with you and be your friend."

She was crying again, but Melanie simply reached for the tissues and pulled her in, the sounds of her soft weeping covered by the rolling thunder coming from outside the bay window.

"Promise me you'll stop shutting me out," Melanie said.

"I promise."

"Promise, promise?"

"Triple-scoop promise."

Rory didn't at all feel deserving of the kind of friendship she had with Melanie. But maybe her friend was right— maybe that's what being a friend was all about. Friendship didn't have to be earned, but something that was given unconditionally.

Chapter Twenty-Five

RORY WAS SCROLLING through the final proofs of the yearbook, making sure everything looked good before giving her seal of approval, when the email came in. The notification blinked at the corner of her screen, and she immediately clicked it open.

Tears welled in her eyes as she read.

The front door creaked open downstairs. "Ry, do you want to ride to this thing together?"

A laugh escaped her chest as she wiped away her tears, sitting up from her desk. She tugged on her sweatshirt and raced downstairs, feeling utterly bewildered.

Tyler was standing in the kitchen when she turned the corner. "What's wrong? Why are you crying?"

She smiled, eyes crazed. "I-I got in."

Tyler beamed at her, and in one swift moment, lifted her in a hug and twirled her around the room. Rory was crying happy tears, her arms wrapped tightly around Tyler's neck.

He set her down gently and cupped her face. "Congratulations. You're amazing."

She scoffed and shoved him. "I don't know about that."

"You are. You are going to kill it at Baybrook. They won't know what's coming."

She grinned at him, still in shock. But as reality set in, her face fell. "But...I won't be able to go. Gabi—"

"Ry, let yourself enjoy this moment, don't worry about it yet," he said, brushing his hands down her arms, then interlacing his hands with hers. "And I have a feeling she'll come around."

She looked down at their hands, her heart aching at the way they fit perfectly. She squeezed her eyes shut and after a deep breath, she let go.

"Haverport is seventeen hundred miles away from North Texas."

"I know."

She felt his hand brush hers again, but she backed away. "Maybe you're right. Maybe...maybe this would just get too complicated. Plus, you're still technically with Zoe and taking her to prom..."

"Rory—"

She cut him off. "Today is not about you or me. It's about Mel. We need to get going." She stepped around him and grabbed her wallet. "And I need to make a pitstop first, if you don't mind."

He nodded, looking broken and defeated. "Yeah, okay."

SHE KEPT her gaze out the passenger window the entire ride to Sandy Cove, her hands gripping the present on her lap, keeping her focus on her friend and pushing Tyler's disappointed look out of her mind.

No one seemed to notice the fact that they arrived together, except Jay. His lips were pressed into a tight line, his eyes downcast as he glared at the two of them approaching the group.

Rory ignored the flip-flopping in her stomach as she glanced around the Scoopers, realizing the most important person was missing. "Where's Mel?"

Calvin pointed to the beach. Rory followed his hand and found Melanie in between two practically identical sandcastles, shaping the tower for one to match the other. When she finished, she sat down, looking satisfied with her creation, then turned her attention toward the ocean before her.

Rory noticed Calvin smiling out of the corner of her eye. He excused himself and stepped down the porch and out to the beach, taking a seat next to her.

The cottage's screen door swung open. "CAKE!" Jess screamed.

"Don't worry, Rory is a good six feet from you," Blake teased.

"That's it," Rory said, planting her hands on her hips as she turned toward Blake. "You're officially the new Ass Hat."

Tyler burst out laughing, which had Rory chuckling as well, relieved at the tension dissipating. He was hiding his disappointment well.

Blake made some kind of snarky comment back to her, but she couldn't comprehend it, her mind way too focused on the way Jay just stood there with his arms tight around his chest. Looking like he was ready to bolt.

Jess went to slice the double layer ice cream cake she made as Melanie's parents came through the front door, followed by Kevin. He sidled up next to Jess and placed a stack of paper plates on the table before looking up at Rory. She didn't mean to frown at him as she pieced together why Kevin was here, but her facial expression must have been telling enough because he winked in her direction.

"Crap, this cake is too cold to cut," Jess said, completely oblivious to how close Kevin was standing next to her. "I'm going to run the knife under some hot water."

Jess escaped into the kitchen, and Rory couldn't help herself—she followed. Jess looked over her shoulder as she approached the sink, her expression unreadable. She flicked on the hot water without saying anything.

"Jess..."

She watched as Jess brushed her blonde bangs out of her face before pressing her glasses up the bridge of her nose and looking in her direction.

"I'm sorry," Rory said softly, stepping closer so no one could hear them through the open windows. "I shouldn't have showed up to your apartment unannounced. You were...clearly in the middle of something."

"You think?"

"I was having an awful day at school. I skipped, actually. It's...a long story."

"Everything okay with you and Gabi?"

She leaned against the counter, ignoring the wave of nausea in her stomach as she thought about the conversation they planned to have later that night. "Not exactly."

Jess lifted her chin toward the crowd outside. "And the boys?"

Rory felt an ache deep in her bones at the thought of it. "Things just keep getting more complicated."

Jess didn't say a word as she rinsed the chef's knife under the steaming water.

Rory took a step closer. "Why did you offer to talk to me?"

Jess shrugged. "Kind of wish someone was around to talk to me when I was going through shit in high school."

She nodded, watching as Jess turned the spigot off. Rory knew she shouldn't try to get involved in Jess's personal life —she'd already made that mistake. But for some reason, this time felt different. Jess didn't seem *happy* per se, yet there was something new there. There was less fury behind those glasses, her shoulders were relaxed, and a new sense of calm washed over her face. Something had definitely changed... and Rory wondered if the boy winking on the porch had anything to do with it.

Rory steeled herself and decided to make the mistake again. "Is everything okay with you? At home?"

To her surprise, Jess didn't glare or make a snappy comment. Instead, she shrugged. "Same as you. Things just keep getting more complicated."

"I'm sorry," she whispered.

"Do yourself a favor, Rory," Jess said. "Don't fall in love in high school. Nothing good comes from it."

Then Jess was out the door, slicing smoothly into the cake outside.

She huffed, her eyes grazing over the group and landing on Ty. He was smiling warmly at Melanie as she approached the porch, Calvin hot on her heels. Her heart somersaulted as she watched Tyler pull Melanie into a fierce hug, saying something soothing to their friend that had Melanie nodding, her eyes watering.

Rory exhaled at the sight, feeling like she was gripping a handful of sand, grains slowly slipping through her fingers. *Too late.*

She was in love with the boy next door.

The one who sat with her on the swings for hours, played touch football in the backyard, hung out in pajamas on weekends to watch countless hours of Disney movies, made her laugh so hard hot chocolate came out her nose. The guy who saved her from making mistakes, made sure she drank water when she had too much to drink, forced her to spend holidays with his family when she was alone, and kissed her in a way that left her without any feeling in her legs.

Rory was in love with Tyler Chapman. And he was about to leave her behind.

Her hands were shaking as she turned away from the group and leaned against the counter. She took deep, calming breaths. These feelings she had for Tyler had gone far beyond any kind of crush she'd had, even for Jay. They were earth-shattering, and when Ty finally left for college, she would have to glue together the shattered pieces of her heart. She wasn't strong enough for that. She had to create distance...had to hope it would make things easier in the end.

Her acceptance to Baybrook eased some of her worries —it was the perfect escape, the next step toward a new Rory. She wanted to spend her days sculpting abstract pieces and perusing student art galleries and deepening her knowledge of graphic design. Despite having no idea how in the world she was going to afford art school, the simple thought of attending made her feel that same kind of contentment. That she'd finally found where she was meant to be.

She'd spent her whole life seeking attention, and she knew her shithead father was in part to blame. The man who—in the end—didn't choose her when she'd stood before him in the flesh.

It was right then and there that she vowed to move forward, to choose herself. Her mother might hate her and kick her out. She may go into debt trying to pay for school. And there was a chance she'd lose Ty forever.

But she would stick up for herself and what she wanted. She'd finally take this new path forming right in front of her like a block of clay, ready to come to life.

THE WARM BREEZE that night was a late-April tease, a small promise that the summer season was around the corner. The group sprawled out on the porch, full from the cake they'd devoured, watching as the last sliver of sunshine faded into the horizon.

A black convertible pulled up and parked on the side of the street. Zach stepped out, moving his sunglasses to the top of his head as he walked toward the group. Blake yelped with glee and jumped up from his seat, hopping down the steps and planting a kiss on Zach's lips.

Jess hummed. "Must be nice."

Rory didn't miss how Kevin bristled.

"You could just break up with him," Calvin said calmly. He was tangled up on the porch swing with the birthday girl, the two of them tucked under a blanket. Despite there being enough places to sit, Rory made a point to sit closer to Melanie. She pulled a cushion off one of the deck chairs and used it to sit on the floor next to the swing, keeping a safe distance from Tyler who sat at the opposite end of the porch, and Jay, who was propped up on the wooden railing. Jay leaned his head back against the cedar shingles, his hat on his knee, scrolling through his phone. She'd done her best to avoid them all day, focusing on Melanie instead of the revelation she'd had in the kitchen hours before.

Jess's phone began to ring. "Speak of the devil," she grumbled.

Jess answered with a muffled *"What"* to her boyfriend on the other line, escaping into the cottage.

Kevin cocked his head in the direction of the house, and Calvin nodded, kissing the back of Melanie's head as he slid out of the blanket and off the swing.

Rory didn't waste time—she swept right into Calvin's spot, curling up with Melanie under the blanket. "I got you something."

Melanie frowned. "I told you not to."

"Do I look like the type of person who actually listens to the rules?" Rory teased. She lifted her present and placed it in Melanie's lap.

Melanie rolled her eyes, untying the ribbon. "That's fair."

Rory watched as her friend opened up the box, revealing two matching coffee tumblers, both from Seabreeze Café.

"I could have made friendship necklaces or bracelets or something," she said. "But lattes have kind of always been our thing, and since we'll both be living in town and going to school next year..."

Melanie grabbed her hands. "You got in."

Rory grinned, nodding her head. Melanie shrieked, throwing her arms around Rory's shoulders.

"Wait, where did you get in?"

Rory pulled herself from Melanie's grasp, turning to Jay. He was finally looking at her, his curiosity taking over that simmering rage for just a moment.

She gave him a timid smile. "Baybrook."

Zach whistled as he stretched out, leaning his head back on Blake's lap. "Damn, that school is not easy to get into. You must be mega talented."

She felt her face flush. "I-I don't know about that. They're just trying to fill this new program."

"Don't belittle yourself," Tyler said pointedly. "The dean literally sought you out."

Jay's eyes went wide. "Shit, he did?"

Rory nodded, feeling embarrassed that all the attention was on her. "Yes, now let's be done talking about this."

"I mean, I'm not surprised," Jay continued. "Those year-book designs I saw were pretty dope."

Tyler's eyebrows knitted together as he whipped his head in Jay's direction. "You've seen them?"

Jay gave him a cat-like smile, leaning back with smug satisfaction. "And you haven't? *Fascinating*."

"Stop," Rory snipped.

Calvin chose that moment to step back out, frowning at Rory. "You're in my seat."

"Actually, I think you were always in *my* seat," she said with a smirk, glad to have someone to distract her from the icy tension.

"Calvin, look, Rory and I have matching mugs," Mel said, holding them up with pride.

"For lattes only," she added. "No herbal tea shit in there."

Calvin shook his head, plopping down on Rory's cushion with a thud. "You're both ridiculous."

"I'm thinking we should get stickers and decorate them," Mel said. "Ooo, do you think Baybrook has a sticker I can put on mine so I can shamelessly show off my talented best friend?"

"They probably tell the artists to make it themselves,"

Rory answered, thinking about the colorful notebook Dean Farrow showed her weeks earlier. She wondered what other creative projects her classmates would be working on. Her hands were thrumming with anticipation, ready to get started on something herself.

"Even better, you'll make stickers for me," Mel said, leaning into Rory's shoulder. "What should they be?"

"CAKE!" Blake screamed, making everyone laugh. Jay included.

"How about *Mrs. Ass Hat?*" Rory teased, nudging her side.

"I thought I was the new Ass Hat?" Blake quipped.

Zach smirked. "Would probably make for a good hat. His ass is cute."

Everyone howled at that, Blake covering his pink cheeks.

"How about one that says *They're Not Sprinkles, They're Jimmies,*" Tyler added.

"That's actually brilliant," Calvin replied.

"What about *The War Room?*" Blake added.

"Or *Warning: Milkshakes May Explode,*" Jay teased, winking at Melanie.

Melanie gave him the finger in response. "That only happened to me once."

"Be careful," Rory added. "You'll be saying that forever."

"Rory, dropping an entire *cake* is different than one milkshake explosion on the wall," Blake said.

"I DIDN'T DROP IT! SHE BUMPED INTO ME!"

They all were laughing now, fighting back and forth. And yet, she secretly loved it. Loved having her family together, no matter how sticky it got.

"How about *The Scoopers,*" she said.

Melanie smiled, wiggling in her seat. "I love it."

"We could sell them at the shop," Calvin said, his brain in business mode.

"Is this our life now?" Jay asked. "Hey, army boy, not everything is about making money."

"Says the guy who's saving up to move to Japan," Calvin responded with a flick of his hand.

Rory whipped her head toward Jay as the group went still. Jay remained silent, glaring down at Calvin.

"That's it," Blake said, hopping up. "New rule: No more secrets. My heart can't take it anymore. Why am I always the last to know everything?"

"You weren't the last to know," Jay said coolly. "Because no one knew."

The group stayed silent as Jay hopped off the railing, making his way to the porch swing. He grabbed Melanie's hands, kissing her knuckles. "Sweet Mel, happy birthday."

She nodded, and then the Scoopers watched as Jay got in his car, escaping into the night.

Melanie looked over at Calvin. "Babe, really?"

"Did you know?" Rory whispered, tears pricking her eyes.

"No," Melanie responded. "But I did know they had a meeting recently."

"About what?"

"Jay told me that he wouldn't be around next summer," Calvin said. "Wanted to give me enough warning to hire and train someone new."

"Because he's moving to Japan?"

"He wants to transfer to a school out there," he explained. "Says there's a program he's interested in."

"What program?"

Calvin just shook his head. "I've said enough. I think at this point you need to talk to him."

Rory huffed, looking out at the ocean past the porch, the waves covered in darkness.

She felt a warm hand on her shoulder. "Ry, want me to take you home?"

Underneath the blanket, Rory squeezed Melanie's knee. Melanie placed her hand on top of her own, squeezing back. A silent agreement.

"No, I think I'm going to stay a little longer," she murmured. She couldn't deal with being alone with Tyler right now, and she wasn't quite ready for whatever big conversation Gabi wanted to have back at home.

Tyler hesitated as he hovered over her, but Rory didn't waver on her decision, so he bid his farewells. Blake and Zach were next, walking hand in hand as they made their way to his convertible.

"You really know how to kill the vibe, Ball," Melanie murmured.

The sound of raised voices had Calvin excusing himself and heading back inside.

"Want me to beat him up for you?" Rory said.

Melanie chuckled, turning to face her. "No, it's fine. He's not the best when it comes to Jay. He's working on it."

"Why?"

Melanie's face softened. "Why do you think?"

She frowned. "Me?"

Melanie just nodded.

Rory groaned, placing her face in her hands. "I bet he's excited for the day I leave. I cause so much drama."

"Maybe you shouldn't be so hot and awesome," Melanie teased. "The boys can't help but drool over you."

"If that were the case, where are all the boys asking me to prom? I mean, not like I'm going anymore, *but—*"

"I hate that you're not going. I don't really want to go either."

Rory blinked. "Then don't. Join me and Vanessa. We'll have empanadas."

"But I already have tickets..."

"So? Why waste your time going if you're already dreading it?"

Melanie chewed on her lip. "Yeah?"

"Yes!" Rory said, her spirits lifting. "We could pick up lattes in our new mugs to start the night. And maybe even get an entire blueberry coffee cake, Vanessa has quite the hook-up."

Melanie grinned. "You had me at lattes."

She squealed, the two of them swinging on the porch, gabbing about their anti-prom plans as Rory squeezed out every last moment she could from the evening, just in case everything came crashing down when she got home.

Chapter Twenty-Six

CALVIN OFFERED to drive Rory home. They remained silent as his truck took them over to Misty Bay, up until he parked the car outside of her house.

"I'm sorry," he said as she unbuckled her seatbelt. "That wasn't my news to share. He just—"

"Makes you want to scream sometimes," Rory finished for him.

Calvin chuckled. "I'm kind of surprised he even asked to meet me and tell me in person. He seems...different."

"He had a lot going on this year," murmured Rory.

Calvin dipped his chin.

"Maybe you should—"

"Yeah," he interrupted. "I'll apologize."

She nodded. "Good."

As she got out of the car and walked up to the house, she sent up a silent prayer into the universe, to whoever was listening, hoping that someday Jay would want to be her friend again. He'd forever be the boy she played spoon swords with, the guy who was always willing to get in trouble with her—like their annual tradition of locking newbies in the walk-in. She wanted to know everything going on with him, wanted to know about this program in Japan. She could only hope things would stop being so weird between them.

Rory reached for the doorknob and let out a long sigh.

She took a lot of chances this year, made a lot of decisions that went against what she thought her life was supposed to be. What she was supposed to do, where she was supposed to go. Deciding against going to a traditional university like her mother had always wanted for her, joining the yearbook, even going after her father. Kissing Tyler. Falling for him.

Her shoulders eased. Whatever befell her as she entered the house, she knew down to her core that she would never regret choosing herself.

She opened the door. Gabi sat on the couch, a box of half-eaten buffalo chicken pizza on the table as she watched *Gilmore Girls*. She looked up at Rory and paused the show. "How was the party?"

A mess. "A lot of fun."

"Good," Gabi responded, patting the cushion next to her. Rory took a seat. "And Melanie is doing okay?"

"As okay as she can be, I think," Rory said. "I don't know that she'll ever be truly okay."

"It's a good thing she has you guys. A family to lean on in the hard times."

She thought back to her conversation with Melanie a few nights ago, sopping wet on her bed, how similar Gabi's words were to what her friend told her. "Yeah, exactly."

"And I think, maybe, it's been good for you, too."

Rory gaped. This was not what she expected. "I don't understand."

Gabi sighed. "I've been so tunnel-visioned about us

having enough money to afford college that I completely lost sight of my daughter and what *she* needed to be okay. And I'm truly sorry, sweetie. I screwed up."

Tears lined Rory's eyes. "But I've screwed up, too."

"Yes, and we'll talk about it," Gabi said with a cock of her head. "But I just needed to start with that. To let you know that I understand why this all went down in the first place. That maybe my actions were the catalyst."

Rory looked down at her hands, twisting them, not sure what else to say.

"So...why'd you skip school?" Gabi asked.

Rory looked up at her. "You're not going to like it."

To her surprise, Gabi smiled wearily. "He called me."

Rory's eyes went wide. "He did?"

Gabi sighed. "Yes, he called me right after you drove off, all in a huff. Said you are just as stubborn as me, that he couldn't believe how low I'd stooped to send you his way."

"Oh god," she whispered.

"I told him that I was proud of my daughter for facing her fears, and glad that my Rory will forever know how much of an asshole he is."

Her tears were falling now, and she let her eyes flutter shut. "I'm so sorry, I shouldn't have done it."

"Gone behind my back? Yeah, definitely not," Gabi said. "But standing up for yourself, for me? I could never be angry at you for that."

Gabi was holding tissues toward her as she blinked her eyes open. She snatched one, blowing her nose.

"How'd you find him?" Gabi asked.

So, Rory told her. How she found her yearbook in the attic and did some online stalking, then about the newspaper clipping and realizing where the estate was.

"They're *loaded*," Rory explained. "That house...it doesn't make sense. You work so hard, it feels unfair."

"With the Barrys, money always came with strings attached," Gabi explained. "I didn't want to get tangled up with them anymore than I needed to because I did not want that life for you. So I only accepted his child support, and nothing more."

Rory gave her a curt nod, then confessed the rest; about how much she'd thought about her father before that, wondering what kind of man he was, wondering if her life would be any better if he were around.

"But I was wrong," she admitted. "He was a dick, and I can't believe he—"

Gabi now had tears in her eyes, reaching for Rory's hands.

"I can't believe he tried forcing you to terminate your pregnancy," she finished, breathless from the weight of it.

"A woman should always have the right to choose what she wants for her body, for her life," Gabi said. "As soon as he showed his true colors, I knew it would never work between us. Especially if my little one was a girl."

The two of them wept, squeezing each other's hands in between reaching for tissues and blotting away tears. When she finally felt like she had control of her emotions, Rory leaned back, looking at the TV screen in front of them. Ironically, Gabi was watching the episode where Lorelai and Rory visited Harvard. Rory's eyes were bright with promise, Lorelai's with pride as they stood at the entrance leading to campus.

You'll always regret it if you don't try.

One last leap. One last big opportunity to stick up for herself.

She looked back at Gabi. "I know you wish this was our

life," she said, pointing to the screen. "That I was the kind of kid who loved the idea of going to college, who wasn't always such a problem, one who followed the rules."

"You clearly haven't seen the whole show," Gabi grumbled.

"I don't think I can do it. Go to college in the way you've always hoped. I-I think it would crush me. And I'm sorry that it'll disappoint you, that I'll never be the Rory you imagined."

"Sweetie," Gabi said, squeezing her hands again. "I didn't name you Rory because I want you to *be* her."

Rory just blinked.

Gabi sighed. "Oh baby, no. I did watch a lot of this show when I was pregnant with you, but I named you Rory not because of who her character was, but who she was to her mother—to Lorelai. Lorelai made this big decision to be on her own, to raise her child in the way she thought was best. She moved her to a different town and even if she had to live in a shed, she made it work. Rory was like this little beacon of hope through all of the crap she had to deal with, and as I watched, I also wanted my little girl to be that for me. To be the thing that drove me to work hard and do everything I could to give her a life she loved.

"But sometimes, your best intentions don't line up with what the other person needs," Gabi admitted. "And I've realized recently that by forcing you to go to college in the way I've always dreamed for you makes me just as bad as Emily Gilmore."

"Huh?"

"Lorelai's mother in the show...? It doesn't really matter," Gabi answered with a chuckle. "What matters is how I realized trying to force you to do something you don't want would go against this streak of independence I had at your age. Yes, my parents hated that I left Florida while pregnant with you and decided to make a life for myself here, and we fought about it for a while. But it was never because they wanted to force me to be around them—it was because they were so sad about how much they would miss us. But they still trusted me enough to make that kind of decision for myself and for my child.

"And I want to trust you, too," Gabi concluded. "I want to be the kind of mom who supports her daughter's decisions. You're almost 18, an *adult*. You should decide what you want to do with your life. And if studying graphic design at an art school is going to be what makes you thrive, what leads you to a life you will hopefully love, then I am behind it."

Rory threw her arms around her. "Thank you, thank you, thank you."

Gabi pulled away, brushing a strand of Rory's hair behind her ear. "I looked at the tuition costs, and it's not cheap, sweetie. It's a private school, and there's no in-state tuition. Between what your father has sent over the years and what I've saved, I can pay some, but you may need to take out loans or find scholarships."

"I'll make it work. We'll figure it out, Mom. We always do."

Rory felt her mother squeeze her tightly at the use of the title after so many years. She squeezed her back before sitting up, looking up at the woman she'd admired since she was little.

Gabi smiled, tears lodged in the crinkles around her eyes. "Together."

"He must have a sick sense of humor."

Rory looked up at Jay, his position mirroring hers at the opposite side of the Scoops counter. Arms tense, crossed across his chest, leaning against the counter.

"It was bound to happen eventually," Rory mumbled. "Us working together."

"Yeah, but scheduling us a few days after the party? That was on purpose."

Rory just smirked and dug her sneaker into the rubber mat on the floor. "Yeah, maybe."

They stood there in silence for a bit longer, a sun beam shining through thick-set clouds outside the window. Scoops was dead, but it was early in the afternoon. Crowds tended to rush in when the elementary school let out. But they still had another hour to kill, and there was nothing else to do but wait and stare at their shoes.

Rory held her hands out in front of her, the nail polish chipping around the edges. She usually stayed on top of keeping her rainbow manicure pristine, but with prom two days away, she was spending every spare minute of her time in the computer lab, making sure every facet of the yearbook was ready to go so they could submit the file after prom with ease.

"So..." she started, heaving a sigh. "Japan, huh?"

Jay looked up at her, an unmistakable gleam in his eye. "Yeah, Japan."

"Is it a business program?" she asked, recalling that he was planning on taking classes to get his business degree.

"No, I dropped that major this winter," he admitted. "I'm doing something new."

"Like what?"

Jay didn't answer her, distracted by a pair of cat ears bobbing up to the window.

"You still have ears on your head," Jay deadpanned. Vanessa wore one of her neon skirts—this one purple— with a *World of Warcraft* graphic tee tucked into the front. Her usual fishnet stockings were gone, and she donned a new pair of slim black combat boots with a slight block heel.

"Yes, thankfully they are still there," Vanessa sassed as she reached up to her human ears, giving them a tug just like their first interaction.

Rory slid closer to the window where Vanessa stood outside. "Hey, Vee. What's up?"

Vanessa beamed, shrugging her backpack off her shoulders. "Brought you a present."

"My birthday isn't for another week, you know."

"Trust me, you want this now," she said, pulling out a spiral-bound book. "You're going to want to kiss my face after you see this."

"I'd pay to see that," Jay mused.

Rory couldn't help herself, she stepped back and shoved Jay in his side, causing him to stumble back with laughter. Seeing him smile made her grin, and he peered around her with intrigue at the spiral-bound book Vanessa was sliding through the window.

Rory flipped it open, and on the inside was a mockup spread of the first page of the yearbook.

"Oh my god," she breathed.

"Print proof of the book," Vanessa said. "The printers offer it as a courtesy in case we hate the coloring of anything. I flipped through it already and think it looks good, but I'll let you make the final call."

Rory flipped through, not able to contain the smile sliding across her face. Each page was perfect, from the designs to the lay of the text and all of Sean's incredible images. So much hard work, now right at her fingertips. She wondered if she would always feel this way about her art at Baybrook, this feeling of pride and satisfaction.

"Wow, Rory," Jay breathed from where he stood right next to her, their shoulders brushing. Almost as if the art had bridged the gap between them. "This is insanely good."

She grinned, teeth and all. "Thanks."

Jay looked up at Vanessa, glancing at her ears before his eyes flicked down to her shirt. "So...you play?"

Vanessa smirked. "Yeah, I play. You?"

"Uh, sometimes," said Jay with a casual shrug, but Rory could see through it. He was nervous. "There's a group that meets at UCONN, Thursday nights, and most weekends. They game, eat pizza, hang out till the wee hours of the morning."

"Is it *they* or *we*?" Vanessa mused.

Jay's face flushed, his eyes flicking over to Rory.

Vanessa smile widened, the silver crystals at the creases of her eyes glinting under the sun. The clouds had cleared. "I already know about the group," she explained. "Two former Haverport alumni are in it, friends of mine."

"Terry and Pheebs?"

Vanessa grinned. "You know them."

"I, um..." Jay looked at Rory first before responding. "Yeah, we hang out a lot on campus. They're actually the ones who convinced me to change my major."

"Did they also convince you to transfer to the University of Tokyo?"

Jay squinted his eyes at her. "Who are you, witch?"

Vanessa threw her head back and laughed. Rory watched as Jay smiled at Vanessa, her heart squeezing in pure delight. Well...this was an interesting development.

"We've been dreaming about it for years," Vanessa explained. "We game together all the time. If you play with them then we've probably streamed together before."

"Oh my god," Jay said, palming his forehead. "You're Kitty Cat."

Vanessa curtseyed. "At your service."

"They always talk about you, saying you were the reason they wanted to wait one more year before the move."

Rory couldn't help it as she butted into their conversation. "I'm guessing this is why you're moving to Japan?"

"Ye—yeah," Jay admitted. "To study game design."

Vanessa started stepping back as she slid her backpack over her shoulder. "I'll see you Saturday, Rory?"

"Yes, text me your coffee order—Mel and I will grab you whatever you want."

She beamed. "Sounds good." Rory caught her friend winking in Jay's direction. She twirled, her purple skirt flowing behind her as she strutted to her car.

Jay exhaled.

"You're in trouble." Rory chuckled.

"Yeah, no kidding," Jay bemused. "That was—so hot."

Rory cackled, and Jay shoved her playfully, the two of them falling into one of their usual fake fist fights like it was the most natural thing in the world. At one point, Jay swung his arm around Rory's neck as part of his attack, giving her a noogie. She poked his side, causing him to squeal as he cowered back.

They were both panting and laughing as they leaned against the counter.

"So that club you joined back in the fall..." Rory began to ask.

"It was the gamers club," Jay finished. "I met Terry in one of my classes and he invited me."

"Why didn't you tell me?"

"Because I was embarrassed? For so long I'd acted like this person I wasn't because I thought it would make people like me. Soccer, girls, parties. But then I went to college, and I felt—"

"Lost."

"Yeah, lost," he explained. "At first I thought I was just homesick, and that maybe having some kind of tether to home would make me feel better."

Rory held her breath, realizing where this was going.

"But it just made things worse."

"I'm sorry," she breathed.

Jay shrugged. "I'm the one who brought you into my mess. But I realized as I was with you that I was still pretending to be someone I wasn't. And as I started to discover who I really was—the things I like, the way I want to spend my time—I was scared to show this new side of myself to you. I thought...I thought maybe you wouldn't like me anymore."

"That's ridiculous."

"Please, listen." She nodded, and he continued. "When you broke things off, I thought I was heartbroken. But at some point, I realized it wasn't heartbreak. It was fear. Because when I no longer had this tie to home, I was free to be who I really was. And that really, really scared me. But it was the swift kick in the ass I needed, to stop using others as a way to make myself feel better, to find happiness in who I really am."

Jay reached for her hand, but not in a romantic way. As

her friend, as the boy who loved to wrestle and pull pranks and make crude jokes.

Rory squeezed it. "That's huge, Jay."

"I know, how mature of me," he teased. "Do I get a medal?"

"How about a punch in the face? I hear you're gunning for a black eye."

Jay winced. "Okay, yeah, I deserve that."

She crossed her arms. "If you've been doing all this self-reflection, then why taunt him?"

Jay pursed his lips. "It's fun."

She rolled her eyes. "Wrong answer. Try again."

Jay didn't look her in the eye as he spoke. "Finding out you chose him over me made me feel like shit, even if we were never really dating."

Rory rubbed her neck. She needed to speak her truth; she knew she wasn't all that innocent either. "This isn't all on you, Jay. It's my fault, too, and I'm sorry. Part of me wanted to use you as a way to make Ty jealous after he started things with Zoe. I'm sorry."

He nodded. "What's going on with them, anyway? It's fucked up, if you ask me."

"Yeah...I know. Let's just say it's not at all what you think."

"So they're not really dating."

"You said it. Not me."

"But that still leaves you in second place, Rory," Jay said. "And a girl who kisses like *that* should never be in second place."

Rory let his words roll right over her. She couldn't deal with Tyler right now. One messy boy problem at a time. Instead, she wiggled her eyebrows. "That good, huh?"

Jay shoved her. "Don't let it get to your head."

"Too late," Rory teased. "So...what happened to that girl you posted on Instagram? Are you seeing her?"

"God no. That picture was actually taken at a party last summer. I posted it to piss you off," he said, looking guilty. "I actually haven't seen anyone since."

Rory smirked—she'd suspected as much. "Which means you're *wide* open for Kitty Cat."

"Shut your mouth," Jay said. In an instant, he had a cotton candy–colored spoon in his hand, ready to pounce. Rory snatched one herself and they started fighting, their battle going on until a line of customers started to form outside the shop.

Chapter Twenty-Seven

"Here they come!"

Rory rushed over to where Vanessa was perched on the couch with her laptop, leaning over the armrest to get a closer look.

Sean's first batch of pictures popped up in the editor's shared drive, images of the Haverport seniors dressed in colorful gowns and sharp tuxedos as they entered the dance. So much excitement. So much makeup. So much love and hope for what the future held after graduation.

"Is it weird that I'm really happy I'm not there?" Vanessa confessed.

"No," Melanie said, plopping down next to Vanessa, her ponytail swinging as she placed a plate of empanadas down on the coffee table. "I'm relieved."

"Isn't it supposed to be, like, the best night of our lives or something?" Rory asked.

"I thought that was supposed to be your wedding," Melanie mused.

"No way," Vanessa cut in. "The best night of my life is when I launch my first video game and it immediately becomes a cult favorite and causes a bunch of nerds to stream it on Twitch. I refuse to let my best night be defined by a dress. Or a man."

Rory gave Vanessa a big, sloppy kiss on the cheek. "I knew I liked you."

"Looks like Jay has his work cut out for him, then," Melanie teased.

Vanessa rolled her eyes, but Rory caught a hint of a smirk on her friend's lips. "He tried talking to me last night through our stream."

"And?" Rory asked, nudging Vanessa's shoulder.

Vanessa shrugged, eyes still on her laptop, like she wasn't giving him a second thought. "I told him he's going to have to try harder than that."

Melanie laughed. "Oh, that's going to do wonders for his ego."

Vanessa frowned. "Why?"

"Let's just say...Jay hasn't always had to work too hard for a female before."

"Hey!" Rory shouted, giving Melanie a death glare.

Melanie rolled her eyes. "He barely had to work for you. You were smitten."

Vanessa looked up at Rory, a silent question in her glance. *Still smitten?*

Rory shook her head. "I realized pretty quickly that he wasn't for me," she admitted, her heart sinking slightly at the thought of hurting him. But she reminded herself of their conversation at Scoops, about how a lot of what he felt was fear of the unknown for what his future would hold. If she was honest with herself, she felt the same way.

She'd officially accepted her offer to Baybrook, but she still had no idea if Tyler had accepted his offer for North Texas. He told her he would always be there for her, that they would always be family. But would he still feel that way hundreds of miles away? Or would their friendship simply fade into a distant memory?

"Should we start sifting through these?" Vanessa asked.

Rory reached over to the laptop and scrolled through what was already available in the shared drive. "Yeah, maybe we decide which ones we like and put them in a separate folder? Then at the end of the night, we choose which of those for the final spreads?"

"Sounds fantabulous," Vanessa said.

"Oh my god," Melanie said with a mouthful of empanada. "This is probably the most insane thing I've ever eaten."

"I've watched my *mamá* make them hundreds of times, and I'm still convinced she uses some kind of voodoo magic when I'm not looking to make them taste like that," Vanessa responded.

Rory's phone pinged at the other side of the room. She snatched an empanada and took a bite as she walked over, tapping the screen.

She frowned. "Walker just sent me a Snapchat."

As soon as she said it, Melanie's phone pinged, then Vanessa's immediately after.

"Holy crap," Vanessa whispered, looking at her screen.

Rory opened up Snapchat and clicked on the image Walker just sent.

It was slightly blurry, but clear enough to notice two girls hidden in a secluded corner outside of the ballroom at prom. They were kissing.

Rory scanned the caption Walker sent with it.

Maybe we should add this to the yearbook

"Rory," Melanie said softly, padding across the room toward her.

She took a closer look at her screen, at the two girls who were kissing. And realized she recognized them both.

It was Helen, her hair pinned away from her face in a classy topknot, her hands on flushed, smiling cheeks.

Zoe's smiling cheeks. In Helen's embrace, her slicked-back blonde hair tucked behind her ears.

"Holy crap, indeed," Rory whispered.

"Dear god," Vanessa said, hopping off the couch, phone still in hand. "This is bad."

"Why is it bad?" Melanie retorted.

"No, not bad as in what they are doing is bad," Vanessa corrected. "Bad as in this is everywhere. Walker blasted it on Snapchat and now it's circulating all over. Four different people just texted it to me."

"That's disgusting," Melanie said. "How could he do that?"

"Because he wants her to hurt," Rory whispered, realization now dawning on her. "He wants to get back at her."

Melanie just looked confused. "Why?"

Rory suddenly felt panicked. For Zoe. For Helen. For the two of them at this godforsaken dance, being outed on full blast for the school to see.

She glanced at Vanessa. "Call Sean."

Vanessa quickly obeyed, putting her phone on speaker. Sean answered in two rings.

"Sean," Rory rushed out. "Where's Zoe?"

"Tyler just whisked both of them out of here," Sean explained, music booming in the background. "Gina is on the phone with Helen now. They're peeling out of the parking lot."

"And Walker?"

"His face is still white after whatever Tyler just said to him before they left."

Rory's heart swooped, her chest tight. A protector. A gentleman to the bitter end.

"Okay, Gina says Tyler is dropping them off at Helen's place."

The three of them exhaled, staring at one another.

"Guys, I'm not sure how much more of this I can take," Sean admitted. "I just sent in a bunch of dancing images. Do you think we'll have enough?"

"Absolutely," Vanessa said. "At this point, screw it. We'll work with what we got."

"I can go home and edit them—"

"Sean, we know how to edit an image for crying out loud," Rory retorted. "Now turn off your camera and make out with Gina a little before you take her home."

Melanie coughed out a laugh.

Sean's silence was telling enough—they could *feel* his embarrassment. "Yes, ma'am," he mumbled before hanging up.

The three of them were silent for a beat, staring at Vanessa's phone.

"Rory," Melanie finally whispered. "Should we...call Tyler?"

Rory shook her head. "I can't deal with that right now. We have a yearbook to finish."

The three of them settled back on the couch and got to work. Melanie helped choose the best images, and Vanessa gave them any edits they needed before sending them off to Rory to place into the spreads. The work was grounding during such a chaotic night, but that didn't stop Rory from glancing out the window constantly, wondering when a certain Jeep would pull in.

Rory was placing the last image of the night into the yearbook when a knock sounded at the door.

"Holy crap, it's finally finished," Vanessa said. "I feel like we need to celebrate."

"Melanie brought over some sparkling cider," she said, pointing to the fridge as she went for the door. She swung it open and felt like she was going to combust.

Tyler was at the door, still in his tux. His bow tie was unclipped, swinging around his neck, the top two buttons undone. He was leaning against the door frame, his hands in his pockets. He looked tired, but his eyes were bright as he looked down at her.

"Maybe hold off on that," she heard Melanie say. "I think we're about to get kicked out."

Vanessa made some kind of purring noise. Rory turned to glare at her, but Vanessa just gave her a cheeky smile in response.

Rory brought her attention back to Tyler. "Is Zoe okay?"

"She's at Helen's for the night," Tyler explained. "And I told them to call me if they needed me."

Rory nodded, a lump forming in her throat. Words eluded her.

As if reading her mind, Tyler brushed his fingers against her. "Can we talk?"

She followed him out onto the porch, where he leaned against the railing. She shivered.

"Cold?" he asked, reaching to shrug off his jacket.

"Don't," Rory protested. "So cliché. Let me just go get my sweatshirt."

"I think I have something better."

Tyler pointed to the small table at the end of the porch. A bright red bag was perched at the center, the handles tied together with a white bow.

"My birthday isn't for another week," she jested.

"Trust me, this can't wait."

She glanced up at him, unable to resist the smoldering look he was giving her. Like she was the most precious thing in the world...even in her baggy T-shirt and leggings. It was hard enough to be standing this close to him with the way he looked in that *tux*. It took everything in her not to let that puny shred of control snap entirely.

The front door swung open as Vanessa and Melanie creeped out, bags in hand.

Rory pressed toward them. "Wait, we need to finish."

"We literally just did," Vanessa retorted. "I sent the file to Penelope for one final look. It goes to print in the morning."

Her shoulders relaxed. "Wow, I can't believe it's over."

"Or just beginning," Vanessa mused, her eyes glancing up at Tyler.

Tyler smirked in response, crossing his arms.

Rory hugged Melanie. "Are you good—"

"Vanessa is taking me to Calvin's," Melanie whispered in her ear. "You better text me later with an update."

Tyler was patient with her as she watched them leave, threading his fingers through hers after the car was out of sight. "Present?"

Rory frowned. "This seems silly."

"Seriously, Ry? I had to wrangle Bea out of bed to help me wrap this thing, and you won't even—"

Rory snatched the present before he could finish. "You seriously think I won't open a present when it's in front of me? I haven't changed *that* much."

He smiled. "That's my girl."

Her heart fluttered at the sound of it. *My girl.* She tried swatting away the butterflies in her stomach as she undid the ribbon.

"Just open it," Tyler said, stepping closer to her. His chest was now against her back, his hand stroking her arm. "Don't overthink it."

"Okay," she whispered, removing the tissue paper on top.

Inside the bag was a neatly folded gray sweatshirt. She grabbed for it, holding her breath.

Her hands began to shake, but as she held it up in front of them, the words on the sweatshirt didn't say *North Texas University* like she'd expected.

"Wait..." she breathed.

Tyler's arms slid around her waist, and he rested his chin at the top of her head.

"This isn't..." she stammered.

The letters on the sweatshirt weren't green, but a cherry red.

Rutgers Football

She couldn't control her still-shaking hands as she dropped the gift and turned toward him. Tyler just leaned in, holding her close, his smile warm and content.

"New Jersey?"

"One hundred and fifty-five miles. Three and half hours by car."

Tears streamed down her cheeks. "Care to explain, Chapman?"

He brushed his nose against hers. "Can I kiss you first?"

She pretended to frown, which was rather difficult when trying to hide the goofy grin on her face. "No. Explain. Now."

He chuckled, shaking his head as he leaned back, eyes not leaving hers. "When I met Zoe's dad, I thought North Texas would be my only chance to play college football. But what I didn't know was that a scout from Rutgers was at the Thanksgiving game."

"That's kind of a dumb game to go to," Rory said.

"It wasn't on purpose," he explained. "He happened to be there with some family, but when he saw me play, he recognized my name from my application and started digging."

An excited tremor rippled through her when he said it.

"At the time they didn't have an open spot on the team, but something fell through for an incoming freshman a week ago and..."

"He called you," she breathed.

He nodded. "He called me."

She beamed. "But...what about North Texas?"

"I told them no." He shrugged. "I thanked Garner for his help. He really did go above and beyond for me. He wasn't mad, just said he was thankful that Zoe had such a good guy in her life."

Her throat tightened. "Crap."

Tyler nodded, catching her drift. "I feel awful. I shouldn't have deceived him like that, but—"

"You were protecting Zoe," Rory interrupted.

"Yeah," he exhaled. "I was."

Rory thought about it for a moment. Zoe. Helen.

"Where is Zoe going to school?" she asked.

"NYU."

Which made perfect sense. Helen said no to her scholarship at Northeastern and decided on Barnard instead. To be in the same city as Zoe. The thought of the two of them having to hide for so long broke her heart. "Why did they hide it? Were they embarrassed?"

"Zoe was on edge about her father's reelection campaign," he explained. "Walker's dad was a big financial backer for Garner's campaign, and one night this summer when they all had dinner, Garner made a joke about the two of them dating."

"Wow," Rory breathed.

"Walker took that as a sign later that night to finally make a move. But he had no idea that Zoe and Helen had gotten together earlier in the summer and were seeing each other in secret."

She very much wished she could punch Walker in the throat. "Why didn't she tell her parents?"

"With so much media attention on them, she was afraid. She wanted to wait out the year until things with the election died down, then tell her parents before going to college."

"And Walker?"

"That's where I came in," he answered. "Playing fake boyfriend meant she was safe from Walker, and she would have someone to help her so she could see Helen."

"Like a date to the movies," she said, remembering how awkward Zoe was when Rory and Melanie ran into them at Haverport Cinemas months ago, how adamant she was about seeing a movie in a different theater. Memories of the past year began flashing before her eyes, moments that she missed. "Those candy grams on Valentine's Day..."

"All Helen," Tyler responded. He pulled her in tighter. "Are you mad?"

She scowled. "Why would I be mad?"

"I deceived everyone, I made some pretty dumb decisions just so I could play football," he said. "I kept secrets from you for months, and I feel awful about it, Ry. I'm so sorry."

"Okay, that's true, maybe you did deceive a few people," she admitted. "But you also sacrificed a lot to help a friend when she needed it. I'm weirdly proud of you for it."

He didn't say anything, his eyes on her lips.

"I don't know what kind of person this makes me for saying this, but I know you," she started. "I know how much playing football has meant to you, even on that first day when you moved to Haverport and sat next to me on the swings and told me all about your dream of playing in the NFL. My stomach was in knots every day you didn't receive a call, knowing that your dream felt so close...yet so far. If I had the same kind of offer from Zoe and her dad, I would have done the same thing. In a heartbeat."

"But I hurt you," he croaked. "Ry, no dream is ever worth losing you. *You* are my dream. You are the thing I desire most in this world. At the State game, after you left and I searched the stands for you, I realized football means absolutely nothing to me if you aren't there cheering me on. I don't want any of it unless you're by my side."

Tears streamed down her cheeks. He brushed them away with his thumb.

"I love you, Rory Michaels. I have loved you since the first moment I met you ten years ago. When I ran into the backyard and saw you sitting alone on that swing, I vowed that I would never let you be alone again.

"When you told me you wanted to move on and be just friends, I thought I missed my shot for good. I thought I needed to forget my dumb vow, to move on and forget you. But I don't think that will ever be possible for me."

He cupped her face in his hands. "Because I will always choose you, Ry. I always have, and I always will. You have never been second place, not once. You are the girl for me."

Then he finally pressed his lips to hers. She smiled into his kiss, her arms finding his shoulders as she pulled him closer, her hands tracing down his neck and inside the collar of his button-down. His hands grazed her face and neck until they snaked around her waist as he leaned forward, tipping her back as he opened his mouth to hers. She slid her tongue against his as he lifted her up, pressing her up against the front door, her legs wrapped around his waist.

He broke apart from her briefly. "I love you," he whispered, kissing up her neck and nibbling her ear. "I will always love you."

"I love you too," she said, sweet relief washing over her at finally being able to admit those words to him.

He grinned, a hum in his throat. "Say it again."

"I love you."

He kissed her cheek, down the other side of her neck. "Again," he breathed.

She chuckled at his insistence. At him finally being *selfish* and taking what he wanted. "I love you."

He brushed his nose against hers again, his eyes closed. "I don't think I'll ever get over you saying that."

She smirked. "You probably will. I'll be too much of a— what did you call me? A *menace?*"

He grinned, his hands drawing circles at her hips, using all of his muscle to pin her against the door. "But you're my menace."

"So if I decide to scream about vaginas with Melanie and Blake in the hallway at the top of my lungs, you'll still love me?"

He chuckled. "Yes."

"How about if I eat all of your beignets? Or I force you to watch hours of Disney movies with me on the couch?"

"Even then," he said, dropping a kiss on her forehead.

"And when I show up to a game without my green bandana because I, um...kind of threw it out?"

He held her steady as he carried her back over to the bright red bag. "You didn't finish opening your present."

Her mouth fell open. "You nut job."

Tyler held her tightly to him with one arm, the other reaching in and pulling out a new bandana. But this one was even better; instead of a simple green cloth, it was crocheted, with white and pink flowers knitted in.

"Oh my god," she said, snatching it from him and tying it behind her ears. "It's perfect."

Tyler simply looked at her, his eyes sparkling, his face glowing. Like she was the light he'd always needed. "You're perfect."

Chapter Twenty-Eight

Rory walked up to Penelope and Vanessa sitting at a table in the cafeteria, ready for the lunch crowd. She smiled at the stack of yearbooks piled next to them to hand out to students.

Penelope looked at her clipboard. "Name?"

Rory frowned. "Seriously, Penelope?"

"We have to be sure we're not handing out yearbooks to people who didn't order them," Penelope replied. "Because if we run out, we'll be screwed."

"Oh, stop that," Vanessa said, reaching into her backpack. "You of all people know that Rory ordered one."

Penelope smirked, eyes still on her clipboard as Vanessa pulled out a yearbook and handed it to Rory.

She brushed a hand over the cover. It looked the same as any other Haverport yearbook on the outside—navy leather with white stripes and *Class of* 2024 in bold letters across the center. It was the only request the school had for the staff—keep the outside the same. But the pages on the inside were their domain, and according to the murmurs she heard in the hallway as students retrieved their yearbooks, people

295

were impressed at how *unique* this yearbook was. Like it was a yearbook just for them—a generation looking toward a bright future, instead of staying stuck in the ways of the past.

She flipped open the cover and grinned, realizing why Vanessa held her copy in her backpack. The first page on the inside of her yearbook was already covered in signatures and messages, all from the yearbook staff.

"We seriously couldn't have pulled this off without you," Penelope admitted. "Principal Barnes said this is the best-looking yearbook he's seen in his twelve years working here."

"It was a team effort," Rory said as she brushed away the tear in her eye.

"Yeah, but your vision brought it to life," Vanessa said, grabbing Rory's free hand from across the table and squeezing it tight. "You're going to absolutely kill it at Baybrook."

Rory smiled, looking down at her T-shirt. It was tan with thin white lettering. *Baybrook School of Fine Arts.* It was always a tradition on the last day of school for students to wear any apparel they had from the school they planned on attending, or part of a uniform if they planned on going out into the workforce. It was a fun way for the seniors to find out if anyone else was going to their same school; Rory already connected with two other art students wearing the same shirt as her.

"Thanks, guys," she replied, slipping her yearbook into her tote bag. "Got your speech ready, Penelope?"

She scoffed, brushing her sleek red hair behind her shoulder so no one missed the name on her shirt. *Princeton.* "Rory, who do you think I am? I've had this thing ready for two months."

Vanessa shook her head, her own UCONN shirt tucked into one of her signature neon skirts. "Valedictorian, Class President. What's next?"

"Congresswoman."

Rory chuckled. "Not even surprised. See you guys at rehearsal?"

They nodded as Rory shuffled away from the table, a line already forming behind her as students picked up their yearbooks. She climbed the stairs up to her locker, the noises getting progressively louder as students broke off from their final morning classes before lunch, last-day excitement ringing in the hallways. Rory opened her locker and grabbed her notebooks, discarded pencils, gym clothes, and folders, stuffing them into a box.

She felt a warm pair of arms brush up against her sides, grabbing the box in her hands. "Here, let me help you," he said.

Rory smirked. "Looking for any excuse to touch me, huh?"

"Can you blame me after waiting ten years?" Tyler whispered in her ear, kissing her cheek.

She smiled, closing her empty locker as she turned to face him. He placed her box on the floor and tugged on her shirt, closing the distance between them. She lifted a hand to his chest, tracing *Rutgers* in bold letters across the center.

"Nice shirt," she said.

He shook his head. "No, you can't have this one."

She pouted. "Why not?"

"Ry, you already stole three of my tees and two of my sweatshirts, not counting the sweatshirt I *bought* you."

"But that one's not as big as yours." She frowned. "Plus, won't you get all kinds of free stuff when you start playing with the team?"

"Yeah but—"

She swatted his arm. "No buts, the girlfriend of a foot-ball player gets full rights to his entire wardrobe."

His shoulders melted at her use of *girlfriend*. "Fine, you win."

"Did you think I wouldn't?" she teased, leaning in to give him a peck on the lips. Before she could pull back, he caught the back of her neck and let the kiss linger, a satisfied moan rumbling from his chest.

"Alright, alright, we get it, you're into each other," Blake said as he walked up with Melanie beside him.

Rory pushed back, tracing a finger down Tyler's chest. "Come on, Blake, we only get a month before Ty leaves us for camp and we have to do this long-distance thing."

"Which probably means the two of you are going to be insufferable at work this summer," Blake replied. "Mel, you should have Calvin set a rule that these two can't come within three feet of each other at Scoops."

Rory balked. "You're saying that to *Melanie*. She and Calvin pretty much invented workplace PDA."

Melanie blushed. "Shut up."

"We'll be polite...when people are around," Tyler said, squeezing Rory's side and kissing her cheek again.

"Gross," Blake bantered, a smile on his face.

"*All seniors please report to the football field in fifteen minutes for graduation rehearsal*," said a voice on the intercom.

"Wow," Melanie breathed. "It's really happening."

Rory reached for Melanie's hands. "We did it."

"I don't know what I'm going to do without you guys next year," Blake grumbled.

"We're literally going to *live* in town," Rory jested. "We'll still hang out all the time."

Melanie smiled, tears in her eyes as she glanced between him and Rory. "Promise?"

Rory squeezed her hands. "Always."

She watched the two of them walk off, heading for the yearbook table to grab their copies.

Tyler leaned against her locker, tugging on her shirt again. "Will you sign my yearbook, Ry?"

She batted her eyelashes. "Only if I can write something vulgar."

He rolled his eyes, handing it to her. "Menace."

"*Your* menace, may I remind you," she teased, opening his book. "Wow, yours is practically filled already. Pays to be the Homecoming King."

"Page three is also reserved, so don't touch it."

She turned to the third page, which was completely blank. She frowned. "Who for?"

"Me," said a soft voice next to them.

Rory stood up straight as she glanced up at Zoe. She looked nervous, her smile tight. But she stood there proud, with her fingers laced with Helen's, the two of them donning their New York school tees.

"Okay, that's fine," Rory replied to Zoe. "But only if *you* write something vulgar."

"I don't think Zoe knows how to be vulgar," Helen bantered. "It will only be sweet messages, probably with flowers and hearts by her name."

Zoe bumped her hip into Helen.

"As long as there are drawings then," Rory said, sneaking a quick glance at Tyler. He was still smiling down at her, completely unfazed by all the students milling around, whispering to one another.

Zoe let go of Helen's hand and gave Rory a hug. "I'm sorry, Rory. For all of it."

She hugged her back. "Why are you sorry?"

"You should have been with him from the beginning," Zoe said softly. "I feel like I really screwed up this year."

Rory took a step back. "I had things to work out too, you know."

Zoe just nodded, looking somber.

"Everything okay at home?" Tyler asked.

Zoe just shrugged. "My parents are pissed...but not because I came out. They're really mad that I lied to them, that I chose not to trust them with such an important part of who I am."

"And your dad?" Rory asked.

"He says I should have been honest about my anxiety with being in the public eye," she admitted feebly. "Refusing to go to his reelection party hurt his feelings, and he wishes we could have discussed it. I've learned...a lot the past few days. About them, about myself..." She paused, her eyes drawn to Helen. Rory watched Helen squeeze Zoe's hand.

"Have you spoken to Walker?" Tyler asked, his face pulled into a scowl.

Zoe shook her head. "I refuse to go near him."

Helen tucked a strand of Zoe's hair behind her ear in comfort.

"This whole thing made me realize that it's never worth trying to be something you're not just to appease someone else," Zoe admitted. "Because if you're not completely honest, then you're not exactly caring for others in return. Or trusting them with being your truest self."

Rory just nodded, her mind drifting to the year she'd had. When she finally allowed herself to be authentic, everything changed. With her mother. With her true feelings for Jay. With her decision about college. With her closest friendships. With the guy next to her who she was head-over-heels in love with.

"It's certainly not the easiest thing to do, but it's worth it," she replied.

Tyler squeezed her hand, a silent reminder of that conversation after prom three weeks earlier, of the words he repeated to her like a prayer. *I will always choose you.*

SEVEN OF THEM STOOD THERE, staring out at the thirty-foot drop below.

"This is nuts," Blake said. "You guys are nuts."

Rory reached for Melanie's hand, her other laced together with Tyler's. "When has that ever stopped us before, Blakey boy?"

"Yeah but...in your graduation gowns?" Blake asked, eyeing the group.

Rory, Melanie, and Tyler were still wearing their navy-blue gowns, caps on their heads. The group drove to Sunset Rock after the ceremony at Rory's request, a hidden gem in town that was a known spot for rowdy teenagers daring to make the big leap into the ocean below. Calvin even closed Scoops for the night, all so the Scoopers could have this moment before the busy summer season ahead.

"Oh yes," Rory said, flicking her head slightly to get the tassel out of her face. "Caps and all."

"But do we really all have to?" Blake pleaded.

"Three—" Melanie started.

Tyler squeezed her hand. "Two."

Rory beamed, scanning the group she loved dearly

beside her. Jess removed her glasses, tossing them next to her bag. Jay returned Rory's gaze and winked.

She grinned. "One."

They all sprinted. Jay hollered as he jumped, curling his body into a cannonball. Melanie let go of Rory's hand and screamed with delight, holding tightly to Calvin. Jess dove with the grace of an Olympic athlete, and Blake cursed loudly into the sky before his body slapped against the water beneath.

Tyler pulled Rory back before she could jump, curling his arms around her and brushing his nose against hers. "So...still best friends forever?"

She grinned, drawing close to his lips, then wrenched out of his grasp and ran to make the jump.

"You MENACE!" he yelled, chasing after her.

She laughed, holding her arms out wide. As her cap soared off her head and a smile bloomed across her cheeks, Rory finally felt ready to embrace the future that didn't feel so scary after all.

Epilogue

Rory sat on the floor at Calvin's house, a cup of tea next to her in a rather ugly mug, the sun painted on it like it was done by a kindergartener. Which, according to Melanie, it was.

"Hmm, I can't decide. I love the colors on this one, but the lettering here is so much clearer," she explained, holding up two different designs in each hand.

Tyler nudged her hip with his foot, his legs tucked in next to Rory as he sat on the couch behind her. "I think the colorful one. It's more you."

"Yeah, but she's right," Calvin retorted. "Our older customers may not be able to read it well."

"Babe, I highly doubt older customers are even going to bother buying stickers that say *They're Not Sprinkles, They're Jimmies*," Melanie added.

"Headband, we have a lot of loyal customers. They may buy simply to support us."

"Then having bigger letters probably won't matter much," Rory said. "You're right, Ty. Colors it is."

He kissed her on the top of the head. "Good."

Kevin stepped into the living room, holding a plate of oatmeal chocolate chip cookies. "Guys, someone tell Gram to stop baking cookies. She's a machine back there."

Melanie snatched a cookie off the plate. "Never."

Calvin frowned. "Weren't you supposed to pick up pizza, like, a half hour ago?"

Kevin's eyes went wide, fumbling with the plate as he dropped it onto the table. "Shit, sorry. I got pulled into cookie heaven."

"Maybe we should call Penny's and add another pizza now that Tyler is here?" Rory asked.

Tyler barked out a laugh. "Just for me?"

"I'm sorry, have you seen yourself lately?" she teased, shoving his leg as she stared up at him. "I thought you were a human garbage disposal before, but training for camp has somehow transformed you into an entire dumpster truck."

Tyler wiggled an eyebrow at her, puffing up his chest. "You don't seem to be complaining."

"Keep it in your pants, Chapman," Calvin retorted.

Tyler chuckled darkly, his eyes on her like molten dark chocolate. They still hadn't taken that final step together, but Rory was content with waiting and making it count. With Tyler, she knew this thing was going to be a lifetime kind of commitment. There was no rush. She wanted to enjoy every second of it.

But that hadn't stopped them from constantly having their hands on one another when they weren't apart, the need to touch him a constant tremor in her being. She still couldn't believe how long she went without touching Tyler like this...and hated that it took her this long to realize how much she needed the boy next door.

The ringing of the doorbell had Rory ripping her gaze from Tyler's, trying to avoid the way her body was responding to the slow circles he traced down her neck as she watched Calvin frown over at Kevin.

"Did you order the pizza for delivery?" Calvin asked.

"I don't think so?" Kevin replied, opening the door. His body went rigid as he gazed at the person on the other side. Everyone had gone silent. Her blonde hair was tied up in a bun, the long wispy bangs she was growing out tucked behind her ears.

But it wasn't her signature glasses missing from her face or the stained T-shirt she wore that shocked everyone.

It was the pile of duffel bags and suitcases she had by her feet.

Jess glanced at Calvin, who was already off the floor and walking toward the door. Her eyes finally landed on Kevin, her look determined as she spoke.

"Is it too late to take you up on the offer?"

Also by K.Sinko

The Scoops Series

Safe Harbor

Always Choosing You

The Offer

Standalones

Sunday Supper

Call Of The Loon

Novelettes

Please Be Mine

Acknowledgments

High school is messy...and so was writing this book. I wouldn't be where I am today without the people in my life willing to get messy with me.

To my beta reader team, you guys are rock stars. Your encouragement and honesty while putting together this story helped to make it shine. Thank you for your kind words and for the giving me the little nudges I needed: Alexis Wierenga, Abby Hancock, Genny Ryley, Amber Strickland, Caitlin Goodey, and Melanie Stewart.

Britt Tayler, I am indebted to you! Thank you for your keen editing eye and your insight. This story is a lot stronger because of it. I look forward to diving into book three with you soon.

Also thank you to Brooke Crites for hopping in with a last minute proofread. I am thankful for your thoroughness!

Jonny Ryley, your artwork brought this series to life. I can't even express how grateful I am to have such unique, original art that perfectly encompasses each of these stories. Thank you for making this gorgeous second cover and for caring deeply about every little detail of your work.

Mom, thanks for talking sense into me when I needed it. This story felt messy from the start, but your advice guided me in those beginning stages and helped make this story special. Thanks for letting me call and vent out all of my random thoughts when I need to.

I can't forget "the sisterhood" and "the thruple." Thanks

for keeping my sanity in check so I wouldn't rip out my hair working on this book. And my brother, Brendan Sinko, for the late night chats, the encouragement, and for generally being a pain in my ass.

Lastly, to all of my readers. Social media marketing isn't easy as an author, but I am so very thankful for Bookstagram and all of the ways I have connected with readers and authors alike. Thank you for all of your excitement surrounding this series; the videos and graphics and reviews and sweet comments don't go unnoticed. You make this job fun and you keep me going. I can't wait for you to read the last book of the series...and for all the other love stories to come.

About the Author

K.Sinko is an indie published author with a deep love for love stories. She is the author of *Sunday Supper, Call Of The Loon, Please Be Mine,* and the Scoops Series—a trilogy of stand-alone romances featuring the of a fictional ice cream shop. Her debut novel *Safe Harbor* became an Amazon best seller for young adult contemporary romance and is the winner of two Indieverse Awards. Follow her on Instagram and sign up for her newsletter to get the latest book updates.

tinyurl.com/ksinkonewsletter

instagram.com/authorksinko

www.ingramcontent.com/pod-product-compliance
Lightning Source LLC
Chambersburg PA
CBHW022024310726
48972CB00006B/1792